Last of a Dying Breed

**Lock Down Publications
Presents
Last of a Dying Breed
A Novel by *Jamaica***

Lock Down Publications
P.O. Box 1482
Pine Lake, Ga 30072-1482

Visit our website at **www.lockdownpublications.com**

First Edition December 2016
Printed in the United States of America
This is a work of fiction. Names, characters, places, and incidents either are products of the author's imagination or are used fictitiously. Any similarity to actual events or locales or persons, living or dead, is entirely coincidental.

Lock Down Publications
Like our page on Facebook: Lock Down Publications
@www.facebook.com/lockdownpublications.ldp
Cover design and layout by: Dynasty's Cover Me
Book interior design by: Shawn Walker
Edited by: Shawn Walker

Jamaica

Prologue

Dear Love,

Hey there. How are you doing? I hope this letter finds you in good health. I hope all is well with you.

I know you're wondering why I'm writing you and I know I'm probably the last person you want to hear from, which I can understand but I need to get this off my chest.

I know I can't make you believe me, Love, but trust me I never meant for it to go down like that. I never knew they was gonna take what I said and use it against you...

It eats me up like a muthafucka. I know you'll never stop hating me, although I pray you do.

...I really wish I could turn back the hands of time and make it okay.

I debated asking you this, but do you regret meeting me? I hope you're able to say no despite it all.

...I hope I can gain your trust and we can link back up again. That's not out of the question, huh? Well, if I have a chance at redemption, I enclosed my info.

I ain't gonna hold you up too much longer. I probably took up too much time already. Until next time, keep your head up and stay strong. You a G so I already know you gonna be alright. I hope to hear back from you, even if you cussing me out.

Peace Out...

I could have burst a blood vessel after having read that fuck shit.

Nigga got me fucked up!

I paced the floors with his letter clutched in my hand, remembering every step that led me to *him.*

Do I regret meeting you? I replayed his question to myself.

"Fuck yea, bitch boy!" I answered out loud before I sat on the bed and fell backwards, staring up into nothingness.

Jamaica

I should have never shown love to that nigga, but the thorough bitch that I was *did*, so I wasn't about to cry about it now. I'd been solid from the womb and there wasn't a man alive that was capable of breaking me.

My eyes then shifted from one side of the room to the other as I processed the day we crossed paths.

Chapter 1

I waited behind the stage of Dance 4 U, the strip club my best friend, Snow worked at, nervous as hell. It was my first night dancing publicly and for such a big venue but making money, hand over fist, motivated me to get my shit together and do the damn thang!

"Ballers and shot callers, Imma need y'all to come out ya pockets for this Caribbean beauty up next. She one bad ass Jamaican gurlll. Let's show some love to Honey Lovvvveee!" The Deejay excitedly announced and I walked onto the platform like I owned that muthafucka.

The initial jitters I felt immediately went away when I saw damn near every man crowd at the stage to get a better glimpse of me. I flashed a smile and then my adrenaline kicked in. It was go time!

By the end of the first song, I had 'em sweating my thong, tongues damn near out of their mouths.

"Damn, shawty! Work that shit, but come over here with it." A nigga to the left of the stage screamed as I was showing my skills to a bald headed man in front of me.

"Fuck that nigga, ma. I got all the money you need right here." Bald head said to me as he flashed a hand full of green in front of my eyes.

Ha! Ha! These niggas were arguing over pussy that neither one of them will ever get.

After debuting my sexy ass off to four songs, I sat down on the bench. My muscles were trembling from all the work on the pole I did.

But it was all worth it.

I glanced in the bucket on the floor and felt a rush of pride. Fuck 5's, 10's and 20's, I was seeing 50's and 100's. *Hell yeah!* Not too bad for my first night on stage.

I opened my locker to grab my bag because the bucket said my work here was done. It was time to go.

As I walked through the locker room, my phone rang.

"Hello?"

"I'm outside waiting on you."

"Where at?"

"Employee's door."

"I'm on my way out." I ended the call.

Jamaica

Next I felt a tap on my arm, "Love, you want me to walk you out?" A security guard asked me.

"Nah, you can walk me to the big man's headquarters, though."

As we headed to the manager's office, the guard said, "You put on one hell of a show tonight."

"Thanks." I left his presence to pay my dues.

I handed Samuel a thousand, plus two-fifty for DJ Sledge. He smiled and told me I did splendid.

I left out and headed down the hall. When I opened the employee's door, I turned around and tipped the guard, too.

Once outside, I saw my peoples. "Thanks for coming through for me tonight," I told her when she let me go.

"You know I wouldn't have missed it for nothing." I knew she meant that, too, and with that, I embraced her again. "And I already called you a cab, too." Snow informed me.

"You not leaving?" I asked as I released her. She looked around the parking lot, plenty niggas were posted up on their vehicles just shooting the breeze.

"You see all these men out here and you think I'm leaving?" She chuckled before she proceeded, "Imma find Mr. Big Dick Willie tonight." She kissed my face and walked off.

"Have fun but make sure you call me as soon as you get home." I yelled at her.

She didn't turn around, but she tossed the deuces in the air as she reentered the club.

I dropped my duffle bag on the ground and locked it between my feet so I could fish my phone out of my handbag. I wanted to make a call as I waited on my cab.

"Damn, shawty!" I turned around in the direction of the voice, only to discover four niggas behind me.

The way they slowly began approaching me made me feel uneasy. I reached down and grabbed my bag and took steps away from them, hoping they'd see my disinterest and fall back, too.

They didn't.

"You the one that shut shit down in there earlier?" He asked but I didn't respond 'cause one of his backup singers did.

"My nigga, that's the shawty that had on the green and yellow!" And just like that a huge smile spread across their faces.

"Oh, hell yea, it's her." He turned around to his niggas and then back to me. "Can I take you somewhere so I can get a personal show?" He laughed like the shit he said was funny.

I wanted to go AWOL, but I bit my tongue. Four against one, the odds weren't in my favor.

"I'm off for the night but you can check me out tomorrow." I tried speaking pleasantly but my face said *fuck off!*

He grimaced, matching my same displeasure for him, them. He looked off to his boys and then back at me.

Snarling, he said, "Ole, ugly, uppity ass bitch! I ain't asking. I'm telling you." He went to snatch my arm, but I jerked away from him.

I thought to run to the nearest group of people but my feet didn't budge. Although it would have been smart of me to haul ass, the G in me wouldn't allow me to run from a nigga. Win or lose, I was prepared to fight.

"One of y'all get the bag!" He barked as he grabbed ahold of me.

I began fighting as best as I could but he was much stronger than me. "Get the fuck off of me!" I cried out.

"Nah, bitch! Not before I get me."

One of his niggas snatched my bag, while my aggressor tried copping a feel of my pussy and shoving his disgusting tongue down my throat.

"Stop!" My voice was slightly muffled. "Get off of meeee!" I finally was able to belt out.

As I felt him drag me off to God knows where, I heard a deep and even toned voice say, "You heard what she said. Get the fuck off her!"

"Nigga, mind ya business!" My abductor said, holding me tighter.

"Yea, you minding the wrong nigga's business," one of his boy's said. "This nigga don't know who the fuck we are!" He directed his statement to his partners.

"I don't give a fuck either." My knight in shining armor spoke up with confidence, lifting his tee shirt up and pulling out a black pistol from his waist.

The sight of his gat turned them into straight pussies. They threw their hands up and the piece of shit holding me, let me go.

I then ran to my rescuer, standing beside him.

"You can have the bitch!" He scoffed.

"What you said, nigga?" My knight asked.

"It's all good, yo!" Scary ass replied with his hands still in the sky.

With his gun trained on them niggas, he asked, "You straight?"

I shook my head *no*, all the while looking at them pussies. "Nah, they got my bag of money."

"Grab yo shit, then, Love!" He nodded his head in their direction.

With the heart of a lion, I walked up to the dude who had my riches, snatched my bag and spat in his face. He mugged me hard but didn't flex. I then walked over to the ring leader and socked his stupid ass in the face. "You fucked with the wrong bitch, bitch!"

In a reactionary manner, he pulled his fist back to lay my ass out, but when he heard the cock of Knight's hammer, he reconsidered. "That's what the fuck I thought." I rolled my eyes and turned away from him.

I then went back to the man who saved me, enjoying the swell of my clit.

Minutes ago, I felt powerless and scared for my life, but now I felt untouchable. Thanks to the mystery man, who knew *my* name.

"Now get the fuck on before I catch four bodies." Knight ordered and them weak niggas fled just like that.

Thankful for his help, I turned toward him but I couldn't see his face 'cause his fitted hat was pulled all the way down, covering his eyes.

As the niggas disappeared so did the small crowd that I hadn't noticed until now.

When the coast was cleared, Knight tucked the gun back in his waist under his shirt.

"Thank you." I whispered, but I knew he heard me.

Wiping his brow, he lifted his hat just a little and then I realized I had seen him several times before at some of the private parties where Snow and I danced.

"Don't sweat it." He blew it off. "Let me walk you to your car."

"I don't have one. I was waiting on a cab before that incident happened."

"Come with me, I can give you a ride, if you want it."

The worst had almost happened and if it wasn't for him, then I don't know how bad it could've gotten. Feeling safer with him, I followed him to his car.

I recalled him being a big money nigga from all the cake he threw at me, so I knew he didn't need my coins. And if he wanted to harm me, he would have done so on any of the nights I performed, privately. At least that was my reasoning as I waited for him to unlock his car.

He opened the door for me and in I stepped. As he walked around to the driver's side, I text Snow and told her I was leaving with the big spender who pushed the Impala. Neither she or I knew him personally but we knew of him from our parties.

He entered the car, removing the gun from his waist and placing it on his lap as he started the engine. Jeezy's album *Let's Get It: Thug Motivation 101* was bumping through the speakers before he cut the volume down.

"I'm sorry you had to go through all that shit just now." He spoke as my cab finally pulled into the lot. He saw it, too. "Want me to let you out, so you can catch your cab?"

"No need." I shook my head *no*. "I rather ride with you. I'm staying over at The Best Western Hotel if you're still willing to bring me home."

He nodded his head and pulled out of the parking lot.

The ride was silent minus the music playing, until my knight sparked conversation.

"In case you're wondering, my name is Tamaine Davidson, but in these streets, I go by Murdoc."

I followed suit. "I am Love, Love Jenkins."

"I already knew that!"

I don't know why I blushed, but I did.

We furthered our small talk until we arrived at the hotel and in front of my room's door.

He placed his car in park. I hoped he wasn't taking it upon himself to follow me inside because although I owed him for looking out for me, he wasn't getting any pussy.

11

Jamaica

Tamaine moved the gun off of his lap and placed it on the console. I stared at it for a second before my attention went to his left hand movement on the side of his door.

"Well, thanks again for saving me back there and for the ride. I guess I'll see you around some other time." I went to exit the car but he gently stopped me, by pulling at my arm.

"Hold up." He located a pen and then pulled out a knot. He scribbled something down on it and then handed it to me.

"What's this for?" I accepted the grip, eyeing it and him suspiciously.

"It's my contribution to that fiy' ass show you put on tonight. I would have shown love in the club, but you had them niggas packed like sardines at ya feet."

He smiled and I did, too.

"All I can say is thank you."

"And that's enough for me." He placed his gun back on his lap and shifted his gear into reverse. "Have a good night, Love."

On that note, I exited the car and closed his door. He waved through the windshield and then pulled off right as my phone started ringing.

It was Snow. I reached for my room key, opened the door and gave her the rundown of what happened once I was inside. She was pissed that she left me alone out there.

"You're good. Hell, if you was out there, he would have had to save two instead of one." We both chuckled. Her ass was just as small as me.

"Mane, thank God for dude, yo!"

"Girl, my momma is definitely watching over me, sending him to protect me right on time." I told her as I started counting my money up.

"She is, but make sure security escorts you to ya car from now on. It'll make me feel better."

I told her I would and we ended the call, but not before expressing love to one another.

After tallying everything up, I calculated my earning at fifteen hundred take home. And considering I paid a thousand to the house and two hundred and fifty dollars to the deejay, I made some serious bank. *Not bad for my first night.*

Afterwards, I counted the wad of cash Tamaine blessed me with. It was two thousand five hundred large. *Damn!*

I then looked at the bill with his scrawl on it and noticed he left me with his digits.

Humph! I'd be calling Tamaine, Murdoc, my knight, fo' sho!

***

I woke up with Tamaine on my mental heavy. And even though I had his number, I didn't call him. Part of me wanted to reach out to him, but I guess I subconsciously wanted to play hard to get. Besides, he knew where to find me, if he really wanted me.

Once I got through replaying thoughts of him and that G shit he pulled, I got out of bed, showered and dressed. I then called a cab to take me to the River Ridge Mall. After the night I had, a little retail therapy would do me good. Plus, I was sitting on racks. I could afford to splurge.

After having spent a few hours shopping, weighted down with bags galore, I decided it was time to go back to my hotel, make a drop off and hook up with Snow, if she was free.

I called a cab and told the dispatcher that I'd be outside by the food court entrance.

As I waited, mad niggas were jocking my fly. Not to sound cocky, but I was so used to that shit that it didn't faze me. I just kept watch of the time and the cab I expected to arrive in ten minutes or less.

"Damn, ma, can I get some of your time?" One guy quizzed.

"Can I wait with you?" Another asked.

"Where yo man at, shawty?" And another.

Tuhhh!

Different men walked past me saying the same ole shit but it wasn't until I heard *his* voice that I looked up.

"Well, hello again, Love."

I smiled before we even locked eyes. Hearing Tamaine's velvety, smooth voice almost melted my panties into liquid goo. He was smiling right along with me and that's when I saw that his bottom row of teeth were all gold. *I liked that thuggy shit!*

I looked him up and then down and flirtatiously joked. "Let me find out you stalking a sista."

"Neva that. But if I was, could you blame me?"

Tamaine looked so damn good that if he was, I wouldn't even be mad. He stood about 5'11", was high yellow with an athletic build and a killer smile.

I lowered my head and smiled stupidly. I felt silly, probably looked it, too. "No, I guess not, but you're good, anyways."

Ha! Ha! I laughed inwardly.

From there, we talked until my cab arrived. I felt disappointed that our time was being cut short, but I proceeded to the back door of the taxi.

"We'll have to get together *on purpose* next time." I reached for the handle.

"Or we can do this now." He walked over to the driver, without hearing my approval first, handed him some money and instructed that he pick up another because he had me covered.

I was impressed by his assertiveness. I liked a man who went after what he wanted and clearly Tamaine was that man.

He walked me over to his ride and opened my door, like he did last night, allowing me time to sit comfortably before closing the door. From there, we had lunch at this cozy spot he knew.

We talked fluidly over drinks once we finished our meals and the more he divulged was the more I wanted to drink *him* in. But his money didn't grow on trees, so he had to get to it.

"I hate to cut this short but I have some things to handle. I'm gonna bring you to your spot but before I do, I'm gonna need them digits of yours." He smiled.

"What you don't trust that I'll call you?" I reached for his phone, so I could input my number.

"I don't trust nothing I can't personally guarantee. Don't take it personal."

"I feel you." I agreed.

Shortly after, he dropped me off and I regretted our time ending immediately. I was digging him. His conversation was on point and he was so easy on the eyes. And being gangsta 'bout his *and* bossed up was an added bonus.

Once inside, exhausted from shopping and then the date with Tamaine had me ready for a nap. I had work later that night, anyways. But before I crawled under the sheets, I text Tamaine: *Can't wait to see you tonight.*

I knew without him telling me that he'd be at my show.

Later that night, I arrived at Dance 4 U. My first stop was in Samuel's office, letting him know the situation that had taken place last night. He assured me that more security would be enforced. Whether it was or wasn't, I had a feeling that I wouldn't need it anyway, at least not with Tamaine around.

From there, it was time to do my thing.

Once my name was called to hit the stage, I got into my zone and just like the previous night, I smoked that shit.

After I collected all of my earnings, I headed to the back. I wasn't greedy, so after my performance, I was ready to bounce. I planned on going up front once I changed to locate Tamaine, so we could pick up where we left off from earlier.

Instead of the security guard waiting for me by the locker room, as I assumed he would, Tamaine was there with one foot against the wall, looking at his phone.

"How you got all the way back here?" I was shocked that he was in the employee's only section of the club.

He stuffed his phone in his pocket and walked toward me.

"When I want something, I go extra hard for it," was his reply.

"Really?"

"Yea, really."

"Give me a second to change and then pay Samuel. I'll be ready to leave afterwards."

"I already took care of your boss, so you good on that?" he said casually.

I was taken aback. "What you mean?"

"What you mean, *what I mean*?" He chuckled. "I handled that now go handle you."

I shook my head at him, but in a good way. I was digging his *take charge* mentality. I wanted to know what made me so special to get this type of treatment but I *was* that bitch, so why not?

I slipped away for a few moments and returned dressed in a pair of short and a tank, representing my Jamaican colors.

"You looked good in everything you put on." He complimented and I blushed.

As we walked out of the building, he let me know that he respected my hustle but that stripping shit wasn't for me.

"Females these days rather sit around and collect instead of going out and getting theirs, so I salute you for ya grind, but you know with a man like myself on your team, you wouldn't have to do this, right?"

"Well, I got to know you before I draft you." I half-kidded. I was definitely caught up but not too far gone that I didn't probe his mind before moving full speed ahead.

"A'ight. Ask me anything. I'm an open book."

And any and everything is what I asked as he stopped off to get us something to grub on before bringing me to my hotel.

Parked outside of my room, I learned that he was 23 years old with no children. His father succumbed to drugs, as my mother had, and he'd just came home from doing three years for a dope charge, amongst so much more.

"So what you do for a living?" I inquired. He pulled the strap out from under his leg and spoke, "I live life, baby girl."

I looked up at the building and wondered if I was really living my life, from a hotel room.

"Your turn to tell me about yourself. Besides dancing, who is Love?"

"I'm me!" And he smiled. "I'm loving, caring, down to earth, loyal to those that are loyal to me."

"Damn, me too."

"See, we have a lot in common." He leaned his seat back as I told him about myself, even down to how my mother overdosed on crack and I was the one to find her after school that day. I had never opened up about my moms to anyone but Snow. "I miss Queen, every day." Tears streamed down my face but it felt good to release my constant pain to someone who cared.

He leaned over the console and held my face in his hands as he wiped my tears away.

"I can share my moms with you." I closed my eyes and relaxed at his remark. "Look, since you don't have anyone in your life, I can be everything to you and more."

My heart damn near beat out of my chest. This thug nigga was romantic as hell!

I gazed into his eyes, searching for any hint of deceit. I found none. Now the moment was purely emotional and I found myself responding accordingly.

I leaned in closer to him and allowed our lips to touch. I let his tongue slowly enter my mouth, as my eyes slowly closed. His lips were as soft as pillows. Engaged in passion, he then slowly pulled away from my gaping mouth and planted a kiss of endearment on my forehead.

"Get some rest, baby girl, and hit me up as soon as you get up." He told me as he released my face.

I almost wanted to invite him in, but I reserved that invitation for another time. I opened the door but before I could exit, he handed me another knot.

"Stack ya paper up, baby girl, you deserve it all!"

I smiled generously, thanking him with another kiss, but this time against his knuckles. "Imma call you *before* I got to sleep," I told him.

"A'ight, I'll be waiting, then." He pulled off, only after seeing that I made it inside safely.

Later that night, I called as I said I would, as I was drawn to do. And we talked for hours, well into the next morning.

He dozed off a few times, but played it off smooth. I thought that was cute. But when he wasn't snoring in my ear, he was dropping some heavy shit on me. I sopped it all up, too. I liked how he was rapping. He was unlike any other.

Needless to say, Tamaine had me open like 7/11 and by the time we said bye, I was ready to say hello again.

Jamaica

Chapter 2
2006

After my first three shows at Dance 4 U, I never went back. Tamaine pitched me the idea of a fairy tale life and I bought it.

He moved me into a beautiful four bedroom, two bathroom house on Blue Ridge Street.

"You don't have to shake your ass. I will take care of you," was always his speech and I trusted him.

"You want me to sit in the house all day doing nothing while you run the streets?" I asked him while we were having a heart to heart conversation.

"You being in the house is for your own good, Love."

"How is it for my own good? I wanna go out and see the world, too! Every other weekend you gotta go out of town, while I stay here and watch the house. Shit, either you gonna teach me the game or you gonna see me shaking my ass again."

He took a seat on the sofa and propped his feet up on the center table. All he kept doing was shaking his head.

"This game shit is not for you," he said. I loved how he was protective over me and my attraction for him only grew deeper within my heart.

I took a seat across from him.

"How the fuck you figure?" I replied with a bit of an attitude. I didn't like being underestimated.

"This is a man's game."

"Whose rule is that?"

That made him laugh, and the tension lifted a little.

"You so damn hardheaded! Why can't you just let me take care of you?"

He still wasn't getting my point.

"It's not that I don't want you to take care of me, I just want to be able to have your back at all times, too." I felt like he had mine, and I wanted him to feel that way, too. I got up and closed the space between us. "When you leave me here by myself, all I do is stress.

My mind be going crazy." He smiled. "You don't have to teach me shit, just let me come with you." I told him as I rubbed on his dick.

"Love..." his words trailed off as I unbuckled his pants and squatted down between his legs. I used my teeth to unzip his jeans as I eye fucked him. Licking my lips with my wet tongue turned him on, causing his dick to grow instantly.

Once I got it out, it was standing at attention. I rubbed it with my left hand as I circled my tongue around the head of it. My right hand was between my legs, rubbing on my warm cookie.

I licked the head slowly and it jumped at me. I looked up at him. He took off his VA fitted hat and showed me his gold teeth. I worked my mouth all the way down to his balls, then I came up. I released the dick from my wet mouth but kept my left hand sliding up and down on it. I licked and sucked his balls slow but steady. I had saliva all over his wood.

Up, down, down, up, my mouth went. I found a way into my panties with my right hand. My pussy was soaking wet, so I slipped one finger inside of my fountain, as my mouth worked its magic.

"Oh shit," escaped from his mouth.

He grabbed my ponytail hard and guided my head up and down. He had taught me how to please him, and I had turned it into an art. Every single time I gave him some head, I made it my job to do it better than before.

His head hit the back of the sofa and his right leg got to jumping. His hands moved my head fast and then slow. When I came up, I sucked the left side from top to bottom and the right side from bottom to top.

"Suck that shit, baby," he moaned and I did as I was told. He had my head moving like a bobble head.

"Baby, I'm 'bout to nut," he told me with heavy breathing. I wanted to feel it going down in my stomach. "Fuck, baby!" He screamed at me as my head moved faster.

"Umm," I moaned.

"Babbbbyyyy," he said and then blessed me with my vitamins for the day.

As he spilled his seeds into my mouth, I drenched my fingers with my own juices. After I swallowed all of him, I got up and pushed my fingers inside of his mouth. He licked them off and I put my lips on his mouth to taste myself.

"You such a freak," he told me.

"I learned from the best." He kissed me again and I pulled away. I got up off of him and walked off to go clean myself up.

"Yea, you can come with me," he said under his heavy breathing but loud enough for me to hear him.

I stopped in my tracks and turned my head around. "Damn, all it took was a mean blow job?" He busted out laughing and threw a pillow at me.

***

My first trip came the next day.

"Make sure you pack an overnight bag, Love, and be ready in twenty minutes or I'm leaving ya ass." That's how he woke me up.

"Thank you, Lord, for this day. Protect us, guide us and keep us. Amen!"

I flew out of the bed and ran to the bathroom to get ready. The hot water was taking so long to heat up that I just jumped into the cold water. I was rushing, washing my body and brushing my teeth at the same damn time. Pussy, armpits and ass, the main parts that I needed to hit.

I dashed out of the shower with no towel, water dripping from my body as I packed me a small bag.

I put on my bra, thong, white wife beater and black skin tight jogger pants with my black and white J's. I picked my phone up off of the charger and it rang in my hand.

"Let's go, set the alarm for the house and come on," he said into my ear. I made sure the back door was locked, I punched the code into the alarm system, closed the door and secured it with my house key.

Tamaine was waiting on me in the car in front of the house. He watched me walk to the car and licked his lips. He was thinking about pussy, I bet. Well, I was thinking about that trip.

He reached over and unlatched my door for me. "Put yo seat belt on."

I wasn't even in the damn car yet.

"Tamaine, let me get in first, damn!" I scrunched up my face at him.

He pulled off laughing. He placed his right hand on my pussy and pinched it, wanting a reaction from me, so I gave him one. I let my seat back and put my right foot on the dash board.

"You a freak," he said, laughing between words.

"And you can't live without me!"

He slapped my leg and put his hand back on the steering wheel. I fixed my seat back to normal.

A few minutes later, one of his phones rang and I got it for him out of the middle console.

"Yo," he barked into the receiver. I tried my best to hear, but I heard nothing. "Aite. I'll hit you up then." He ended the call and glanced over at me. "Put that nigga Jeezy album in."

I opened the glove box and got *Can't Ban the Snowman* album and popped it in.

His head bounced to the beat as it came out of the speakers. I wanted to know where we were heading but I wasn't going to ask, so I sat back and listened to Jeezy preach.

I'm back
I'm back Mr. Magic City
Blowin' color purple make it rain on ya forehead
I thought I had a fan the way I blow that money
You would have thought I had a plan the way I throw that money

I fell asleep unknowingly and when I woke up, there were nothing but trees flying by and cars driving beside us. Murdoc looked over at me and chuckled. "You can't hang, sleeping beauty."

As soon as I heard him call me *sleeping beauty*, my face turned somber as I recalled the last day with my mom.

"Wake up, sleeping beauty," Queen rubbed my back as she tried to wake me. "You have to get ready for school, baby." That's what she lived for: to make sure I was well taken care of. Not even her vicious crack habit interfered with that.

"Mom, can I stay home with you today?" If I had it my way, it wouldn't be up for debate. My mom was my best friend and I enjoyed every minute of her time.

"No, but we can stay up late, watching all of our favorite movies" Queen smiled beautifully as she picked my clothes up off of the floor.

"Okay, I'm getting up right now," I jumped up off of the bed with a boost of energy, as I looked forward to leaving school before I got there.

"Love!" Murdoc called out for me, but I was too dazed to respond. He tapped me slightly on the arm. "Love, you aite?"

I didn't want to fall into a grieving mood so I forced the memories to the back of my mind and ignored his question.

"Where we at?" I rubbed sleep from my eyes.

"We on 29 heading South. Straight to South Carolina, baby."

My mood changed and I got all excited. I had never been out of Lynchburg before. *Never!* I couldn't wait to see what this next state looked like.

Jeezy was still bumping through the speakers, so I twisted the volume down so I could talk to him.

"Are you going to tell me what's going on now?" A smile appeared on his face. "A whole year and you still can't tell me what you do?"

He gripped his chin and exhaled. "I'm selling drugs, Love." I had always suspected it but his confirmation said that he trusted me to know his business.

"Now, how hard was that?" I asked.

He removed his eyes off of the road and fixed them on me. I stuck my tongue out at him. He returned his eyes to the traffic and told me what I wanted to hear.

His first dope charge was over 7 grams of crack cocaine. He had gotten pulled over because his ass was driving drunk. He didn't even remember getting stopped by the police until the next day when he woke up in a cell. They had already found the crack, so he'd told them how he smoked so they wouldn't give him a distribution charge.

They gave him a possession instead. The judge gave him five years. He did three and that's when he met his good friend, Jerry.

He said, "When I got home from doing my bid all I had to do was leave my number with his sister and wait."

He called Jerry's sister, left his number and six months later he got a call from Jerry to meet him in South Carolina. The rest was history.

"Being the man is too much. All I wanted to do is live good, enjoy life and be able to provide for my family," he said as he touched my leg. "I always refused to serve the street niggas, I would rather break it down and serve the fiends."

My mom was a fiend. Damn!

"If you in the streets, why not serve the street niggas, too?" I wanted to know everything about this man's game.

"The crack smokers need you, the street niggas can replace the main man in two ways: death or jail, plus you can always find you a new connect."

I understood exactly what he was saying, but I couldn't stop thinking about me joining the game. I was old enough to figure out what I wanted to do with my life and at that point, I wanted to hustle, fuck shaking my ass, again.

After we got to SC, he used his phone to place a call.

"Aite, I'll see you in twenty flat."

SC wasn't anything different than Lynchburg. Shit! It had good and bad parts just like any other place.

We met up with Jerry at a car shop named Choppa City, where I watched as they took the inside of the Impala's door off. When they finished, they stuffed cocaine wrapped in bleach with black pepper paper towels inside of the panels. They lined everything back up perfect, and the window went up and down without any problems.

Tamaine paid Jerry his money and we hit the highway back home.

"You want me to drive?" I asked him when we stopped to get gas.

"You think you can handle it?"

"There ain't nothing that I can't handle, baby." I told him as I sat in the driver seat. I adjusted myself and waited for him to enter the car.

Hours later, we made it home safe. I parked the car in the driveway and woke my King up with a kiss.

"How did you find the way back?"

"GPS, baby!" I held my phone up and exited the car.

I then dashed for the front door. I had to pee so damn bad!

When I came from out of the bathroom, Tamaine was still outside. I watched him through the kitchen window as I cooked us something to eat.

He took the doors apart, got his shit and then put the doors back together.

By the time dinner was finished, so was he. He threw the packages on the kitchen counter and I shared his food out. *Lemon pepper shrimp with seasoned rice.*

We ate at the kitchen table and talked with each other.

My life had really been complicated, both of my parents died when I was young and I was left to continue my mother's childhood pattern of being in foster care.

Devastated by my mom's death, I stopped talking. I wouldn't talk at school or at the center. The only time I would speak was when I visited her grave at the community center on Polk Street, so having Tamaine in my life was a blessing. He allowed me to open up and express myself to him about all the shit that I had been through.

All I had was him, and he knew that. All I needed was him, and he felt that!

"So you want to hit the block with me, too?" I lit up like a Christmas tree.

"Hell yeah!" I jumped up, almost knocking the table over. "All I want to do is have your back," I told him as I sat in his lap, with my feet locked behind the chair.

"I know that's all you want to do, baby." He kissed me on my forehead and scooped me up off him.

"So run it down to me."

"Aite." He looked at me with a smile on his face before he continued.

"There is 36 ounces in a brick, but in the streets they call it a whole chicken or a bird. A half a bird is 18 ounces, that's 504 grams. An ounce or a zone is 28 grams. A half, otherwise known as half time is 14 grams. A Mike Vick is 7 grams, also a quarter. Then there is 3.5 grams, that's an eight ball but they say 8th Street."

I listened to him as he got his hands on the boxes of Arm & Hammer baking soda. The hot water on the stove was bubbling when he reached under the kitchen sink and got a big ass glass bowl.

"This right here," he said as he brought it up to my eye level, "is a Pyrex bowl. It doesn't break even with hot water."

I stood to the side so I could see just right.

"Half a chicken," he told me what was in the bag, pouring the white substances inside the bowl. "It was all solid but I broke it down by hitting it against the outside wall. No lumps the better it gets done and faster, too." I shook my head. "I only got a brick today."

I let his words soak inside of my head. After telling me that, he went to work.

He made sure again that there weren't any solid chunks inside of the bowl and then he poured two whole boxes of baking soda inside of the container. Using a metal butter knife, he stirred it all together.

The scent was so strong I had to cover my nose with my shirt.

He picked up the bowl so it would be closer to the stove. He held the handle of the pot and emptied it into the bowl. His hands were moving so fast.

Stirring it all together, I watched how it soaked up water and the baking soda, together. He ran over to the sink and turned the cold water on and then went back to the big bowl.

"Put more water in the pot, put it back on the stove and turn it on high." I moved as his sentence was finished, trying not to be in his way as I followed directions.

"You getting a free lesson," his crazy ass told me.

"Glad you think you're the teacher." He eyed me and chuckled at my comment.

He had the bowl in the sink as he let the water run off of his fingers into the bowl. The color wasn't white anymore, but the shade of butter. Within seconds, it wasn't liquid anymore but solid chunks.

"This right here, baby," he said looking at me, "this shit right here is the truth!" Shaking my head at his excited ass was all I could do.

Seeing enough, I walked off. I was in need of some rest. I went to our bed. The strong scent had me dizzy.

Jamaica

Chapter 3
Let Me Try

I talked Tamaine into letting me hit the block with him, and I was ecstatic.

"This shit is not for you," he lectured, but I couldn't even remember all that he said 'cause it went in one ear and flew out of the other.

We were at our kitchen table and he was cutting down what he had created into small pieces with a razor blade. He would then drop a piece in the side of the sandwich bag, tie a knot around it, position it inside his mouth and use his teeth to cut it off.

"Damn, why don't you use a knife or something to cut it?" I asked him.

"Too much time," he said as he spat it out into his hand and dropped it on the table.

After the crack was bagged up, he put all of the small pieces in one bag, tied it and gave it to me. Looking at him all confused, I questioned his ass? "Where am I going to put it?"

He laughed at me, but I didn't find that shit funny.

"In ya pussy," was his reply. I didn't question him. I put the bag inside another bag and put it where he said. With a little wiggle, it slipped in perfectly. I could even walk just like normal.

From there we headed to his house on Jackson Street. It was a trap spot and crackheads came to both buy and smoke their dope, but they had to pay to party.

"Murdoc, all I got is $15 to my name," this female told him.

"So what the fuck you telling me?" He asked her with his hands in his pockets.

"I can't go home and do this shit," she had tears in her eyes. "I don't want my daughter to see me getting high."

"I don't give a fuck about that shit! That's your muthafuckin' problem," he took his left hand out of his pocket and pointed at himself, "not mine."

The way he talked to her gave me chills. I was glad he didn't talk to me like that.

"You want the shit or not?" He growled.

"Can I smoke it here and pay you double next time?"

He took a step back and looked at the figure in front of him before he spoke. "Bitch, take ya fuckin' money somewhere else, before I beat ya ass for disrespecting me!"

She didn't utter another word. She held her head down and I had to wonder if it was from shame or not getting what she wanted.

I noticed the lady was old enough to be my mother. My mind always went back to my mom, especially when I saw someone who faced an ugly drug addiction like hers. I couldn't help it.

Hours had passed and so many people had stopped by. His three cousins on his dad's side, even his boys from the hood. They smoked weed, talked shit and just chilled. Most of the time after having seen so many addicts pass through, I would be in my own world thinking about my mom and her addiction.

"We going to Park Ave., okay?" Tamaine told me after we had sat around getting money for a few hours. I was cool with it because whatever he said went.

Park Ave. on a hot summer evening jumped like fire crackers on the 4th of July and then some. Crack heads were everywhere.

"Damn, this shit smell like water," he said, smelling the bag after I had taken it out of my pussy and gave it to him.

"You know it!" The extra bag that was on it was for my own purpose. The way the shit smelled in the kitchen I didn't want my pussy smelling like that.

From there, I watched his every move. Even though other drug dealers were out there, most of the customers came to him.

"This shit is the fiya." One returning fiend told him.

"I already know!" He bragged.

Niggas were posted all over the streets. Whenever a car or a fiend came down the block, niggas' hands were already on their package tryna get that Jolla for themselves, but they looked out for each other when it came to 12.

I had them extra eyes for Tamaine, looking for the police and his unknown haters, too.

"I like having you out here with me," he said after he had finished making a sale. He knew, unlike anyone that he may have trusted, that I for sure had his back.

I took the bag back from him and pushed it inside of my panties, sitting it right under the entrance of my heaven. So, God forbid, if the police pulled up all I had to do was push it up in me.

The power of a pussy.

"And I'm loving being out here with you, too." I was the only female out there with her man, and I liked that.

"Where ya strap at?"

He patted his side. "You sure you don't want me holding it for you?" I asked him.

"Naw, boo, I got it!" He slapped my ass as a fiend from earlier turned the corner. I dipped my hand in my oven and pulled the bag out handing it back to him.

"Murdoc, can I get 2 for 30?" The short black lady asked.

"Come on, Mary, you killin' me here, yo."

"Shit, you know I bring that money, though." She had a New York accent.

"Yea, that you do."

"I got the John parked 'round back," she said as she pointed around the corner. "Imma suck his ass dry by tonight."

"You wild!" Tamaine told her.

She laughed as he gave her two pieces off of that fiya.

"I get high. He gets pussy!" And with that she walked off.

Hearing everyone refer to him by his alias made me question its origin. "Where the hell you came up with the name *Murdoc* and why you use that name?" I asked when the fiend was a distance away.

He looked over at his boyz at the top of the hill before he focused back on me. "Shit, I was watching some show and the name came up, so when I hit the block, I didn't want to use my real name out here so I ran with Murdoc. And it's harder to identify someone with a name that's not on their birth certificate."

"Five 0! Five 0!" A nigga from the top of the hill yelled.

"Give me the strap!" I barked at him. He passed it to me and I tucked it in the waist of my jeans. I dropped my big tee shirt back over my jeans and walked off, leaving Murdoc standing there. If he ran, then that gave 12 reason to fuck with him. So he played cool and I walked away from the spot.

Niggas was throwing their shit in the bushes and running into apartments. Me, I just walked and didn't look back, for all the police knew I was just out enjoying a walk.

I reached the top of the hill when my phone rang.

"Shit clear!"

I turned back around and headed toward my man. When I reached him, I said, "That's why you need me with you all the time."

All he did was smile and reach for his gun.

When he was almost out, he looked at me and suddenly said, "You know, I think I'll come out here at night and you can come out here in the daytime."

Now he was talking what I wanted to hear, but I had a better solution.

"Nah, one of us can always be in the car sleeping. We'll never miss the money and we'll be out here together, still."

I could see that he liked my suggestion, because a wide grin came onto his face. He kissed me on my lips and grabbed my ass.

"I'm done for the night, so let's bounce so I can beat the pussy up real good and start the day tomorrow just like we planned."

On the ride home, we talked about our new mission and how we were gonna take the game over.

"Oh, yea, we gotta be careful because the police station is only six blocks away from where we hustle, Love."

"Fuck 'em!" was my statement. "Ain't no time for me to get scared now!"

Chapter 4
Money, Baby

I could recall my very first 8 ball of crack. It was given to me by Tamaine. I broke that shit all the way down, right there on the block, without a scale or a razor blade. I was a natural.

I used my mouth and the plastic bag that it was in. And by the time I was done, my entire mouth piece was numb as hell. I didn't care, though, my mind was on getting money.

There was a lot of drug dealers, but not everyone had what me and my boo had.

All the smokers came to us. Our names spread like wildfire. It was unbelievable, but we kept that fucking fiya product.

We took turns with the block, some days I'd pull an all-nighter and half of the next day, and he would relieve me. The niggas on the block gave me mad respect. For one, I was Murdoc's girl and two, I was the only girl brave enough to stand out there and get it in.

Tamaine said Dre, a big time nigga from the block, told him how he saw the way I handled the situation when 5-0 had pulled up that time. He expressed his mad respect for me, but I was just doing what any thoroughbred bitch would.

As Tamaine noticed others peeping me, he decided it was time to teach me how to use a gun.

"You gotta learn how to use this bitch," he said, showing me the Glock .40. "As a female, you got the upper hand on the block. There ain't too many female officers, and the male police can't search you, so you have enough time to haul ass."

"Meaning?" I asked him as he loaded the Glock up, wearing leather gloves.

"Shiddd, you gonna take off running, you get far enough and out of sight, you toss that bitch!"

I soaked his lessons up, bit by bit.

"As I was saying, another reason I need you with that thang on you at all times is because no nigga expects for you to be strapped, so you got the upper hand on their underestimation." He cocked the barrel back and continued teaching me on how to properly dump on nigga.

"And after you do that, all you gotta do is pull the trigger. That muthafucka gonna talk for you!"

For two hours nonstop, he taught me how to load and unload and everything in between.

"And when you cock the hammer back, what you do?" He quizzed me.

"I pull that fuckin' trigger and don't stop until I am satisfied."

A smile was plastered over his face, and I was happy that he was teaching me street life, raw.

***

Sunday had arrived and in keeping tradition, I visited my mom's grave.

Before doing so, I dropped Tamaine off of on Park Ave. so he could handle his business as I took care of mine.

As soon as I arrived at the cemetery, I felt emotional. Not a day passed that I didn't miss Queen. I was only a small child when she left me but the time we shared impregnated me with a love comparable to none.

I told her what I had been up to. It made no sense to lie since she was with me everywhere I went. I'm sure she was disappointed in my choices but the way her love was set up, she'd never turn her back on me.

I knelt down at her tombstone, caressing the scribe embedded on the slate. "Mom, I've been missing you so bad. Your beautiful smile, your scent, the strength of your hugs. Everything about you…"

I continued pouring out my heart, as I always did, until I got a call from Tamaine.

"Hello." I answered, wondering why he'd bother me but the urgency in his voice told me what time of day it was.

I listened to him as he screamed into the phone. Instinctively, I walked toward the car at full speed, alarmed at what I was hearing.

I ended the call, telling him I was on my way but I swiftly turned around because I had forgotten to tell my moms something. I yelled out. "Our love is bulletproof."

I locked eyes on her spot in the earth and then I jumped into the Impala and hit the gas as I raced to my man. I hit all the back roads trying to get to him as quick as possible.

I dialed his number when I got close. "Where you at?"

"By Ed's house." He was out of breath and then I heard gun shots.

My left hand was on the steering wheel as I reached over and pulled the .45 out of the glove box.

"I'm right here." I replied but by this time, the call was disconnected.

"Fuck!"

Boom!

I almost lost control of the car as my back window was blown the fuck out. I bust back out that bitch, hoping I hit whoever the fuck that shot my shit out.

What the fuck is going on? I questioned as I pulled into a war zone.

My mind was racing, but Tamaine had prepared me for shit like this, so there was no way I was gonna let him down.

I was leaning down, but I could still see the road. As soon as I passed Ed's house, Tamaine jumped in front the car. I mashed on the brakes almost sending me out the fucking windshield.

"Lay on the hood!" I yelled.

He held unto the car as I sped away from the scene. I turned the block and stopped so he could get in the car.

"What the fuck happened?" I asked him as I handed the .45 over to him.

"Go to Shannon's house." He was heatedly looking back behind us.

"What the fuck happened?" I repeated myself.

"Me and the nigga, KC, got into it over a fucking sale. Muthafucka ain't want the garbage he got, so the nigga got in his feelings and started talking shit. I let the nigga have his words 'cause I wasn't strapped."

Two blocks away, I was backing into Shannon's driveway as Tamaine continued to talk.

"The sale came back again and the nigga clapped at the pipe head, so I walked off but he wasn't letting shit go that easy."

"Fuck that shit! That nigga done fucked with you and he jacked the car up. I know you gonna let us pay that pussy a visit." I was mad as hell, muthafucka could have shot me."

Shannon must have heard us pull up because she opened her front door and we exited the car when we saw her standing there.

He walked up on her. "I need to park this right here," he said pointing to the car, "and borrow yours?"

"For how long?" She was already tweaking. Her lips were shaking, as she rubbed her hands together.

"For the night!"

"Give me a block."

He didn't say shit else, she walked back into the house as he pulled the block out of the bag.

Tamaine rationed out seven dubs. That equaled $140.

In exchange, she tossed him the keys and then he handed her the fiya.

"Rick gonna come and replace that shit!" He yelled to her, but she was no longer at the door. "Let's go!"

I got into her burgundy Ford Taurus and started the engine.

Later that night, we paid KC's mom's crib a visit. It was past midnight. We had searched the block looking for his ass, but no luck, so we decided to hit him where it would hurt.

Tamaine leaned out of the passenger window and emptied his .45 into the house as I reversed down the block.

"Pussy ass nigga got me fucked up!" Tamaine said as we left the bullet riddled house.

The next day, KC didn't turn up on the block 'cause I was waiting for his ass. Fuck a sale! I was ready to catch a body. His!

Days turned into weeks and weeks into a month. News spread around the city but muthafuckas didn't really know who had done the shit to KC's crib.

Word had also circulated that no one was home, so that was a blessing on their end, but it still sent a message to his bitch ass, nonetheless.

I was posted up as usual when Tamaine said, "You can't be out there on the block like that with me."

"Why, Tamaine?"

"'Cuz this nigga is somewhere plotting, so just give ya number out and go from there!"

I resisted his instructions, at first. But then I figured he was protecting me from danger and since I loved my life, I took his advice.

I built my clientele up over a few months and then I dipped from the streets and started using my phone to conduct business.

With that, my relationship with Tamaine got crazy. Seemingly out of the blue, he became very overly protective and insanely jealous. After that, the mental abuse followed. And right around the corner from that came the physical abuse. The nigga started changing more than a chameleon and I didn't know what the fuck was going on with him.

One morning, he started tripping really hard.

Jerking me awake, he asked accusingly, "Yo, what time you got back last night?"

"What the fuck?" I said as I tried picking the blanket up off of the floor.

"Bitch, you heard me!"

"Bitch? Oh, that's how we're doing it now?" I questioned his choice of words.

"Did I muthafuckin' stutter?" he spat.

I threw the blanket back on the floor and walked off. Shit, I shouldn't have done that. The nigga wrapped his hands around my neck from the behind.

"Get off m…" I screamed only to be slammed face first into the wall. A picture of us together fell off of it beside me.

"What. Fuckin'. Time. You. Got. Back?" he said into my ear. He let up with the pressure from around my neck so I could answer him.

Blood trickled from my nose unto my shirt and then the floor.

"Brenda called for a block at," I brought my left hand up to my nose and pinched it shut, trying to stop the bloody mess, *"one o' clock. I bagged it up, drove the four blocks to her house and back."*

"I bet!" Unfounded distrust dripped from his response.

"I tried to wake you up, but you didn't budge." He let go of my neck and I turned around with my hands in the air to face the man who claimed he loved me. *"The money is on the kitchen table."* I pointed in its direction.

His eyes showed no sign of apology. I stepped over the picture and left him standing there looking at the blood on the floor. I couldn't believe he was the same person that I had put my life in danger for.

From that moment on to make him happy, I'd let him go to the block by himself and I would only answer the phone in the day time and when he was awake.

I learned that Tamaine had found a new habit. PCP, to be exact. That explained his episodes of wilding out on me. On top of that, he'd stay out all night and all day, then he would come home and accuse me of cheating, which I never did.

I could handle everything, including the drug use, but that beating my ass shit I just couldn't get down with.

One night, we made a run together and on the way back home, we stopped at the Exxon to get some gas. He sent me inside to go pay for it.

On the way out of the store, a Chevy Caprice pulled up in front of the store with four niggas inside. The driver held the door open for me on my way out, so I told him thank you but kept it moving.

I got in the car and waited so Tamaine could finish pumping the gas. When he got inside of the car, his fist connected with my ribs without warning. I bent over in pain, only to have him two piece me in my head. Using my hands, I tried to cover my head to block his blows.

"Bitch, you got me fucked up!" He told me as he let the engine come alive.

I kept my head in my lap, holding both my head and my rib.

"What are you talking about?" I cried.

"You real disrespectful, bitch! You was flirting with them bitch ass niggas!" He floored the gas pedal and we peeled out of the gas station.

At no point did I make a plea to prove my innocence. It didn't matter.

In the end, he knew he was wrong and he thought dicking me down would remove all the scars that he gave me. After every ass whooping, he would beg me not to leave him and tell me how sorry he was, that it would never happen again.

I distanced myself from his sex and when we did do something, I would fake my nut or I would wear a pad just so he wouldn't touch me.

I really wish I could have read his brain before he got a hold of my heart.

The ass whoopings became more frequent and much more violent as the months passed. And that muthafucka would act like I was supposed to just forget that he had fucked me up.

"My mom wants us to come over for Christmas," he told me two days after he'd blacked my right eye for some imaginary shit he'd made up in his mind. I was supposed to be sleeping with one of the niggas from the hood.

I wasn't in the mood to visit anyone but neither was I in the mood to duck his fists. So I got dressed, covering my swollen eye with a pair of black shades. As I did so, I thought, *I know my mother is looking down from heaven, shaking her head.*

Murdoc must've seen the sad expression on my face. "What's up?" he asked.

"I'm going to visit my mom's grave." Fuck waiting on his feed-back. I just slammed the door on the way out.

After spending a couple of hours at my mom's gravesite, I left feeling better than before. Even from heaven, she had a way of making me feel her unconditional love.

A half an hour later, I arrived at home and Tamaine's car was nowhere in sight. He didn't even call much less text me to let me know he'd be gone.

It was cool with me, though.

I did the laundry, cooked and cleaned the entire house and there was still no sign of him. I ate, took a shower and still he never showed up, at least not until early the next morning.

As soon as the bedroom door creaked open, I turned and looked at the alarm clock, 6:06 a.m. He climbed into the bed, I was pretending to be asleep, 'till he put his hands on my body. The room was dark, but that didn't stop my nose from working. Irish Spring. He smelled fresh, like he'd just taken a shower.

With my eyes still closed, I spoke into the darkness, "Hey."

He pulled me into his arms and kissed my forehead. "I'm so sorry for all the shit I've been putting you through," his voice was hoarse. "You don't deserve this shit from me. I'm not worthy of you."

Even though I'd heard it before, this time felt different. His words had emotions coming from them. I wrapped my arms around him and I rested my head on his chest. He had me mentally and emotionally drained, but my heart still fluttered for him, so I went with my heart.

Christmas day, after spending a few hours shopping, we went to his mom's house. Everyone was there: his mom and her husband, his stepbrother and his girlfriend, one of his aunts and her three kids.

His mom, Ms. Julia, was in the kitchen finishing up the last of the food when I entered the room. From the time that I've spent with her, I'd grown to love her beautiful spirit. I really wish my mom was still alive, they would have clicked.

"Thanks for the gift," she said as she called me over to her with her hand.

"No problem." I walked over and hugged her.

"Why is it that you still wearing shades in the house?" She got right to the point. I inhaled some air, the food smelled so good that my stomach growled like a mad dog. Not knowing what to say, I just stood there. She reached over and took them off of my face, and I didn't stop her. She gasped when she saw and pulled me into her embrace. Feeling the motherly love from her, I broke down and cried in her presence. She patted my back like I was a baby, and I let her. "My son did this to you?" She let me go to look at my face again. The tears just poured like a river, but I nodded my head confirming that he did. "I raised him better than that. He knows no woman deserves to be abused. None!"

My mom probably would've killed his ass if she was alive. "Don't sit around and let him do this to you. I understand that you might love him, but love doesn't include pain and hurt." Her words made me cry harder. It was nothing but the truth. "If any man put his hands on me, I'd kill him and tell the judge I did it."

That made me smile and seeing me smile made her smile, too, but she continued to lecture me. "Yes, he is my son, but you don't need him if he's beating on you."

Every word made sense.

"I'm truly sorry that you're going through this shit with his ass."

QBanga, his step brother, walked in and saw my face before I had the chance to slide my shades back on. All he did was shake his head in disbelief.

"Give us some time, Q," his mom said firmly. She didn't have to repeat herself. He bounced, silently.

She put my shades back on and asked me to help her with the finishing touches for dinner.

Overall, we had a good time. Ms. Julia gave Tamaine the cold shoulder the entire time, and I figured he knew why. I helped her clean up the kitchen after everyone had left.

During that time, we talked about my family, mostly my mom, and she told me no matter what I could always depend or call her if I needed her for anything.

"I know I am not your mom, but you can call me Mom, if you like." That alone made me love her more. I knew God placed me in Tamaine's life for a reason. Now I had a mom.

Tamaine was sitting in the living room when we were done cleaning the kitchen, talking to QBanga.

"You ready to go?" He tugged me into his lap. His mom stood back and watched. She knew I loved her son. He took the shades off and kissed my fucked up eye.

Ms. Julia looked at Tamaine in a motherly way. "You better start treating her good, don't let the devil control you to the point that you abuse the ones who love you, boy." She warned him before saying good night and leaving us.

QBanga had his head down. I wasn't sure why, though.

"I'm ready." I told him. Tears welled up in his eyes. His mother's words had touched him, apparently.

When we got home, I gave him his gifts. Two pair of Timberlands, one peanut butter and the other black. Two pair of Air Force 1's, one white and one black, both high tops and two fitted hats both with the VA logo.

"Thanks, baby," he told me as he dropped to his knees. His left hand dug into his pocket and came out with a black box. "I know how much I love you and I have a fucked up way of showing you, but know my heart beats for you, only."

His mom's words must have really...

He cut my train of thought off.

"I want to spend the rest of my life with you, so will you marry me?" he proposed.

Not wasting any time, I screamed and dropped to my knees. "Yessss!"

I hoped after I became his wife, he would stop the abuse and learn to appreciate me more. I was hopeful, at least, because deep down I truly loved him.

He kissed me and put the ring on my finger at the same time.

And I dreamed that better days were ahead.

Chapter 5
2007

Shit was absurd when the New Year came around. Days would go by and Tamaine wouldn't even show his face at home, not to mention the fact that he never called when he'd be M.I.A. I would drive through every hood looking for his no good ass, but he was nowhere to be found.

I know now that his proposal didn't mean change after all.

I kept hearing my mom's words over and over in my head. *"No matter what happens, promise me that you'll take care of yourself. Never settle for less! Never let a man belittle or take advantage of you!"*

Literally, every single thing switched with that nigga. When he did come home, I would find condoms in his pockets as well as text messages from other bitches in his phone. Questioning him about the shit wouldn't have did anything but caused a fight. One where I'd end up getting my ass kicked. So, I bit my tongue but began to plot.

When he ran the streets doing what he did, I ran the streets chasing money with the drugs that I would steal from his packages.

I ran into Dre, the big-time nigga from the block a few times, and every time he saw me he would tell me how he respected my hustle as a female. He would also make a few comments like: *Don't let shit get in ya way with ya paper* and *You got a mean ass street hustle for a nigga to be doing you dirty.*

I knew he was referring to Murdoc. I didn't consider it telling me dirt on him but more as a look out for myself.

The only time Murdoc called me, his fiancé, these days was when he was in danger or in trouble with the law and as the loyal, down ass bitch that I was, I was there.

And whenever he was home, all we did was fight because I eventually confronted him about the other bitches that I was sure he was fucking with. It would start with angry words but always ended up with him putting his hands on me.

"Who the fuck is you to question me, huh?" He held me down on the bed with my face in the blanket. Every time I would lift my head up to get some air he would put pressure on my neck so I would have to stay down. He also had my hands pinned between his knees on my lower back to suppress me.

"I'm," down my head went, "sorry." When I came up for air, he pushed my shit back down again. I got tired of fighting with him. "Fuck it! Kill me!" I huffed loud enough for his ass to hear me. I was fucking tired of living with his abuse.

I didn't know what he put over my head, but all I could see was darkness. I closed my eyes to welcome it. I wanted to see my mom, anyways. I held my breath to make the process go faster, but he let the load up of me and rolled me over unto my back. I was almost there. I saw flashing lights. But then...

Whap!

He smacked the shit out of me, and my eyes flew open.

Whap!

My head twisted to the left, facing the wall. Gripping my face with his left hand, he choked me with his right hand. I didn't want to fight back because I knew it would be worse, so I laid there looking up at the man who proposed to me not too long ago.

He bent down and licked my face with his tongue until he got to my ear. "You belong to me, so get ya shit together before I kill you!"

This wasn't the same nigga that I had met years ago.

I had to get away from him fast, but how could I get rid of him?

He had finally let go of me and fixed his clothes. I remained still until I heard the front door slam with a bang. As I fumbled to get up, I got a glance of my reflection in the mirror. My hair was all over my head, but that was the least of my worries. My face was severely swollen. I then checked my teeth. All there. That was a blessing because I thought a few would have popped out from the blows to the face.

Pain rushed all through my body. I staggered into the bathroom to get to the medicine cabinet above the sink for some pain killers. I swallowed like five Tylenols with a handful of water and then I blacked out, hitting the side of the tub on my way down.

When I came back to my senses, I was tucked inside of my bed with an ice pack on my forehead.

The room was dark, but the door was cracked so a bit of light found its way in.

Trying to sit up was painful. "Ohhh," I exhaled loudly. "Fuck!" I gave up trying to move.

I was so focused on the pain that shot through my body, I didn't become aware of the fact that someone else was there.

"Love, can you hear me?" Ms. Julia's voice was so welcoming. "I'm glad you're awake. I've been waiting on you for hours." I could hear the tenderness in her speech.

"What happened?" I licked my lips. They were so dry that they cracked when I spoke.

"Tamaine called me and told me you weren't answering his phone calls."

He puts on such a fuckin' show! I thought.

"I asked him why and he told me what had taken place." Her hands were massaging my arms gently and slowly. I closed my eyes but opened them when she stopped stroking me. "I am going to fix you a bowl of that food that I've been cooking," she then disappeared from beside me.

I fought the pain that rushed through my body until my back was against the headboard of the bed, as stabbing cramps lingered all over my back.

Ms. Julia returned with a nice bowl of stewed chicken and white rice. "Just relax, I'm going to feed you." But I wanted to do it myself so I told her *no.*

"Please just let me do it." I could tell that I'd hurt her feelings, but I had to do that for myself because I refused to let that nigga turn me into an invalid.

With all the strength I had in me, I lifted the fork to my mouth. It took me almost two hours to finish the bowl, but I did it.

"How about you stay with me and my husband for a while, Love?"

The question caught me off guard, but that was the only way it seemed like I could get away from Murdoc's crazy ass.

"Okay." I agreed without second guessing.

I told her what to pack up for me.

As I eyeballed her, it looked as though my mom was still alive, the way she cared for me and all. And thinking about Queen made me smile.

It was after seven when we got to her house. Tamaine had called me four times before I'd gotten myself situated.

"You're welcome to stay as long as you like," Ms. Julia said as she ran my bath water.

"Thank you so very much."

Giving me the clearance that I needed, she left. Sitting in the warmth of the water stung the bruised parts of my body at first but then it was all soothed away slowly by the heat.

I relaxed a little and a sense of comfort came over me. My phone rang on top of the toilet, but I didn't have to look to see who it was.

I let it ring and ring until it got on my last nerve. Then I reached over and powered it off.

I soaked my body for an hour and every time the water got cold, I would turn the hot water back on. Feeling at peace, I said a prayer. "Lord, give me the strength to leave him alone. I love him, but I love me more." I said the words, but I knew that was a lie. I loved him more than I loved myself. "Lord, I feel like I can't live without him." The tears splashed into the water beneath me. "Change him back to the way he used to be, please!"

A sudden knock at the bathroom door caused me to jump up, scared to death.

"Yes?" My voice reflected the shake from the startle I experience ed.

"Are you okay in there, Love?"

"Yes, I'm okay, Ms. Julia." I sighed in and eased back into the tub.

I finally began washing washing my body when I heard, "This too shall pass, Love," she was still at the door.

I remembered one night, for some strange reason I couldn't sleep, so I crept out of my room toward the kitchen only to hear my mom crying and talking. Her door was cracked, but I couldn't see inside 'cause it was pitch black.

"I'm tired of smoking this shit every day, I'm tired of living a lie. I need help, I need it now!" Her voice cracked, and her cries grew louder. *"Lord, I've tried everything to get this shit out of my life. If I continue to keep doing it, I just hope it will take me away from pain."*

"It will!" I responded to Ms. Julia.

I wasn't gonna sit around and let Murdoc's dog ass kill me because I loved him. My mom gave up on life, but I wasn't gonna let Murdoc be the death of me.

I got myself together and exited the bathroom and thanked God my bathroom was inside of my bedroom. I didn't want to see Mr. Gates, Ms. Julia's husband, again until my face was healed all the way.

The way his mouth had flown open when I walked through the front door showed his immediate anger. He worked his hands together, wringing them tightly. He looked from his wife's face to mine before he even said a word.

"He wanna fight a woman but not a man? He's such a bitch!" That was the first time I had ever heard him curse.

I turned my phone back on when I got in bed. I had twenty text messages on my regular phone.

Love, I'm sorry. Please talk 2 me.

Don't leave me like this!

I had eighteen more just like that.

Ms. Julia walked in the room to say good night and she said that she had spoken to son, but she'd never told him she'd taken me in or knew where I was.

I knew he was wondering and flipping out 'cause I'd left the car and packed up some of my clothes. His ass was getting some of his very own medicine. I bet if he could have gotten his hands on me at the moment, I would be a dead bitch for not answering his calls or returning his texts.

"Thank you," was all I could say.

"If my daughter was alive I would want someone to do the same for her if she was in trouble." Ms. Julia sighed heavily at the thought of her child.

That night, I slept so well that I didn't even want to get up to use the bathroom in the morning, but I did. My face looked worse than it had yesterday, but I still smiled. Even though my face was battered, I refused to let him take my spirit down, too.

"Love, breakfast is ready," she spoke as she entered the room with a tray in her hand. *Fried apples, turkey bacon and fried eggs with a glass of orange juice.*

"Thank you."

"Don't thank me, it's the least I can do," she said with love in her voice as she placed the tray on my bed and opened the curtains. "Beautiful, Sunday!"

Time had run away from me. I had to visit my mom again but with a fucked up face. Ms. Julia had seen the sadness, so I told her what was wrong as I filled my stomach up.

"I'll take you after church. Get some more rest and we'll go when I get back."

"Thank you." I didn't know what else to say to her.

"If you need anything while I'm gone, text me and I'll get it when church service is over and by the way, Tamaine doesn't have a key to my house. So don't worry."

Thank God.

"You'll be here by yourself," with that, she was gone to praise the Lord.

After eating breakfast, I checked my phone. All of my missed calls were from Tamaine.

My battery was dying, so I got my charger and plugged it up and left it on silent. All he kept saying over and over again in his text messages to me was how sorry he was and that he would go get help.

I cried and cried until I had cried myself to sleep.

Months passed, and I still hadn't moved back with Murdoc but by now he knew that I was staying at his mother's.

We still trapped together almost every day but I was holding out on going back to him completely.

But as a little more time went by, he became the gentle loving man that he was when we first met. We spent a lot of time together, and my love for him began to blot out all of his transgressions. I felt like I was falling in love with him all over again.

"I want you back home, where you belong," he said with pleading eyes.

"Give me a few days to think about it and I'll let you know."

"Cool, I can wait." He responded with a smile.

We had to crawl before we started walking again. I hoped that all that bullshit we had been through so far would make us stronger.

I loved this new understanding person he had become, and I prayed he would remain that way.

For the next two days, I received red roses along with touching, heartfelt notes. His sweetness melted me like soft ice cream on a hot summer day.

When he asked if I had decided if I was coming back home, my answer was quick.

"Yes, I'm coming home with you, baby."

His mom was happy that he'd changed and sad that I was leaving because our bond had become real tight. A mother and daughter type of love.

I just crossed my fingers and hoped that her son wouldn't revert back to man that had drove me to her house with his abusive ways.

Jamaica

Chapter 6
Trappin' Time

Moving back into the house with Tamaine was extremely different, at least it was for the first six months. We did everything together. Where he went, I was there but sweet shit doesn't last forever, and I discovered that I couldn't teach an old dog new muthafuckin' tricks.

The more money we made the less he started coming home. I knew he had other bitches but I resigned myself to the idea that shit like that came with the game. More money. More bitches. Same gotdamn shit as before!

Murdoc wasn't doing much for me beside giving me a nut every now and then, if I let him. He ran the streets night and day, and every dime he made out there, he spent it on unnecessary shit. I guess flossing became just as addictive to him as crack was to the smokers.

***

December of 2007

I was on the verge of leaving his black ass again but then I found out I was pregnant. I was so dehydrated that I'd gotten sick really bad. I couldn't keep anything down that I ate, so Ms. Julia drove me to Lynchburg hospital and there we found out I was three weeks pregnant.

"Oh, I'm going to be a grandma." Ms. Julia hugged me with enthusiasm.

I text Tamaine to let him know I needed him home ASAP. He assured me he would be there before I arrived.

Ms. Julia talked my head off the whole way back to my place, but none of what she talked about worried me. I was just hoping that Tamaine would be excited.

"Make sure you call me and tell me what he says," she said, smiling as she dropped me off.

True to his word. Tamaine was already home.

"I sure will." I leaned over and kissed her cheek.

Tamaine was sitting in the living room, rolling up a blunt when I walked in the door.

"What's up, baby?" He acknowledged me as he licked the blunt.

I sat across from him. "I'm pregnant!" My tone was low but firm.

He took his lighter from out of his pocket to dry his relaxer. He then put it in his mouth and set fire to the end. I took my J's off and put my feet on the table.

"You ready for this?" He coughed as smoke escaped from his mouth and nose.

"We," I pointed back and forth, "knew what we were doing, so we have to be ready, together." I told him feeling sick to my stomach.

I dashed out of the room with my hands covering my mouth. I got to the bathroom just before I emptied my stomach.

"Ughhhh." He stood behind me, holding my hair out of my face and rubbing my back.

"My baby pregnant, fa real," he said with a laugh. I took my head out of the commode to look up at him. A big ass grin was covering his face.

"Bluuuhhh!," I dropped my head back down.

He flushed the shit down. "Let me get you a washcloth so I can clean you up."

I grabbed my ponytail so it wouldn't get in my way. It felt like everything that I'd ate was flushed, so I stood up slowly wiping my mouth with my left hand.

"You better brush ya teeth before you try to kiss me." I took the wash rag out of his hand and threw it at him. Then I brushed my teeth. He couldn't stop laughing and smiling at me.

"I hope it's a boy," he said as he stroked my flat stomach.

With the toothbrush inside of my mouth, I responded. "I want a girl, first."

"Shit, how many you want?"

I held up both of my hands, showing him all of my fingers.

"What?" He yelled at me. I brushed my tongue looking at him. "Ten, fa real?" I nodded my head *yes*. "Remember that when you pushing this one out."

I spit the water out of my mouth. "Whatever."

He had his hands wrapped around me from the back, seeing our image in the mirror in front of us caused me to smile. In that moment I felt complete.

"I love you."

He pulled my head onto his chest and then bent down and kissed my forehead. "I love you, baby ma."

"Baby ma?" I held my left hand up to remind him that he'd proposed to me.

"I love you, wifey." He corrected himself.

Just hearing him saying that had me melting. I turned my body around and kissed him.

***

Two weeks later

The devil returned in Tamaine. He was all the way back to his old ways, from coming home late with less money in his pockets to cussing me out and snorting powder.

I found dollar bills rolled tight with cocaine inside of them. I knew it was cocaine 'cause I tasted it and it made my tongue numb.

He would be real paranoid, looking out of the windows of our house every five seconds. His palms were always sweating and he couldn't sit still. I stayed as far out of his way as possible, but he would always have an outburst.

"I'm not ready for no baby, so get rid of that shit," he yelled at me from across the room, out of the blue.

"Well, guess what? I'm not getting rid of it, so fucking..." he cut my words off with a two piece to my belly. I dropped to my knees holding my stomach. "Get rid of it! Or I will!" I was hunched over in pain, praying that my baby was okay. "And I mean it, too, bitch!"

Every time he finished beating me, he would leave. Today was no different. I laid right there on the cold floor in the fetal position praying.

"Lord, this ungrateful piece of shit doesn't love me!" Tears flooded the floor beneath me. After a good ten minutes, I picked myself up. I went to the bathroom hoping that nothing would be in my panties. Before I got my shorts off, I said a few words to the man above. "Don't let me down like this."

I held my breath as I sat on the soft cushioned seat. I unfolded the toilet paper and wiped, nothing. For twenty minutes, I stayed in the same spot, wiping and hoping no blood would show up.

I tapped my stomach. "Stay with me. I'm going to get us through this shit!" I hit the shower and began to plan our escape.

I wasn't worried about Tamaine coming home. That day, I had made up my mind that I would be fighting back, baby and all. I wasn't fighting back for myself but for my unborn.

The next day, on the block, I ran across my real nigga, Dre. It was time to trap off my own supply and not Murdoc's. I didn't tell him my plan then and there but I stored his number in my trap phone for a later time and under a smoker's name 'cause if Murdoc had found out I even had his number, I wouldn't be breathing.

The following day when Tamaine was out, I picked up my phone to call him. As I pressed send on his number, I rubbed my belly, "This is for us!"

"Hello?" he answered.

"This Dre?"

"Who this?"

"Love."

"Oh yea! What's up, baby girl?"

I felt butterflies and I laid my hand over my stomach. "I need to holla at you."

"Aite."

Twenty minutes later, I was sitting at the car wash on Lakeside Drive, talking to Dre. I kept me and Murdoc's business out of it, but everything else was the truth.

I needed a plug or some work, but either way I needed help. He was really hesitant, until I told him I was pregnant and I had to get a place before the baby was born. I had to cop small because I had to see what his product was like first, so I got me an eight ball.

He came through and only charged me a $100.00. *What a come up!*

The next day, I got me a crib. It was a two bedroom, one bathroom, kitchen, living room with a basement on Mclvor Street for $425/month.

I paid the deposit and first month's rent.

Two weeks had passed and still no Tamaine, thank God. That nigga wasn't worried if I was alive or not. His actions alone showed that he didn't give a fuck about me.

I moved into my house with nothing but my clothes. I was starting from the bottom. I didn't need shit from Murdoc, including the money we hustled together.

One night, I got a sale for $100. They didn't have the money, but they did have a '98 four door, gold Honda Civic. I took it.

Dre's dope was that damn good. Motherfuckers sold their ride to get high. *Damn!*

I took the car that Murdoc had got me and parked it in front of his house and left. I never even got a phone call from him, questioning why I did that. Nothing.

I didn't need the distractions, so it was all good. It was time to come up any fuckin' way.

In a short time, I went from 8 balls to quarters and then a half to an ounce.

"Damn, baby girl, you doing ya thing." Dre told me after I handed him $800.00.

"At least you know I'm not playing no more."

Seconds later, my phone rang.

"Love," I answered after seeing Ms. Julia's name on the screen. "Yes."

"Hold on," the phone got quiet and then I heard, "Love!"
Damn! Murdoc's voice.

"What?" I answered annoyed.

Dre gave me the *call him* sign for me to hit him before he bounced.

"I'm locked up."

I stopped putting the dishes away. *"Locked up?"* I repeated. "Where at? For what?" Suddenly I was worried.

"Calm down. I'm downtown for drinking and driving," he said calm as ever.

"How long have you been there?"

"Two days."

"Two days, nigga? So where the fuck was you at before that?" I heard him breathing hard. "Not right now." He had the fucking nerve to tell me, so I ended the call.

I dialed his mom's house number and I sat on the floor by the stove.

"Hello," she answered on the second ring.

"I have to move all his furniture and things into ya basement." She was silent, so I continued to talk. "I am not living there no more."

I removed the ring off of my finger that her son had gave me and looked at it disdainfully.

"Why?"

"Oh, he didn't tell you?" I asked her knowing damn well he didn't, so I told her.

"Is the baby, okay?"

"Yes." I answered her firmly.

"Ok, I'll call his stepbrother and stepfather."

We planned to meet up the next day at his house to move everything out. I finished putting my dishes away and cleaned my living room. I'd gotten a deal on the kitchen set, living room and bedroom set for twenty-five hundred from Rent a Center.

When everything was spotless, I headed to the bathroom to take a hot bath and relax for bed when my cell phone rang.

"You have a prepaid collect call from, 'Murdoc'. His voice came after. "To accept press zero."

I pressed zero.

"Baby, I know you mad but listen to me, please," I took my clothes off as I ran the tub water. "I need you to come see me tomorrow at eight a.m. That's my visitation."

"You need me to..." he cut me off by raising his voice.

"Damn, I'm begging you."

"Tell me where the fuck you was at? And don't fucking lie to me either." I heard him when he chuckled because he knew if he was out I wouldn't be talking like that to him.

"When you fucking get here tomorrow. I'll. Fucking. Tell. You!"

"The caller has hung up." The operator relayed to my ear.

***

The next day

I was up at 6 a.m. getting dressed to go see his ass. By 7:15 I was out of the door.

I parked my car in College Hill parking lot and walked to the jail across the street. I entered the lobby where there was a desk with two officers and a computer.

"I'm here to see Tamaine Davidson," I said.

"Your ID, please." The fat male officer asked me, while the skinny lady was filing her false nails down. I pulled my ID out of my back pocket and handed it to him. "Take a seat, over there," he said, pointing toward the waiting area.

I was the only person there, but not for long. By 8 o'clock the place was packed. Everyone from babies to grandmas were present.

The skinny officer then came from around the desk and called out the names from a list in her hand.

"Jenkins, booth 1, Austin #2, Taylor #3," as she said the names I got up and followed the other ladies.

After six names, we walked through a scanner. The first three ladies got through just fine but the lady before me had to leave her belt at the desk.

"I'm pregnant," I told the officer before I walked through it.

"Come around," she said, waving me over to her. She had a metal wand that she glided over my body. The other ladies walked through as the rest stood by the elevator.

The door opened and we all entered together. The old lady pressed six and the door slid shut. As soon as we got off of the elevator, I noticed there were sections blocked off by a wall on each side. Men in orange jumpers were behind the glass with phones in their hands. I walked to the last booth in the first section and there he was, smiling.

I picked the phone up.

"You looking good pregnant."

I sat on the stool. Not in the mood for his bullshit. I ignored his ass and hammered him with my own question. "So tell me where the fuck you been at?"

"I went out of town to meet up with this new nigga to cop some shit. The nigga had me on a goose mission for two days, so I headed back to the 'Burg." He couldn't even look me in my eyes.

I put the phone down and got up to leave.

Boom!

He'd punched the glass and gestured for me to sit down and pick up the phone. Looking at him made me sick, but I sat down and picked it back up, anyway.

"If you gonna lie, tell that shit to somebody that's gonna listen." He dropped his head but when he tilted it up and looked at me, tears were running down his face.

"I've been fucking..." the words seemed to stick in his throat as tears continue to roll down his face. The hand that I held the phone with was shaking uncontrollably and his eyes danced around from my face to my hand. "I was fucking with this bitch."

"Does this bitch got a name?" Rage had my feet dancing under me.

"Keisha."

The name didn't ring in my head, but I wanted to know who this bitch, Keisha, was.

"She's my stepfather's sister's daughter!"

My mouth dropped open, not believing what I was hearing.

"Your cousin?"

"We not blood, Love!" He screamed at me.

"Nigga, it doesn't matter what the fuck you say, y'all are related!" I had my index finger pointed at the glass in his face.

He went on to tell me how they'd been fucking around for months. Neither his stepfather nor his step aunt knew anything about it. He said he told Keisha that their little fling had to end because I was carrying his seed and he wanted to be with me 'cause I held his heart captive.

Keisha then flipped the fuck out and he terminated her with an ass beating from hell. He said he fucked her up so damn bad that her lips looked like twenty bees stung her at one time.

"She can't even see out of her eyes, yo," he said like I should have given a fuck.

"You act like you in love with the bitch! Shit, did you ever feel sorry for me when you beat my ass?" There weren't no more tears from his ass now. "Hell no!" I answered the question for him.

"Six minutes left." A female guard yelled behind him.

He continued to state that after he'd assaulted her, he'd left but he'd gotten stopped two blocks from our house by the police.

"And?" I twisted my lips.

"They charged me with domestic violence, assault and battery. I go to court Friday at ten."

"This Friday?"

"Yea." His voice was low. I didn't know what to say to the shit I just learned.

To hear him tell me all that shit, I felt something break inside of me. *What the fuck have I done to deserve all that shit from him,* I thought.

"Time is up." The damn guard yelled.

"I love you, Love."

I dropped the phone and turned around to exit the place without saying a word to him.

When I got back downstairs and back to the lobby, I asked how I could put money on his account. The lady said all I had to do was fill out a money slip form and give her the money. I'd get get a receipt and the funds would be on his account before the day was over.

I gave her two hundred dollars, got my proof of deposit and got the hell out of that place.

On my way home, I stopped at the Dollar General and picked up a few writing materials along with some post cards.

I hadn't eaten shit all day, so I drove to the Chinese place, King's House on Memorial Ave. and got me some stewed chicken and broccoli before I went home.

Then my text went off. It was Ms. Julia.

Love, we'll meet you over at the house at 3.

Damn, I'd forgotten all about moving the things out of his house.

I text Ms. Julia back: *Ok, I just got back from seeing your son. I'll talk to you when I see you.*

In a bit of a rush to eat, I didn't even chew my food, let alone taste it. I swallowed it. The baby must've been real hungry, I thought.

Hours later, we transported the whole house except for the building itself to his mom's place and his other crib on Jackson Street.

Days later, I went to his court date on Friday where they gave him six months, with nothing suspended.

"Don't worry, I'm gonna ride this wave with you," I said, during our visit after he'd gotten sentenced.

I gave him my word, and my actions had my words' back.

Every Wednesday morning, I was there sharp and on time. When the calls came, I answered even in my sleep. I took pictures of myself daily and I made sure he had mail.

I was six months pregnant with a little girl and trapping harder than the devil in red. Once I was hell bent on something, there was no stopping me. I would sleep in my car with my phone hooked up so it would stay charged. And every time my trap phone rang it was a scale, so I was never at a standstill.

Tamaine told me on a visit how he'd had all his money over at Keisha's crib.

"Let her have that shit! We good over here!"

I wasn't pushing any weight, I was just serving the fiends: two dollars, five, ten, twenty sacks, whatever they desired I had it. I appreciated them and they loved me in return. Making them happy was my goal and keeping my finances heavy was my formula.

In two days, I'd only had three hours' worth of sleep, but I was going to have a baby girl and she had to be straight. Plus, there was Tamaine.

As months passed, Tamaine only had twelve days left before he got released.

Auto Extra off of Old Forest Road had an all-white 1993 Chevy Bubble Caprice on 24's on sale for 5 stacks and I wanted him to have it, so I copped that thing for him.

I knew I was doing things right 'cause after I got that joint and drove it through the hoods, Dre called me.

"Mane, niggas mad right now!" His comment had me baffled.

"Why's that?"

'Nigga's was stacking their money up so they could buy that pretty thing I heard you pushing." His statement caused me to laugh in his ear. "They hating hard on you lil' mama."

"Fuck 'em! Let them hate!" He burst out laughing and ended our conversation.

If you got haters, that means you doing something right.

Two days before my baby daddy hit the streets, I went and picked up the Chevy from the car shop behind Kenny's on Park Ave. I had a blue and Orange two tone paint job done, plus the checkered dash board to top it off. Inside was the same as the outside but with a thump.

I took that shit for a spin and had heads doing 360° turns.

On his release day, I picked his ass up in that bad boy.

"Who's shit is this?" He asked as the jail gate closed behind him.

I was leaning against the passenger door and his eyes was like *wow!* "Whose you think it is?" I held my arms wide open so he could hug me.

"What's up, baby?" He kissed my big ass belly and then my lips. I held him for a few seconds and then out he went.

"A welcome home gift from us to you." I rubbed my stomach. He walked around the car twice, touching and rubbing that shit down. "This is dope, Love. I mean, I heard you doing big things. Ya name is ringing all through that jail."

That didn't surprise me. I was the only female out there doing what niggas was wishing they could do. See I was a born hustler, natural survivor, seed of a gangsta and I put that on my momma.

"Let's get the fuck out of here before these muthafuckas change their minds!"

He jumped into the passenger seat. The nigga started the car before I even got inside and the system banged.

Sometime later, people from across the street in the College Hill apartment complex came out to see if it was a live marching band outside, but it was just us.

I looked over at Tamaine, wearing a smile of pride. Yea, the nigga cheated on me but I overlooked that shit like nothing happened because I was a sucker for him. I knew it and couldn't help it.

I was in love with him all over again. He was my one weakness, and I would have killed the Pope if he asked me to.

Damn!

Chapter 7
Nothing Last 4 Ever

Even though I was way pregnant that didn't stop him from fighting me. He started creeping again with the bitch, Keisha, who put him in jail.

I went through his phone and busted them out. See, what was done in the dark always came to light.

"I'm not going through this shit with you again. You want that bitch? You can have her, but you won't have me, too!" I called myself taking a stance.

Whap!

The first blow to my face caught me off guard. I stumbled by the stairs but regained my balance. I turned my body toward the basement so he wouldn't hit my belly and I took the blows to the back of my head like a boxer.

My hands helped me out a little but not much. Next thing I knew the nigga was trying to push me down the stairs. I held my arms out to hold onto the wall. He pushed me twice and I rocked back and forth.

Instead of just standing there taking punches like a beating bag, I ran down the stairs, praying that I didn't fall.

When I got to the bottom, I looked up at him with hate. He didn't come down there 'cause he was too busy looking for my drugs and money.

I locked myself in the laundry room until I heard the twin pipes on the Caprice. My head pounded from all his lies, fuck the beating.

Mental abuse was worse.

I called his mom and she came over. When I opened the door for her, she held her mouth with her hand.

"I'm fine!" I said before she had the chance to say a word.

"No the hell you are not!" She screamed at me and I hugged her as I pushed the door closed.

"The baby's still moving. He can't stop this show, Ma." That was the first time I ever called her that, and she smiled to hear it.

"I'm gonna call the police," she was reaching for her phone.

"No," I took it out of her hands and refused. "Hell no!"

"Why?" She was looking at me like I was stupid.

I had to tell her the truth, that was the only way. So, I sat her down in the bathroom while I nursed my face the best I could.

I gave it to her raw and uncut and not one time did she interrupt me.

I watched her close her eyes and I figured she was saying a prayer for me. I told her about our first trip together and how I'd gotten my own connect.

"Please don't judge me," I said in tears in front of her. 'I've got to do this for my child. I refuse to have her go without, but I'm gonna try and get a job after I give birth."

"Okay." She stayed and helped me pack all Murdoc's clothes and clean the place from his searching ass.

Unfortunately, he found the whole chicken of cocaine that I had and the $15,000 I had with the brick, I had $10,000 inside my daughter's room under her mattress but he didn't look there.

I heard his mom talking on her phone in the kitchen, lowly. "You ever come near her again. I'm going to call the police on you my damn self." I heard the pain in her voice. Never in a million years did I want his mom to be against him. "From this day forward, I don't even know who you are. And you're not welcome in my house anymore."

By the time I emerged from the bedroom, her face was wet. I took her hand and sat it on my stomach, her granddaughter moved for her and that made her tears dry up.

Murdoc never came back around. Dre told me how he'd seen him and some high yellow bitch out at Club Phase 2 stunting in the car that I tricked out for him.

When I told Dre what happened, he didn't second guess me. That was one of the realest niggas I'd ever met. He then gave me a whole brick and charged me half price.

"I heard you bustin' ya hammer at fiends, too." He said with a laugh.

"Damn right, my nigga! If I let one muthafucka get away with it then they all gonna try me." He understood what I was saying. "And that goes for them street niggas, too. I've been through too much shit to let another human being take me down. Dealing with Murdoc has turned a bitch's heart cold to these streets."

"Get ya money back up, yo, and stunt hard on that nigga, along with the rest of them hating ass niggas out there," he said after he dropped off the bird to me. But before I closed the door, he hit me with the realest statement ever.

"Love, you gonna be the Queen of Lynchburg mark my words!"

That's all I needed to hear, and it motivated me.

Jamaica

Chapter 8
August 2008

It was in the heart of summer when I gave birth to my baby girl, whom I named Tameia Queen Jenkins. She came into this world kicking and wailing and looking just like a mixture of me and her daddy.

"Love, she's beautiful." Ms. Julia told me when she flew from my pussy.

She'd been with me from the jump. She'd called Murdoc to the hospital per my request when I went into labor. I didn't want him to miss his first child's birth, but I later wished I hadn't.

After he saw her come out, he left but that was fine with me.

Ms. Julia cut the umbilical cord in his place. I wished my mom was there, but I had Ms. Julia for the moment.

Looking at Tameia for the first time made me bawl, but with happiness. I finally had someone to love that I knew would love me back. My child.

Snow, my long-time friend from the center I grew up in, showed up with a lot of gifts. She was so happy for me. We caught up on everything that was taking place in her life. She was engaged and I was to be her maid of honor. She'd found herself an older black dude in his 40's.

"Girl, he treats me so good. He rubs my feet, cooks, cleans, works, I don't have to lift a finger if I don't want to."

I was so happy for her because she was rightfully due that. As for myself, I was going to find happiness on my gotdamn own. It was all about me and the little princess I had just given birth to.

As I laid in there listening to Snow talk with so much excitement, I couldn't help but recall seeing Murdoc through rosy glasses of my own. But those days were long gone. That muthafucka wasn't shit, and I was not going to fool myself into thinking otherwise.

I smiled for my girl and her situation but I knew that in order for me to have what I needed for me and mine, I had to put on my game face and become the force in the game Dre prophesied I would be.

Jamaica

Chapter 9
What a Bitch

After spending three days in that damn hospital, I was ready to get home to my own space. So when I got discharged from the hospital, Ms. Julia dropped me and Tameia off at home.

Reality hadn't hit me until I'd put her to sleep that night. I found myself crying in the bathroom as my body slid down the wall. I knew my world had changed, but I was hoping that it had changed for the better.

That same night a sale hit me up.

"I have $400. Can you hook me up?"

"Of course!" *Four hundred dollars? Who's turning that down? Not me.*

I'd been fucking with this fiend named Ann for almost a year.

When I was sick or needed to make a run she would drive me, so I presumed shit was sweet. I gave her the address to my house, not thinking nothing bad about it.

With my daughter beside me on the couch, because she had woken up, I served the bitch the 4 grams she was looking for. I broke all the rules. Every last one! The 1st rule was broken by letting the bitch know where I rested my head. The 2nd rule, I served her inside and the 3rd, I did it in front of my daughter.

Something told me that I would later regret that but I wanted that cheddar too bad to let the opportunity to slip by. I just hoped Lady Luck would protect me from my recklessness.

September 2nd

Weeks passed without any repercussions, but just when I relaxed and began not to worry over my mistake, that bitch, Lady Luck, turned her back on me.

I was sleeping peacefully, when a loud, intrusive knock woke me up. Me and Ms. Julia was fast asleep in the bedroom. I'd been up all night making them chips, while she watched her grandbaby for me.

The police had the kind of knock that even if you're deaf you were still going to hear it, and it was one of those knocks that morning.

"Ma, the police at the door." I whispered to her as I woke her up.

"How you know?"

"I just know. Tell them I'm not here." I had a feeling that my time was running short.

"Okay." She picked Tameia up from between us off of the bed still sleeping in her arms.

I watched her leave the room and I glanced at the photo of my daughter on my nightstand. I heard them ask for me and she responded that I wasn't there and that I had a doctor's appointment.

"Give her this card for me when she gets back home."

"I sure will," she told them and closed the door.

All damn day, I didn't even answer my trap phone. I text Snow and told her what was going on and she reminded me no matter what that she had my back.

I called Tamaine and told him he had to come to my house. He showed up thirty minutes later, with a hicky on his neck. I didn't even question him about it. I wasn't fucking him.

I explained the situation to him and he said no matter what we had going on that he had me and his daughter's back.

The crazy part was that he was scared shitless for me but I wasn't even anxious for myself. I had expected it. I just didn't expect it that soon.

Around seven that evening, I called the number on the card that the-officer had left. The lady who answered the phone informed me that someone would be there momentarily to see me.

As soon as I put the phone down, there was that knock again from earlier. Ms. Julia and her son's face showed nothing but sorrow. I unbolted the door and yanked it open. The fucking street was flooded with police cars. Blue and red lights flashed but that didn't faze me at all.

"What's your name?" The white officer standing at the door interrogated me. He had his hand on his gun.

"Love Jenkins." Bitch ass cracker already knew my name.

"Step outside!" His team member demanded.

My feet didn't even hit the front porch before five bitch made crackers rushed me. "You're under arrest!"

They had me faced toward the wall with my hands behind my back as they cuffed me.

"May I ask why I'm under arrest?" My face was mashed against the wall by one of them pussies.

The officer to my left spoke. "Your name came up in our investigation, so we're taking you downtown to find some things out."

"Can I kiss my daughter before I go?"

"Yea, you can. This will probably be the last time before you do it again. But that all depends on how you play ya cards."

Ms. Julia brought my daughter to me. She was wide awake, just looking at the bright colorful lights that flashed around her. I kissed her soft lips and Murdoc whispered in my ear, "Imma meet you downtown."

They stashed me away in the back of the squad car with my hands still cuffed behind my back. I already knew what time it was.

My name rang more bells in the dope game than six churches on Sunday.

Jamaica

Chapter 10
They 'Bout 2 Find Out

The ride was quick. Instead of taking me to the booking center, they took me to building 9 on Court Street. They escorted me into the building through the side door. The first door to the left had the word *Narcotics* spelled out on it. The one to the right said *Homicide*. They housed me in the narcotics' room but moved my cuffs in front of me.

The only furniture in the quartered section was a black desk and two chairs. A camera in the far right corner of the ceiling looked dead at me. I held my middle finger up to it.

I had a pair of short shorts on, showing off my new tattoo: my daughter's original foot prints and a white wife beater with my J's.

I slouched in the chair as I let my legs shake. Then a tall, black haired, blue eyed, white, skinny bitch entered the room.

"My name is Detective Gant. Do you know why you are here?" The bitch asked me.

I gave her that look like *bitch, if I knew*. She took the seat behind the desk with a brown folder in her hand.

"So you still don't know..." her face was in the papers. I paused her ass.

"If I did, I would have answered you the first time." She moved her eyes up to me.

"Okay, smart ass! On July 3rd, a confidential informant working with Lynchburg Police Department made a controlled drug purchase from you for $60.00." I sold so many $60's that day it could have been anybody.

I just looked at the bitch hoping she would hurry the fuck up and do what she had to do.

"On August 20th, the same confidential informant working with the LPD made a controlled drug purchased of crack cocaine from you for four hundred dollars." She took her eyes from the paper and looked me dead in mines. "Your newborn baby was next to you on the sofa during the drug transaction."

Ann got me! That was the only sale I made that day.

"Your charge is 2 counts of distribution of crack cocaine and 1 charge of child neglect."

I was taking care of my child and they gave me a child neglect charge? What a system!

"You can get out of all of this if you cooperate with us."

"Cooperate?" I asked her to make sure I'd heard her correctly.

"Yes!" She closed the file on the table and pulled a tape recorder out of her pocket. "Tell us who you get your drugs from and all of your charges will be wiped away." The bitch was dead ass serious, too. I looked at her then at the folder and then to my daughter's footprints. I didn't even say a word, so she continued. "We have you on audio, along with the baby crying." I kept my face solid, poker player all day. "You can walk out of here free and go back to your baby." My face dropped and my eyes studied my tattoo. "Or you can go to jail, the choice is yours!"

I'd miss my daughter, but loyalty was a must. "Book me."

"Think about it, Miss Jenkins."

Fuck!

I took my eyes off of the footprints and stared her in those blue eyes of hers. "Is you going to keep talking or you going to take me to jail?"

She studied me hard and rolled her eyes. She then put the papers back in the folder, grabbed the recorder, stood up and walk to the door. "Just know child service will be in contact with you," she said before closing the door behind herself. I didn't even look in her direction. *Fuck her!*

One thing about me that the system was going to learn was that I was *the last of a dying breed* and loyalty was priceless.

Chapter 11
Do the Crime, Do the Time

There it was, seventeen days after I had given birth to my child and I was a sitting duck in a jail cell, waiting to be judged by another human being.

It was either break down or woman up. I man'd up!

I called Murdoc once they denied my bond. "They ain't give me no bond."

"Who this?"

"It's ya baby ma, nigga! I said they ain't give me no bond." I heard him relaying the message to his mom. "You aite, though?"

"How the fuck you expect me to be okay and I just gave birth? I'm still fucking bleeding!" Angry at his question, I told him to pass the phone to his mom. When she got on the line, I got teary eyed and shit. I cleared my throat and exhaled. "Ma, I'm not coming home."

"Love," she tried to stop me, but I had to talk fast and get shit situated quick.

"Just listen, please," she said *okay*, so I continued. "I'm going to be in here for a minute," I heard her gasp for air, telling Murdoc to get the baby. "Please take care of my daughter for me." A running water hose didn't have shit on my eyes. "Social Service is gonna contact you. I am gonna give you full custody of Tameia until I come home. I refuse to let her into the system or let your son take her. At least with you, he can visit or whatever. But I need you to promise me that you'll always know where she's at if she goes with him and you'll treat her like your o..." I didn't even get the word *own* out good enough before she spoke.

"I promise." That's all I needed to hear and know.

"Put the phone by her ears for me." I heard her shifting the phone around. "Tameia, I love you," my shirt looked like I'd just took a swim. I was soaked in tears. "No matter what, always know that!" The lady walked back over to me and signaled with her hand that I had to hang up. I nodded my head at her. "I love you!" And I put the phone on its base.

"You gonna be photo'd and dressed out, so I need for you to stand over there on those footprints and look at the camera in front of you." She used her finger the whole time telling me what I was going to be doing.

This process took twenty minutes. I had to do fingerprints, too.

Stripping me out was crazy. I had to take all of my clothes off, bloody pad, too. I had to squat, open my ass cheeks and cough in front of a female officer.

"Here is some pads for her." Another female guard said, handing her some shitty brand for me.

They gave me white panties, one white sports bra and a bright ass one-piece orange jump suit, that had buttons from my neck to my pussy.

"When can I use the phone again?"

"Tomorrow when you get to the block." She was really nice to me, so I didn't push the issue.

After I was dressed and padded up, I was escorted to a room that had a bed on the floor and a toilet with a sink beside it.

When she closed the door, the tears came back.

Back and forth, I paced the cell for what seemed liked hours.

All kind of thoughts ran through my head: *How much time was I going to get? My baby girl? How my mom would be going ham if she was alive?*

That night I cried myself to sleep. I woke up sitting on the bed with my back against the door.

"Man on the floor!" Someone yelled.

I rubbed my swollen eyes with the back of my hands. A section in the door flew open and the person had disappeared.

A tall, black ass nigga in the same shit as me stood at the door.

He put his face to the slot and spoke, "You Love?" I nodded my head *yes*. He said, "Jigga, Lil David, Loe, Garry, and a couple niggas in D pod said keep ya head up!" And then he was gone.

I didn't know none of the names he had mentioned.

In twenty seconds, he was back with a tray with food on it.

"What time is it?" I asked.

"It's 5:45 in the morning," was his response. He left the tray on the metal trap.

The breakfast that morning was two pancakes, two boiled eggs and some watered down syrup in one of the sections of the tray. I drank the two bags of milk and ate one pancake, but I crushed the two boiled eggs.

I had to change my pad so I stuck my head in the slot but it wouldn't fit so I just put my face to it so someone could hear me.

"Miss!" I yelled loud enough to get the attention of the lady at the desk.

She walked over to me and I explained my situation to her. She left and came back with some more pads for me.

"You can flush them in the toilet?" I turned around and looked at the shit but when I turned back, she was gone.

That same day, I was placed in general population with sixty-two other female inmates. There were plenty of bunk beds. Mattresses on the floor everywhere, two toilets, two showers, two phones and two desks. One TV was attached to the wall, two sinks and a podium for the guard to stand watch.

"How I use the phone?" I asked a short light skinned, pretty bitch.

"Where the paper they gave you at from down stairs?" she said with a mellow southern accent.

I gave her the paper, and she showed me how to use the phone. The other inmates were doing their own thing.

I called Ms. Julia, first. She was so excited to hear from me. She informed me that money was already on her and Murdoc's phone. The baby was doing great and they would be down there to see me in the morning. They'd figured it all out.

Tameia was asleep, so I talked to Murdoc 'cause he was around.

"Hold ya head up. I'm gonna ride this with you, baby." His tone wasn't solid. It was all cracked up, and he was breathing too hard for me to take him serious.

"I hear you, but don't worry about me, take care of our daughter."

Sixty seconds left. The operator came on over the phone.

"Kiss her for me, please."

"I love you and I will!" he said, but I didn't respond.

I ended the call. My second night in jail wasn't bad. The high yellow, pretty bitch was cool. Her name was La'Tasha but she went by Flowsicka.

We talked the whole night. Both of our beds were on the floor so we put them beside each other. She said she'd heard my name in the streets from both the fiends and the street niggas, but she'd never seen me.

"Love stay with the fiya!" That's what she said the fiends said. And I did. "The street niggas, they love how 1 hunnid you are! Claiming you go harder than a lot of niggas!"

I couldn't wait to get this shit behind me so I could hit the streets running again. *Damn!*

Flowsicka had been in there for a week, but only had to do six months for a pound of weed. I told her all about my life from start 'til then and she did the same. We clicked just like that.

When morning came, we were still up talking.

After breakfast, I took a shower, washed my ass and brushed my teeth. I'd braided my hair into two since I was downstairs.

Around 10, the guard yelled. "Jenkins.

I looked at Flowsicka and she said I had a visit.

It was just like how I'd visited Murdoc. Behind the glass was Tameia and her grandma. When Ms. Julia held her up to the glass, I kissed it. She smiled and that took the cake. My swollen eyes opened. Her grandma was crying, too. she put her in her arm, gave her a bottle and picked the phone up.

"Thanks for coming to see me." Snot ran down my face and I used the jumper to wipe that shit away. We talked and she said that social service had already come by her house that morning. We touched on a lot more and the time flew by fast.

I cried like a baby when she left. I couldn't wait for them social service fuckers to come see me so I could tell them my daughter was going with her grandma. *Fuck their system!*

The guard didn't take me out of the booth 'cause I had another visitor. Murdoc. He looked so sexy, just like how I met him.

"How are you doing?" My head went down with the phone by my ear. "Pick that shit up, Love." I lifted my head up and smiled. I needed that from him. "You too strong for this shit to break you!" I never said a thing our whole visit. I listened to everything he said, though. All of his promises and dreams and how he wished he could do my time for me.

Our visit ended and time moved along.

A month later and shit was bitter. Murdoc stopped coming with his mom and our child to visit me. Every time. I tried calling him, he would ignore my calls, except for the one time he answered. "Damn, you can't even come see me?" I blasted at him as soon as he accepted the call.

"Mane, I've been fuckin' busy," he whispered into the phone. So, I turned the volume up on the jail phone.

"When the last time you seen ya daughter?"

"I'm over here now with her."

"Let me talk to ya mom, then."

"She downstairs asleep."

I heard a door squeaked, so I asked him where he was in the house. He never got to respond to me but I heard a female's voice yelling, "Baby, you want..." and the call ended.

I knew his ass wasn't at his mom's house because I'd just finish talking to her before I rang his line. She said he hadn't been over there in weeks. Every time she called him to get the baby, he said he would but never showed up.

All the loyalty, love and support I expressed to him during his little time and when he was free and I wasn't, it went out the window.

Murdoc's driver license was suspended, but he always drove. One day, we were on our way to make a sale when the police hit the lights behind us. I had 4 dubs in my mouth as I sat in the front seat.

"Mane, I ain't pulling over!" he said.

Thinking fast, I told him he could pull over but take off running.

"What you gonna do?" He started wiping the steering wheel down with the bottom of his T-shirt.

"Let me worry about that."

He turned on Taylor Street and hit the brake so fast that I almost went through the windshield, but my seat belt kept me in place. He was out the car before it stopped moving. I watched as he ran through someone's backyard. He had two shirts on but by the time he was out of my view he was shirtless.

I swallowed the dubs down with my spit. Police cars were everywhere.

"Who was driving?" Dick rider #1 asked me.

"I don't know."

"You don't know, but you sitting in the front seat with ya shoes off."

They were pulling me out the car like an animal.

"I was walking and dude just stopped and asked me if I needed a ride."

They were describing him over the radio. "Black male, shirtless."

Two hours turned into six and I was sitting in Blue Ridge. They didn't find Murdoc, and they couldn't prove that I knew him either and I was sticking to my word, *"I was walking and dude just stopped and asked me if I needed a ride."*

With nothing to charge me with and no history of a record, they let me go. When I got home, Murdoc was there waiting on me. I told him everything. He said Shannon had called her car in stolen. But overall, I had his back.

My best friend, Snow, had written me a letter. So to take my mind off of his sorry ass, I penned her back.

Snow,

Girl, thanks for the pictures of the baby. I'm glad that Ms. Julia allows you to see her. How are you doing? How is ya other 1/2?

Shit is crazy but you already know I'm holding my head above water with my toes flat. I know this letter is all over the place but stay with me :) Thank you for standing beside me. My 1ˢᵗ court hearing is next month on the 11ᵗʰ at 9:30am. I'm not nervous at all, fuck it, it is what it is. I met this cool ass bitch, Flowsicka. I know ya ears be ringing off the hook 'cause I talk about you all the time.

Thanks for the money and I got the book Trust No Man by Ca$h, I haven't started reading it yet but I will. I got you on the next letter. I love you and loyalty is always priceless.

XoXo,
Love

At my court hearing, the only people who showed up was Ms. Julia, Dre and Snow. No fucking Murdoc in view. I was given a court appointed lawyer to represent me. I'd told Ms. Julia and Snow that I wasn't going to pay no lawyer no hell of a lot of money 'cause I was guilty.

The next day, my lawyer, Matt Forbes, came to see me, He let me see and hear my motion of discovery. Hearing my daughter crying on the recorder had me feeling like shit.

"This is your first time ever in trouble, so it won't be as bad."

"This shit is already bad, I'm in here trying to provide for my family, fuck you mean?" Heat was coming off of me.

He didn't even pay my statement any attention. Instead, he continued his speech. "The most you can get is five years."

"Five years!" I jumped up off of the stool in the booth and slammed my left hand on the glass, holding up five fingers. "Five fucking years!" All I could do was shake my head.

"Ms. Jenkins, calm down," he said in a smooth tone.

I sat back down and looked at this white, red headed man. He couldn't be older than thirty, if that. When I was seated, he flipped some papers over in his file.

"You can work something out with the Lynchburg Police Department."

I dropped the phone and covered my face with both of my hands. Snitching was something that never entered my mind and with that, I let that white muthafucka have it.

"Bitch, I'm not saying shit." I said that shit real slow so his ass could understand every word that was coming out of my mouth. "If that's what the police waiting on, tell them I said hold their breath." The guard was outside of the door waiting so when she saw me at the door, she knew I was ready to go back to the pod. "Fuck the system! They can kiss my black ass," I said on my way out the door.

I then told Flowsicka all about the visit.

"Mane, half the streets get picked up 'cause a snitch sell their soul. The police don't do no work." She talked with her hands. "And a nigga will tell faster than a bitch, too."

My next court date was in December. I plead guilty to all charges. Every week, Ms. Julia made sure she was there to see me with Tameia. Social Service didn't come see me 'cause I saved them the trip. I wrote a letter saying I gave full custody to Ms. Julia and got it notarized and mailed it to them.

Sentencing day came quick. On Friday, February 13th, I was sentenced to five years' incarceration with three years suspended for the dope charges and child neglect.

My driver's license was suspended for six months, shit, I never had the chance to get it. Once I learned how to drive, I said fuck that card. The court imposed an 18-month term of probation and a $100.00 fine.

Out of the 24 months, all I had to do was 17. When the judge handed down his judgement, Snow screamed out no so damn loud that they escorted her out of the court room.

Ms. Julia had tears running down her pretty face. She mouthed to me, *stay strong!*

Murdoc had fallen of the map. I didn't even cry. There was no reason to. I'd expected the shit to be worse. Seventeen months was nothing. I told myself, *You're a real bitch. You can do that lil' time standing on your head.*

No doubt, that was true. But the flip side of that coin was that I had my daughter to think about.

Chapter 12
2009

Flowsicka had left me to go home two days before I got shipped to a level 4 Women's Correctional Center in Troy, Virginia. Fluvanna.

The population was 4,000 inmates. I was housed in Building 1A intake. Our uniforms were a light sky blue so the officers called us The Smurfs. Our hair couldn't touch our shoulders and if it did they would tell us to go to comso and get it cut. If we didn't, then we would be put in the special housing unit also known as the SHU.

My first visit was so special because Tameia was trying to walk. Ms. Julia, her husband and Snow made the trip to see me.

Every time I tried to get Tameia to come to me she would cry. She didn't know me. Ms. Julia tried to convince me that she would in time because they had my photos all over their house and referred to me as mommie.

Snow filled me in about Murdoc. He and Keisha were an item even though he was beating her ass bad. She said he was selling and doing Ecstasy pills like crazy. I'm glad he left that *white girl*, cocaine, alone.

He had the nerve to tell her one day in River Ridge Mall how he was holding me down with everything from mail, money to visits. She said some other shit I couldn't even believe.

I asked his mom if I sent a letter to her house would she give it to him when he decided to visit his daughter and she said okay.

We took four pictures together as a family and before they left, Ms. Julia's husband whispered in my ear. "You a hell of a woman. Don't do your time with that boy on your mind."

When I got back to my room after I stripped, squatted and coughed, I took all my pain and hurt out on the paper.

Murdoc,
You don't deserve to get a word out of me but I need to get this shit off my chest. Here I am doing a bid and you are nowhere in sight. Fuck me? Nah fuck you! Fuck you and that bitch that you fucking. I heard you got the bitch wearing my clothes, sleeping in my bed and

driving my car. Damn, she wanna be like me that bad? You're one disrespectful, ungrateful fucker. Every dog got a day coming and before I close my eyes your ass gonna pay. I don't care if it cost me my life. I'll die a happy bitch paying you back, you pussy ass woman beater!

I sealed the letter up and dropped it off in the mail box.

Flowsicka had gone home and kept her word with me. Every week I got a letter and a $50 money order from her with pictures of her and her boyfriend, Maurice.

In one of her letters she mentioned to me that her nigga had a brother named Murda and he wanted to get to know me, so I told her to hook me up.

My first letter from Murda was him telling me all about himself.

He was 39 years old and I was 21. He had 9 kids, 8 baby mothers, 5 girls and 4 boys. The pictures that were enclosed in my letters of him were okay. He wasn't fine like Denzel Washington, but he wasn't ugly like Dave Chapel, either.

He did 7 years in prison for drugs and he'd been out for 4 years. He moved from Harrisonburg to Lynchburg with his brother a year ago. He had a chick that he was messing with but it wasn't serious and they had an open relationship. When he wanted pussy, he got it. When she wanted dick, she got it. It was how they get down.

On top of things with him, my peoples, Dre, always sent me a card every month with a $500 money order but no return address was on it so I could never send a thank you card.

With Snow, Flowsicka, Dre, Ms. Julia and her husband in my corner, I didn't want or need for shit, but my freedom.

Chapter 13
January 14th

I was released from prison. Flowsicka and Snow were there to pick me up.

"Mane, I'm so damn glad you finally home!" Flowsicka told me from the front seat as she blew her Bob Marley smoke out the window.

"You?" I was so excited that I kissed the ground when I walked through the gates.

"Tameia is so big. She walking and saying Da Da now," Snow informed me. "And on another note, your baby daddy got robbed a week ago by some niggas named Face and Mookie." She talked to me but kept her eyes on the road. "Said they caught the nigga coming out that crack head Dicky's apartment over there by Fort Avenue across the street from the 7/11, late one night."

After I finished changing into the new clothes they had bought me, I threw the prison clothes out the window. "And?"

"They stripped him down to his socks., emptied his pockets, made him squat and cough." I couldn't believe my ears.

Flowsicka made smoke rings and bobbed her head up and down to the music.

Man fuck these niggas
Imma spare everything but these niggas
I flip the gun and gun butt these niggas
Take the knife off this AK and cut these niggas

Steady Mobbin by Young Money was coming out the speakers.

Me and Snow glanced over at Flowsicka's ass and laughed. I loved how their relationship started. Me.

When Flowsicka got home, she kept it trill with me. Snow knew all about her from the county jail so they linked up and formed a beautiful bond, too.

Still bobbing her head, Flowsicka said, "His ass gonna get his one day, fa sure."

"Yeah, that's just the beginning." Snow blurted out. "After they took the nigga's money and dope, they patrolled him over to the car where Keisha was waiting on him. They said Face had the burner to his head and Mookie pulled the bitch out of the car and pissed on her."

My mouth was literally hanging open. *A nigga piss on me, I swear on my kid's life Imma sew his asshole shut, cut his dick off and shove it down his throat.* That bitch, Keisha, wasn't built like me so that's what her pussy ass got.

I was between the two front seat anticipating her next words. "Said the dumb bitch started crying but when Face cocked the pistol her ass shut the fuck up. As Face held them hostage, Mookie searched the car and found some extra money they had in the glove box."

Flowsicka was shaking her head and coughing her lungs out. I pushed her up so I could pat her back.

"That's why I don't smoke," I said between pats.

When she stopped she said, "The weed ain't do that I was gonna tell you that them niggas did all that shit without a mask. The smoke hit the wrong spot."

I turned my head in Snow's direction to make sure it was a fact.

She had her eyes on the road but a smile had taken its place on her face. She lifted her right hand in the air, and I knew she was swearing it was the truth.

Flowsicka spoke the unthinkable. "Them niggas went to every hood and told the story themselves, together."

"How long ago this happen, again?"

"A week ago but listen to this shit. The nigga Face told Murdoc that he was gonna make you his bitch when you touched land."

I sat back in the seat and put my feet up on the center console.

"That nigga better cancel that wish 'cause it won't happen." I didn't fuck with my daughter's father for my own reasons but I wouldn't cross that line to fuck with his enemy. That was a law I wouldn't break.

Moments later, I dozed off to sleep but woke up in the cemetery when the car came to a complete halt.

"I figured this would be ya first stop," Snow said to me as I adjusted the jacket on my body.

"You did right," I said, feeling satisfied.

The cold air welcomed my skin, but I brushed it off by zipping the jacket up to my neck. I knew the area well but seeing a big ass tombstone that I'd never seen before me had me second guessing that I was in the wrong section of the cemetery.

Flowers were all over this grave. I searched the ground for my mom, but I didn't find her until I got to that big headstone. And there she was. Someone had hooked her up so I read the writing on the tombstone: *You was my everything! You made sure I had everything and anything. Not a day goes by and I don't think of you. We love you very much. Love and Tameia.*

It was perfect and the flowers were fresh. I held back the hurt in my heart. I didn't want to seem weak in front of my mom anymore.

"Just touched land from a little vacation. Ya baby girl ain't innocent no more." The flowers danced with the breeze of the cold air. "I am gonna get myself together and bring ya grandbaby to see you soon." I took a deep breath and focused my attention on her. "Watch over me, Ma," I said in a calm voice. "I'm 'bout to show the streets that I'm The Last of A Dying Breed." I walked off only to stop a few feet away. "Oh yea, our love is bulletproof."

When I got back to the car, Flowsicka was leaned all the way back in the back section and Snow was talking on her phone.

"You like her tombstone?" Flowsicka asked me with her eyes closed.

"It's beautiful!" I looked at it again from out of the tinted window.

"We went half on it together for you." Snow continued to talk but looked at me through the rearview mirror, as we were now in motion. "We thought you would love it."

Flowsicka was so high that the words flowed from her lips out of nowhere.

"I'm at niggaz' throat with that killer

I'm realing in bulks of that scrilla
I'm realer than most of you niggaz
Never change even when I had a hunnit to my name"
In jail, that bitch would flow all the time and I could see that she still had it.
"I was out there in traffic tryna get it switching lanes
Ya'll just see the pretty face but ya'll ain't never feel the pain
U ain't have to take those loses fucking 'round with this game
Went to jail and that shit taught me a lesson
Watch how you move and be careful who you step with
And I just want to go to heaven
I ain't living right barely see the face of a reverend
Even tho I'm doing dirt sometimes I got a bless em
I'm eating over here but the extras is a blessing
I throw it to my fam now I'm eating with my brethren
Gotta get my brothers right cuz those the niggaz that I flex with"
"Damn, Flowsicka, you still got that shit on lock?" I questioned her as I took the jacket off.

Her eyes were still closed but her mouth wasn't for long.

"You know all I do is spit that real shit and smoke that good shit. *No Sleep Entertainment.*" She pulled the big iced out chain from out of her clothes and showed me the logo: No Sleep. "Just like ya boy, Jeezy, I'll sleep when I die." That had all of us laughing.

"Ya'll both know I'm not about to be kicking it with ya all day. I got a man at home to go take care of." Snow joked.

"Aite, drop me off at my crib in Jubilee," Flowsicka told her.

I told Flowsicka I would link up with her later after I'd gotten my shit together.

"Next stop, Ms. Julia's house," I said.

"I already knew that," Snow told me smiling hard as ever.

The city view had changed a lot. There were a lot of new stores around the neighborhood.

A burgundy ol' school sitting on 4's passed us.

"Who's shit is that?" I pointed toward it, across the way.

"Oh, that's that dude named Marcus shit from Madison Street. He locked up, though, for taking a charge for one of his niggas."

I took my eyes off of the show stopper and faced my bitch. "Yea?"

"Yea!" she said dead ass serious like a heart attack.

"He got 34 years!"

I couldn't even process the number in my head. My face must have given me away so she repeated it again.

"Thirty-four fucking years, Love, and he got 2 kids."

I was just hoping that he had a rider on his team to travel with him, but knowing how these lame ass bitches were, I figured he didn't.

I prayed silently that *that* nigga he took the charge for was showing him some love.

Snow kept her ears to the streets herself. She had a good nigga who worked a 9-5 every day to take care of her. He didn't want her shaking her ass, so he made her quit that job long time ago. All the pretty bitch had to do was stay pretty and fuck on demand.

"How is Pedee doing?" I asked, mentioning her boo's name.

My girl had a big ass smile on her face, "You know he doing good, ready for me to get pregnant," she rubbed her flat stomach.

"What are you waiting on?"

"Time." She ran her fingers through her hair. "Time, Love. I'm waiting on that perfect moment."

Even though Tameia wasn't planned, I was glad that I had her. She was the only reason I never gave up when my days inside my cell got hard. Seeing her pictures and touching her during visitation gave me hope. A bright one.

My mom gave up on me but I damn sure would never give up on Tameia. I had a whole lot of catching up on with my daughter. I'd missed her first steps, her first words, her first tooth. I couldn't take it back but I was willing to make it all up to her.

Jamaica

Chapter 14
Welcome Back

We got to Ms. Julia's house just in time to see Murdoc and his bitch together in the car that I had hustled my ass off in. Snow turned her system up when she parked in the driveway and I came out rapping Jeezy's *Welcome Back*.

Murdoc's mouth was stretched from side to side, wide open. The little time I did had given me some extra curves in all the right places.

Whoever his guest was in the car couldn't take her eyes off of me as I performed. Snow was my hype bitch. She sat on the hood of her ride and threw her hands side to side as I continued to rap. I sang Welcome Back like I was the nigga, Jeezy, himself.

I stared Murdoc down and mouthed to him. "I'm back!"

Ms. Julia came outside and when she saw me she screamed and ran into my path. The joy in my heart was priceless and the smile on her face couldn't be moved.

Happy tears splashed from my eyes. Snow was crying and so was Ms. Julia.

Mr. Gates was now outside with Tameia in his arms. I let Ms. Julia go and moved in the direction of my child.

I held my arms open when I got to her and said, "Mama." She smiled and dove into my arms.

I heard Murdoc's tires as he screeched away from my homecoming. I wasn't concerned about him anyway. I just continued to hold onto Tameia like my life depended on it.

After a while, Snow said her goodbye but planned to catch up with me later on during the week. I told her as soon as I got a line I would hit her up.

Focusing back on my baby girl, I noticed Tameia's was a grandma's and grandpa's baby for real. They had her spoiled rotten.

Instead of calling me *Love*, they referred to me as Mommie and hearing Tameia say call me the same had me floating on a cloud.

QBanga showed up with his hands full of bags. "Welcome home, sis," he said as he scooped me up off of my feet. His ass wasn't little anymore even though we were the same age. He was a little taller but bigger with muscles.

"I got you a phone, some J's, shorts and tights," he put me back on my feet, "wife beaters and a few hoodies. Mom picked up ya bras and panties."

We all laughed and then Tameia had pulled on his pants so he could give her some attention. His face lit up just holding her. He placed kisses all over her face and swung her around. Her cries of joy and happiness were beautiful.

Ms. Julia grabbed my hand and we picked up all the bags that QBanga had had brought in and left him with his niece.

"I know your release papers are to stay here but I really want you to know you can stay here as long as you need."

I saw the love on her face for me. I wrapped my arms around her and cried. Between sobs all I kept telling her was thank you over and over again.

When I got settled, I spent the day with Tameia. She took to me fast, like I never left.

I had 72 hours to let my Probation Officer know that I was home. So, in the meantime, I text Snow and Flowsicka from my new phone.

Tameia was in the bed fast asleep by 8:30 so I called Murda and he answered on the second ring.

"Hey." I cooed.

I could hear him fighting to keep his composure under control. "Love?"

"Hey, baby," hearing him swallow made me smile. "You gonna come see me or what?" I said with the sexiest voice ever.

"What's the address?" I gave it to him and hung the phone up.

Ms. Julia was in the kitchen when I got downstairs. I'd never kept a secret from her so I told her about Murda, right then and there.

"If he makes you happy, then go for it! You deserve it," her words touched my heart, they always had, "but be careful."

I was blessed to have her in my life.

My phone rang as she was washing a cup out in the sink.

"I'm outside," Murda said when I answered.

"I'll be back in the morning before Tameia wakes up." I kissed her on the cheek and headed for the door.

He was on the porch waiting for me. At 39 years old, Murda gave a young nigga a run for their money with his looks. Pictures didn't do his ass any justice. His body was muscular and lean. His swag couldn't be fucked with at all and the waves spinning on his head had me sea sick.

"You just gonna stand there?" I noticed his eyes glow as he spoke, and his statement turned me on.

I walked to him. His six-foot frame hovered over my 5 foot 1 inch body just right.

I looked up into his eyes. "I'm home." In my J's, I tipped up for a kiss, and he kissed me back. He ran his tongue over my lips and slowly sucked the bottom. I slipped my tongue into his warm mouth as his hands held onto me for dear life. I pulled away. "You still gonna do what you promised me on my first day home?"

"You ain't said nuthin', lady."

He led me to the car and opened the door for me. I reached over and unlocked his for him.

This day was planned months ago.

When I stepped into the hotel room, I gasped for air. Rose pedals were all over the floor, leading to the bed.

"What's that on the bed?" I turned around and asked him.

"Liquid chocolate, strawberries, a little vibrator and a bullet." I turned back and looked at the bed. I had to see it all up close. And some K-Y Jelly," he said behind me laughing, that had my pussy jumping bad. "Lay down" he said in a tone that made me melt.

He took my shoes and my clothes off piece by piece, laid me back down and then dripped chocolate all over me. He fed me strawberries and licked me from head to toe.

He sucked on my nipples, slow and gently. My pussy was soaked from all the good foreplay. The first lick he gave my pussy I came. He ate me out but held the vibrator against my clit. I couldn't take it, so I begged him to fuck me. He took his clothes off so fast and his crocodile jumped at me. He pushed my legs apart and moved in.

My body sank onto the bed. My legs were shaking, bad.

He said, "Relax."

I listened to him and let my legs go freely. The first stroke made me stop breathing. I clawed the sheets with my hands trying to take it.

Four long, strong strokes from him had my back arching. I came again. I had my hands on the back of his head, his tongue danced with mine. It felt like his dick was in my throat, the way he was pounding away.

I came two more times within five minutes. I told him I wanted to get on top and I rode him slow and then fast. Looking into his eyes, I saw love, not like I'd thought I'd seen with Murdoc. That shit was different.

I felt my body tensing up again and I knew I was once again letting my wet juices go. "Face down, ass up," he said into my ear. He had me on all fours as he dug my pussy out.

I had the bullet on my clit, next thing, I was screaming, "I'm cummmmin' again."

I collapsed on the bed face still down. He gave me the vibrator and told me to put it back on my clit. He rubbed the K-Y Jelly on my ass hole. I'd promised him that, too. I could see the excitement all over his face. He took the vibrator from me and ran it up and down my ass. I went wild. When he stopped at my ass he applied pressure until half of it went in. I pushed back harder onto it. I used my left hand to rub on my clit until I nutted. Again.

We stopped for ten minutes, my body was tired. I gave him some head and he rose right back up and he got a new condom. He turned me backwards, spreading my ass cheeks and added more lubricant.

To get my mind off of the pain that was about to come, he talked to me as he stroked my pussy with the bullet, while he tried to get his dick up in my ass.

I didn't know how long it took but I knew I heard a pop sound when the head went in. I cried out in pain.

"You want me to stop?"

"No, just stroke my pussy with that shit." I racked his dick all the way up in my ass. I tried to climb the bed like a spider woman, but I never got anywhere.

I felt my clit pulp up. He took the vibrator off of my clit and stuffed it inside of my pussy blocking it with his middle finger. My body rocked side to side, shaking uncontrollably. I came so hard that a milky substance was running down my legs. That shit must have turned him on 'cause he pounded me so aggressively that my body went limp. I didn't know what was happening but I knew I was on the verge of cumming again.

So was he for the first time.

"Arrrghhhh! Love!" He hollered out my name. I knew the neighbors would remember it.

His strokes felt as if he didn't want to have mercy on me. And all of a sudden he dropped on top of me. My body kept twitching.

"Welcome home, baby," he said as he rolled off of me. I reached over and smushed his face.

"Thank you!" I said with a smile on my face, wishing Murdoc could see me now.

Jamaica

Chapter 15
Nigga, Please

Before the sun even had time to come up, I was back home, in front of my door. Murda opened up the car door for me. As I stood up to get out of the car, my ass was hurting bad.

He met me on my side, closed the door and leaned me against it. "You ain't talkin' all that shit no more."

I couldn't help but to smile. During our little bonding during my bid, through the phone calls and letters, I'd talked a lot of shit about sex, too much shit but now my ass was paying for it. Badly.

"Naw, I'm not."

He moved in and tasted my early morning breath. "Still taste sweet, lil' lady."

I folded my arms around his body and took his scent in. He was still fresh.

"I got a lot that I got to get done today, but know that I'll keep you in my thoughts."

"And I'm keep you right here, lil' lady." He took my hand from around him and put it on his heart. His heart beat was steady.

I was feeling him. He knew the struggle, bitter and sweet. I was young and wet behind the ears so with him being seventeen years older, I knew he could teach me a thing or two. That was what I wanted, plus I knew he wouldn't play with Murdoc at all 'cause that nigga thought he was untouchable.

I used the key that Ms. Julia had given me earlier to enter the house.

Tameia was fast asleep in her bed when I peeped in on her. I then climbed the stairs that led me to my room.

Oh, my ass was hurting so bad, I swear he wore my shit out like a CD.

***

Hours Later

"Mommie, Mommie." I felt a little hand on my face caressing it. "Wake up." I didn't say a word. I just looked over at Tameia and shook my head with happiness.

"Hey there, pretty girl," I spoke in a baby voice like hers. She bent down and kissed my cheek.

There was no way I was planning on leaving her again. I scooped her up and planted kisses all over her face, she giggled with joy and it warmed my heart. All the shit that I'd gone through I would go through it 10x's over again to have her in my life.

A short time later, I made breakfast with my child for the first time. She bounced around the kitchen without a care in the world, and I worshipped it. Ms. Julia was up reading her morning paper when I joined her in the living room. Tameia sat in front of the TV watching Scooby Doo.

"Thank you for everything that you have..." she slashed me off before I could even finish.

"You are family," she said with her eyes on Tameia.

Ding Dong!

She got up to get the door and I went to watch TV with my child. I sat beside her and ran my fingers through her curly afro.

"So that's how it is?"

I knew his voice anywhere. I didn't turn around to face him, but Tameia leaped up like a frog toward her father.

"DaDa!" She screamed. "Mommie is here." The love in her voice made my heart dance.

"I know," he replied.

I got up to exit the room so I could shower when he blocked my way.

"Tamaine," his mom's voice was low, but I heard the power behind it. She looked at him as if to say *Boy, don't start no shit.*

I wasn't scared no more and I didn't have a belly in front of me, either. The fear he once placed in my heart was no longer there. Ms. Julia got Tameia out of his hands and gave him that look that said *You better not.*

When she and Tameia were out of sight, I watched how his eyes danced over my body from head to toe. Here I was standing in front of the nigga that I would have killed for or even taken a bullet for, but he broke my heart.

He stepped back to get out of my way and I gladly took the space to get as far away as possible from him. But he had a different game. He followed me up to the room where all my belongings were.

No word was spoken. I pretended like he wasn't there because I knew silence killed him. I picked my phone up and saw that I had a missed called from Murda, so I text him with a smile on my face.

Good morning. Message sent at 8:02 a.m.

Murdoc's eyes burned a hole through me, but I picked an outfit out of the clothes that I had so I could go see my P.O. My phone then vibrated on the bed, I picked it up and read the message.

8:04 a.m.: *Breakfast?*

I smiled, I thought I'd fed him breakfast, lunch and dinner last night.

8:05 a.m.: *U still hungry? LOL*

The moment I pressed send the blow came from out of nowhere.

Wham!

I released the phone from my hands and blocked the next one that was meant for my right eye. That nigga was fighting me in his mom's house with his daughter downstairs.

Everything happened so fast, I didn't have time to react. I was on the bed with his hands squeezing the life out of me, but my days of getting my ass whooped were long over.

I kicked him in his dick and that alone gave me enough time to bounce up and two piece his ass. Both to the side of his temple.

He dropped to the floor in slow motion. It wasn't until he hit the floor when his mom burst through the door with Tameia enroute.

The first thing she did was look at me. I was repining my hair back up in its ponytail and grabbing my phone off of the floor. I knocked him the fuck out.

"Imma kill him or he gonna kill me," I told her as I picked my daughter up and headed back downstairs.

We went into her room and I closed the door.

"Where's DaDa?" she asked me when I sat her down on the bed.

"Talking to grandma upstairs." I pointed to the ceiling. She pulled her Barbie from under her blanket and twisted her hair. I then called my P.O. and scheduled an appointment to see her that day.

My cheek bone hurt from the blow that nigga landed so I rubbed it out as I talked to the lady on the phone.

My appointment was for 11 a.m. that day.

Tameia didn't say anything while I was on the phone, but she pulled the arm of her doll off.

I picked an outfit from her closet to wear so she could accompany me to see that lady. I used the downstairs bathroom to get her ready. We played and talked baby talk the entire time together. After she was dressed, I sat her down in front of the TV in the living room.

Ms. Julia and her no good son was descending the stairs, she was first. I stood up ready for another round, that time I was going to be using anything in sight to help beat his ass.

Tameia ran to him. I twisted my neck from side to side as I cracked my knuckles. His mom just looked on.

"DaDa, can I come with you?" And just like the piece of shit he was he turned her down.

"Come to mommie, baby." She did as I instructed.

He walked out of the door and slammed it. Both his mom and daughter jumped but I didn't. My days of jumping were over, and before the week was over, I'd be packing heat. It was either gonna be me or him and the way I was feeling with all that anger, I had a feeling Tameia would be helping me bury her father.

I went and saw my P.O. She didn't piss test me. She just told me I had to find a job and take parenting classes. I advised her that I already completed the parenting class and I had the certificate from prison.

She told me to bring it on my next visit. And if anything changed to call her first. I promised I would.

Tameia was fast asleep when I got back to the car with her grandma.

"I can't stay there with y'all." I studied her face, but she showed no emotions.

After a minute or so, she finally spoke, "I understand."

I told her what I planned to do and even though she didn't approve, she didn't disagree either. She said she had my back no matter what and I found myself telling her thanks again for the billionth time.

Jamaica

Chapter 16
Tear Me Back Down

After telling Snow and Flowsicka what had happened between me and Tameia's father, I called Dre.

"You been home for almost three days now and you just hitting me up?" he teased.

"My nigga, it's been a hell of a three days, too," I told him between laughs.

I was so glad to have that nigga in my life, real talk. He kept it real and trill with me on my lil' bid that I had no choice but to fuck with him harder.

We chopped it up like I wasn't gone for 17 months.

We agreed to meet up later at Friday's on Timberlake Rd. to pick business back up at ten.

The time following to my meeting with Dre I spent it all with my daughter. I got her to sit still with a bag of candy in front of her to do her little afro.

In between, I would text message Murda.

Me: What U doin'?
Him: Nothing. Handling business but missin' U
Me: Swing thru the spot U dropped me off @
Him: Aite

By the time I finished Tameia's hair, she was fast asleep. Getting up early had worn her out good. I picked her up and carried her to her bed. I kissed her forehead and walked out.

Ms. Julia was sitting in the living room reading her Bible. She closed it when I sat across from her. I knew she had a lot on her mind. From her son to the safety of her granddaughter and me, wanting to get back in the game. She had her hands full. I broke the silence.

"I don't know what else to do with myself." I put my phone on the table. From her expression on her face, I knew there was no denying that she was worrying about me. "I know you want me staying here with you and you'd love if I got a 9-5, but I can't."

Her son had already tried welcoming me home with an ass whooping. Anytime he felt like beating my ass all he had to do was show up to her spot and it could go down.

She opened up her hand and moved it toward me, I put my hand in hers. "My child, no matter what you do, I'm here for you."

Her words gave me strength, I knew that Tameia would be well taken care of with or without me. Then my phone rang and interrupted our time.

I answered. It was Murda. "I'm out front."

I told Ms. Julia that I'd be back soon. I ran upstairs and grabbed a stack of the money that Flowsicka and Snow had blessed me with.

When I got back downstairs, she was gone. I locked up with my key.

Murda was standing outside of the car when I turned around. He pulled me by my hand and into his arm. I looked up at him and smiled.

"I heard what that nigga did to you, too," I let my head fall into his body. Damn, Flowsicka must have told her boo, and he told his brother.

"It's nothing," I said, taking in his scent.

"It's nothing to you, but it is a lot to me."

The seriousness in his voice made me feel safe.

I withdrew from his embrace and traveled to the passenger side, thinking back to one of the letters that he wrote me while I was down.

Love,

How you doing, did you miss me or is that wishful thinking? Nah, you missed me. In fact, I got you smiling 'cause we know it's true. Yeah, I got that much confidence, but I can't sleep on you b/c in truth you keep one on my face, too.

Real spit, I'm curious to find out where this path we chose to embark on will lead us.

You don't know me or my capability so the attraction is based solely on personality, loyalty, trust, honesty and not the physical or the shiny things and I like that!

Yo, I wrote to you because for once I want someone genuine in my life. I'm not seeking a woman I can share my existence with although it would be nice, but that's not what I'm after! I want to build something 'greater'. Something love can't compare to but undivided loyalty protects, provides and progress to a relationship man and woman have yet to create let alone will ever be able to define. That type of loyalty can exist, but the billion dolla question is are you the one it can happen with? Time will tell! But until then let's breathe easy, get to know each other, the real us and when you touch down that first embrace will tell it all.

We drove and talked for what seemed like hours. He told me how hurt he was when I mentioned to him that I didn't want him to pick me up from prison or accept his money.

When I looked at his sexy brown eyes, they were comforting and compassionate but strong.

"I want a commitment from you." We were on 16th Street when he said that. Butterflies took over my stomach hearing that word.

"Commitment?"

"Yea, lil' lady, a commitment."

Nine kids, eight baby mothers and 39 years old, and he wanted a commitment out of me. My mind couldn't handle what he was saying.

"That little young nigga shriveled you up." I let him settle his hand on my thigh. "Let a real nigga show you what real love is."

His words rang in my head, and I couldn't stop thinking about why he didn't choose one of his kids° mom for a commitment.

Ever since we had started talking, he'd made my heart melt and forget about everything in the world except for Tameia and him.

His words kept playing themselves over in my head. *You see lil' lady, all we know is the real us in the raw. No act. No physical attraction to cloud our judgement. No power to be drawn to. Just two people with the chance to meet through pen and paper with the ability to be ourselves and expose the real us and make shit happen as man and woman. FYI, I'm attracted to potential and you got that.*

"I don't know what to say." That was the truth.

"I cut ol' girl off a month ago. I told her it was nice meeting her but my woman was about to land and I couldn't jeopardize losing her."

His eyes were on me for a second before he returned them to the traffic.

On 12th Street is where he told me how he really felt. "I'll never let you down, neglect or betray you for as long as air graces my lungs. Our bond will never be broken. Our future is promised, if you want one with me?"

As we rode around Lynchburg, I took the city in slowly. As we rolled through some of the hoods, White Rock, Timbridge Hill, Wise Street, Park Ave., Rivermont, Jubilee, College Hill Top and Bottom, I wondered for a second how would niggas feel having me as their Boss or The Queen of the City?

"Do you hear me?" His voice was soft.

"Yes, I hear you."

Looking over at him and touching his hand with my own, I repeated myself, "I hear you, baby, I'm here now." He smiled real hard and that dimple showed in his face when I said that.

Flowsicka had told me how Murda and Maurice was selling Choppas to some New York niggas every other week up top. She said how hard it was to get guns up there plus a bullet alone on the Streets costed $5, so Murda and Maurice made a trip every week.

"Before I left this shit," I said, referring to the city, "I had the fiends on lock in every hood," we stopped at the light on 5th Street. "I want the key to this bitch." The light changed and traffic moved.

When I was down, I'd heard a few names within the jail; Davis Boys, Jolon Carthorne, The Carters, but no bitch's name. Fuck playing games with these streets. I'd made up my mind to step my game up to another level as soon as my feet had hit freedom.

Murda must've thought everything I was saying was just words 'cause he hadn't seen me in action. He wasn't from Lynchburg so I had to show him.

We made it back to Ms. Julia's house and he told me had to take a trip back home to Harrisonburg because his oldest child, a girl, was graduating from high school. He wanted to know if I wanted to chill in his spot on Greene Street.

I agreed to get a copy of the key before he left town.

"How many bitches you brought there?"

"None," I felt relief from his answer but I had a feeling the nigga was lying.

"Don't let ya mind overdrive you, take my word for my word. I'm a man of my word," he said, reading my thoughts.

That's what these old niggas do?

"I don't know what kind of clowns you used to entertain, but I'm an OG, lil' lady. Been there done that."

I'd been through hell and back with Murdoc and I damn sure wasn't going to go through that shit again, OG or not. He parked in the driveway to the house. Mr. Gates was home.

"What you got lined up for later?"

I didn't want to hide anything from him, but I didn't want to let my cat out the bag, either.

"Gotta meet up with an old friend later." I watched as a wry smile appeared on his face. "It's just business."

"Why you just can't let me take care of you?"

I'd learned from experiences, first hand, that allowing a man to take care of you was when that nigga gained power over you. And after that, it was a wrap.

"Let me get my change up and we can take care of each other."

"I like that about you!"

He didn't have a choice.

In the end, he gave me the key to his crib and told me to call him anytime no matter what 'cause he would be on his way to my rescue.

He must have felt something 'cause that night my life changed once again.

I wasn't supposed to be driving at all, so Flowsicka got one of her home girl's information for me to memorize so if I got pulled over, I could give it to the police. Name. Date of Birth. Social Security Number.

Tameia was asleep when I got in Ms. Julia's Nissan at 9:30 that night to meet up with Dre. I noticed that nigga had gained some weight when I approached him at the bar. He stood up and wrapped his arms around me.

"You eating good or someone pregnant for you?"

"Both!" He released me and I told him congrats.

"Welcome home." He called the bartender over and order me a drink. A Jamaican Lizard.

I wasted no time. "I want back in the game." I took a seat and he followed, so I continued, "I'm done with the fiends!"

I stopped when the bartender brought me my drink. "Shit has changed," he said.

"Can't that much have changed in 17 months other than the prices."

He smiled, took a drink and shook his head. We talked business like I was a man, for real. He saw the hunger I had in me from the first 8 ball I got from him years ago. Now I was starving.

My loyalty had shown itself, so had his, so we said next week we'd link up and do business.

After two drinks, I told the nigga I was heading home. He said he was gonna chill for another hour or so, so I bounced. I didn't want to be out too late and get pulled over, if I could avoid it.

Listening to the radio, on my way home, I sang along to Seckund Chanse's Hop Out.

I've been gone for a minute
Now I'm back up on the block again.
Ready to aim
Hand back up on the glock again

When I pulled up in the driveway, the lights in the house were all out. Nothing surprising there, but when I exited the car, a pair of hands gripped my body. Fear came over me instantly. I wanted to scream, but I couldn't. Cold steel was pressed to the side of my head.

"You ain't talkin' shit now, bitch?" he taunted. "Walk, bitch! And if you as much as scream, Imma blow ya brains out, right here."

I did as I was told and then shit went black. I didn't know how long I was out or where I was. My mouth was taped up and my hands were behind my back tied up. The smell was hideous, I started to gag. My head was hurting so bad that my eyes throbbed.

When the light came on, I closed my eyes but reopened them slowly.

There was a sofa in the corner and I swear I saw a rat looking at me from the corner wall.

Wham Bam!

The first kick landed in my stomach. I tried to move but my feet were strapped, too. I closed my eyes tightly. Finally, I was going to be with my mom.

Wham!

Wham! Wham!

My face bounced off of the floor. My arm went numb and then my face bounced again from the strikes. Blood filled my mouth, so I swallowed.

A right hook caught me in my eye and another under my chin. I clamped my eyes shut and prayed for death to take me, quickly.

One hand was around my neck as the other ripped my jeans off from behind me. I knew what was next, and I couldn't do nothing to prevent it. The pressure around my neck had me barely breathing.

His tongue licked my ear and my skin crawled. I drifted off into space as he shoved his dick into me from the back. I held my breath but with every thrust, I would get some air but his grip on my neck got worse and tightened. Eventually I passed out.

When I came back, I was shocked to be able to move my hands freely even though pain rocked my body. I was free and outside.

My eyes were swollen shut and my legs were weak. I kept telling myself that I could push through this, over and over again.

My hands were against a wall, so with all my strength I knocked against it, hoping someone would hear me and help me. Just when I gave the wall my final touch, a door flew open.

"Oh, my God!" I heard a woman scream before I passed out again.

When I gained consciousness, I heard a voice say. "We're at the hospital."

I tried moving my leg but it hurt so bad that I didn't move it far.

"Love," I recognized Ms. Julia's voice. "She's awake," she kept saying over and over.

Nurses and doctors ran into the room. I could only see a little.

"Her heart rate is coming up," a male's voice said.

"Where Tameia?" It took me forever to ask where my daughter was.

"She is safe, Love." Hearing that, I closed my eyes.

"What did she say when she got up?" That was Snow's voice.

"She asked for Tameia. I told her she was safe and she didn't say another word."

My eyes were extremely heavy from the punches that I'd gotten.

I tried lifting my hands up, but they didn't move far.

"Love," Flowsicka's voice echoed through the room.

Pain was shooting from my head to my toes.

"Who did this to you, Love?" Ms. Julia asked. I could tell she had been crying from her tone.

I couldn't open my eyes enough to see well so I shut them fully. Someone was rubbing my feet and hands. It hurt but it felt good at the same time.

"Love, baby girl, who did this to you?" Ms. Julia asked again.

I wanted to know who was in the room so I asked and then discovered it was just Snow, Ms. Julia and Flowsicka.

I answered. "Tamaine did this to me!" I said in one breath. I heard them gasp for air. "But don't repeat it." That came out low but I knew they heard me.

Back to sleep I went.

Chapter 17
When It Rains, It Pours

It was designed by the universe for me to go through that shit with Murdoc. Honestly, once I heard his voice, I knew I had hell to pay that night.

"She hasn't opened up her eyes in days! Two days, to be exact." I heard them talking on and off as I was coming to.

When I awoke, I said, "Snow." I heard her talking to Flowsicka.

"Love, Love." Snow's voice was soothing, "I'm right here, baby girl, talk to me."

"Where is Tameia?"

"Her grandma got her. Me and Flowsicka are here."

I unlocked my eyes at a snail's pace, and they each stood on one side of me.

"You know that nigga gotta pay for this shit, right?" Flowsicka's remark made me love her more. A little jail time had helped me score a best friend, indeed.

"So much has been going on, Love," Snow notified me.

Basically, my P.O. had been up there to see me, and the police were called. They questioned everyone trying to find out who would have done this to me. I didn't say much, but the doctors were able to determine sexual interference from the attack.

"No, he didn't." Snow was shocked.

I confirmed. "Yes, he raped me." Snow covered her mouth with one of her hands as the other massaged my shoulder.

"What the fuck?" Flowsicka cried out, moving away from the bed with her hands palmed behind her head.

"For right now, y'all the only ones I'm telling."

The nurse marched into the room with a chart in her hands, and Snow moved out of the way so she could check up on me. She didn't stay long, so I told my girls the story that I had told the police.

I gave them the statement, stating that I'd gone out for a run that night to clear my head because I'd just finish having sex with Murdoc and I'd felt like I was doing the wrong thing. And then I was attacked.

They asked me 20 million questions, and I kept saying the same thing over and over again. *No* or *I don't know what happened.*

I was protecting Murdoc's ass only because I didn't do the police thing. I was going to handle the problem myself.

"Thank you, Ms. Jenkins and if you remember anything else, please contact us." One of them said on the way out the door.

"Why are you protecting him, Love?" Snow howled at me with tears in her eyes.

I had one answer to that. "Because he is Tameia's father."

Just then Murda barged into the room. I looked from him to Flowsicka and then back from her to him.

"Baby," I saw the pain in his eyes for me. I closed my eyes and enjoyed his touch on my skin. I knew he felt he'd failed in his responsibility to protect me like he'd promised me when I was in jail.

"Who did this to you?" He asked me beyond an upset tone. I knew I couldn't tell him. "Love!" He barked and my eyes flew open. I had to lie.

"I don't know."

Flowsicka left the room when I said that.

Murda didn't leave my side unless he had to use the bathroom. He had flowers delivered to my room for the week that I was there.

I ended up with a broken finger on my left hand, two black eyes, a broken nose, a fractured rib and a gash in the back of my head.

Instead of going back to Ms. Julia's house, I went to Murda's crib on Greene Street.

"You know I don't have to stay." The stare that he gave me told me dead the conversation about where I was resting my head.

I informed my probation officer about my new address. She said all I had to do was call in once a month to let her know I was okay.

But in case something happened, I should let her know, ASAP.

The swelling on my face had gone down a little thanks to the two different kinds of prescriptions they had me on. Ms. Julia dropped Tameia off with me in the mornings and picked her up at night every day for three weeks.

Snow and Flowsicka came by every other day to keep me company, while Murda did him in the streets with his brother.

I'd got in touch with Dre and told him all about the incident except for Murdoc raping me.

"Flowsicka, mane, I can't seem to hold nothing down. I'm always tired and lightheaded," I finally spoke out. She didn't say a word, so I continued, "Me and Murda had sex, but that was when I first got home and we used a condom."

The night that Murdoc raped me he hadn't used one. I remember feeling his liquid all in me.

"Have you told Murda yet?"

"No," the tears gushed from my eyes, "No I haven't!"

"Stay here. I'll be back. I am going to get a pregnancy test for you."

I cried harder when she left.

Tameia was fast asleep in the extra room. I hadn't even introduced her to Murda. Every time they were here together, I kept them apart, but he saw her when she would be sleeping.

"She looks beautiful, just like you," Murda would tell me every time he would see her.

Flowsicka got back from the store fast. I told her to check on Tameia as I took the test. I knew I was already pregnant before I took it.

I just knew it.

I pulled my shorts down and pissed on the stick. I held it in my hands and closed my eyes. One line, I'm not pregnant. Two lines, I am having a baby. I prayed for the best, but expected the worst.

Two lines.

I held the stick in my hands for what seemed like forever, as my eyes leaked water. I felt worse knowing that I was taken advantage of. Flowsicka came in the bathroom with me. I looked up at her and she glared at the stick.

"You have to tell Murda, Love."

"I will."

After I'd got myself together, Flowsicka left to go handle some business of her own. I called Ms. Julia and told her to come over, right then and there.

I paced the living room until she got there.

I was screaming like a mad woman inside. The rage that I was feeling couldn't be explained.

As soon as she stepped inside the house, I showed her the pregnancy test result.

"Oh, God," she hollered, clutching my hands tightly.

I fell into her arms and cried, asking God, "Why, God? Just why?"

We stayed that way for a long time before I dragged myself away from her. "Can you get Tameia and keep her until I get myself together, please?"

I was exhausted mentally, emotionally and physically.

She agreed and I kissed my little angel and thanked Ms. Julia but before she departed, I told her, "It's your son's. He raped me that night." She didn't say a word. She got in her car and drove off.

Back inside the house, I called Murda's phone. "I need you," I said when he picked up.

"I'm on my way, lil' lady."

I should have told him from the gate, but I couldn't because I didn't want him hurting Murdoc. Not that I cared about him, but because of Tameia. Plus, I didn't want. Murda in any trouble. He had kids, too,

When he came home, I sat him down on the sofa and started talking. He didn't say a word at first, but his eyes expressed anger.

"And now I'm pregnant!" I yelled, sliding down the wall.

"So you fuckin' lied to me to protect that nigga?" he screamed at me. I deserved it, so I didn't say a word. "Huh, Love?" I cried harder and harder. He had every reason in the book to go off.

"Fuckin' talk to me!" He was standing over me, then.

"I'm sorry, but I didn't know what to do." My voice was low. I felt weak.

"You didn't know what to do, huh?" He scoffed. I pulled my knees up to my chest, wrapped my arms around them and dropped my head into them. "He raped you and you didn't know if you wanted to tell your man?"

Choking back my tears, I found the strength to say, "I'm so so sorry that I didn't tell you."

Last of a Dying Breed

"You must still fuckin' want that nigga!" Was all he said and slammed the front door behind him. The loud sound made me jump.

Truth was, I didn't want shit to do with Murdoc. I hated him.

For two days straight, Murda didn't come home. I called his phone but I never got an answer. I text him but he never responded, so I packed my shit and called Snow to come get me.

Before I left Murda's crib, I wrote him a letter.

Murda,

I'm so so so sorry, I should have told you from the gate but I didn't because you have kids out here that need their father, plus Tameia needs hers, too, even if he's a dead beat. I can't take back 3 weeks ago. I wish I could but I fucking can't.

I'm hurting like hell here. The pain is unbearable but this too shall pass. And for your information I don't want that woman beater, raping ass nigga. The only man I want is you but I guess the road is only one way. Thanks for brightening up my days inside that hell hole months ago and for giving me the best sex ever. I love you, know and remember that.

XoXo,
Love

By the time I finished his letter, it was soaked with my tears.

115

Jamaica

Chapter 18
Get Right

Snow dropped me off at the motel on Wards Rd. across from KFC after I told her about the baby.

"You sure you don't want to stay with me?" She'd asked me like a hundred times.

I told her I would call her if I changed my mind, so that put her at ease before she left me.

I called Dre and gave him my address to come through, so we could do business. He promised me that he would be there in two hours.

Before I took a shower, I called Murda's number but he didn't answer so I called Flowsicka. She said he was okay from what her boyfriend, Maurice, had told her.

I asked her could she get me the phone number for the abortion clinic in Roanoke and she said she would text it to me.

I took a shower and cried. Well, I cried more than I took a shower. It seemed like I was meant to go through all this shit, which hurt like hell. I wondered for a second if that's why my mom took the easy way out, 'cause she couldn't play the cards she was dealt.

Both of Queen's parents died when she was only two months old. She was put into the system and there she learned that her father killed her mother and then himself after he found out she was cheating.

I punched the wall, trying my hardest to release some pain but all I did was cause more physical damage to myself.

When I emerged from the shower, my toes and fingers were wrinkled. I then saw that I had a text message from Flowsicka. It was the phone number for the clinic. I placed the call as I got dressed.

The lady asked me so many damn questions that I wanted to say fuck it and hang up, but I didn't. My appointment was made and set for the following Monday at 8:45 a.m.

Dre was beeping in on my line, so I gave her my thanks and then I clicked over.

"Yo."

"Open the door."

I opened the door with the phone still in my hand at my ear. He picked me up off of the floor with his arms wrapped around me and I pushed the door closed with the tip of my fingers. Having his arms around me made me feel good.

"You too strong to be breaking down, yo." He walked me over to the bed and sat me down. I didn't know if it was the baby or my emotions but I couldn't stop crying for shit.

"Get that shit all out, yo," he said, leaving me to get a rag for my face from the bathroom.

And that's what I did as I told him everything. He said I was wrong for not telling Murda first. I made it look like I still had feelings for Murdoc. He said if Murda had feelings for me, then he would come around. Until then, I shouldn't be stressing 'cause I was carrying a baby.

I didn't tell him that I'd just made an appointment to kill it. "Shit gets worse before it gets better, Love," I heard him loud and clear, but I couldn't stop wondering if that was the last of the worst for me.

"Look at all the other bullshit you've been through." I looked at him with surprise. "The streets talk, all, that other shit didn't kill you, so don't let this!" He tapped my leg in a friendly way before he continued. "Females like you don't come around often, so dust ya shoulder off and do you, the right way."

I was far from fine but I knew I had to move on with my life and stop crying over spilled milk. I had Tameia to take care of and first thing in the morning, I was going to see my baby. But now it was time for business.

No matter how much Dre talked to me about not jumping back into the game, I brushed his words off.

"How much you gon' let me get a chicken for?" He tried to get up off the bed but I pulled him back down and jumped to my feet. "Look," my voice was raised above normal. I had to let him know I was dead ass serious. "I've been fucking with you for years, my nigga." I stopped for a second so it could sink in his head. "For years, yo. Now you acting like you can't fuck with me, but weeks ago shit was a go." I was walking back and forth at a furious pace. That nigga had me mad. "Say something, Dre!" I stopped to stand in front of him.

His head was down looking at the floor, but very slowly he raised his head, looking at my body. No matter what time of the year it was I had shorts on. Tameia's footprints could be seen all the way up my thigh. I watched him licked his lips and shake his head from side to side.

"Do this for me." I sounded like I was begging.

"It ain't gonna be 17.5, like ya nigga Jeezy say." That made me laugh.

"Just don't crack me too hard." I gave him my puppy face and with that, he started laughing, too.

"Ya first one, Imma let you get it for 20. The next one after that will be 25."

"You ain't said shit but a number, my nigga. I am gonna show ya ass."

"You still cocky as hell," Dre said calmly.

"I call it confidence," I retorted.

For an hour, we sat down and discussed how and when he was gonna holla at me. I ran my plans over to him but he was only concerned about my safety and his money.

What he didn't know was that I'd already had 10 bands stashed at Ms. Julia's house. I made that shit before I did my bid. I told her to spend it, but she didn't.

With my shit lined up, I went to sleep feeling really good.

Early next morning, I called Snow. "Bitch, get ya ass up and come get me, we got a long day ahead of us."

"The day ain't even start, yet," she responded in a grumpy tone.

I had to laugh my ass off 'cause she was never an early bird person.

"It's 5 a.m. but I expect to see you at 6, so don't be late."

I hung the phone up and took a shower, only to have my head inside of the toilet bowl, throwing up. That baby was kicking my ass, bad.

Snow didn't arrive until 7 a.m., and she was talking cash shit, too.

"You know I had to suck the skin off Pedee's dick before I left the house or he wouldn't let me go."

"This early in the morning?" I asked shocked as hell.

"You know morning sex is the best sex," she said, rolling her eyes in her head and touching herself.

Not in the mood to hear about her sexcapades, I changed the subject.

"I gotta go see Tameia, get an apartment, buy a few things and rent a car." Then I thought about not having a license, so I rephrased the end of my statement, "You gotta rent me a car."

An hour later, we were at Ms. Julia's house. Tameia was up, raising hell and crying when I walked through the door. When she saw me, she lit up with joy and ran to me screaming, "Mommie!"

I told Ms. Julia that I was taking her with me for the day.

She was cool with that, so I packed her up a few pieces of clothes and some snacks.

Snow had her car seat in her car, so I strapped her in and off we went.

I text Murda's phone. *What can I do to make it up to you? It's my stupidity, you have all the right to be boxing me around in the ring, right now. I should have told you! I love you.*

By midday that day, I'd found a two-bedroom house of Leesville Rd. for rent. It was privately owned, so I called the owner and she showed up to give me a tour.

She didn't do a background check or anything, and I was glad she didn't. I told her it would just be me and my daughter. I paid the deposit and first month's rent that day and she gave me the key.

I took Tameia back to her grandma's house so I could clean the apartment up and go shopping for a few things.

Lil' mama didn't want to leave me. She cried so bad that her little body trembled.

Ms. Julia gave me the 10 bands that she had for me before Snow and I hit the road again. I dropped the money off at my apartment and headed to Walmart on Wards Rd. to purchase some much needed things.

Me and Snow cleaned the apartment up better than a cleaning team probably would have. All I'd gotten was a blow up bed, a comforter set, bathroom supplies and some cooking utensils to cook up crack.

"Bitch, what you gonna do with a big ass Pyrex bowl, Love?" Snow wasn't about that life, only thing she knew was the pole.

Her nigga, Pedee, was into the streets, though. He just didn't let her know and it wasn't my place to tell her.

"Girl, I'm gonna stack it to the ceiling, shawdy."

She knew what I was saying, so she dropped the conversation.

Working nonstop for almost three hours on my empty apartment, had it not so empty anymore. I was still missing a lot of shit but not for long.

"Girl, we got to get to Enterprise before they close so you can get me a car."

"What we waiting for?" was her remark.

While she was inside getting the ride, I was outside sitting in the driver's seat of her black 745 BMW, texting Murda again.

Damn, you whooping my ass with your silence. I'm sorry. I'm sorry, so so so sorry. You already gave me 2 black eyes, a missing front tooth and you still kicking my ass with me not hearing from you. Damn, babe it's a knock out. You won. Just text me back.

I sat there watching my phone and praying that Murda would respond to me but he didn't.

Snow's knock on the window brought me back to my senses.

"Follow me 'cause I'm not driving that shit," she said, pointing to the 2010 black Dodge Charger.

"Oh, hell yea!" I screamed with excitement.

When Snow pulled off out of the parking lot, I couldn't wait for her to pull over so I could push that big boy. Two streets over, she stopped and parked. I took all my shit out of her car and ran to the Charger. I kissed her all over her face with joy.

"Can I go home now?" she said when I let her go.

"Girl, you know you don't want to," I said, laughing at her face 'cause she was serious.

"Bye, call me later." She kissed my cheek and got in her car.

I watched her pull off into traffic before I got inside my new ride. My phone buzzed alerting me that I had a text but it was from Snow. She said I had the car for a month, all the paperwork was in the glove compartment and she loved me. I replied: *I love U 2, thanks!*

Jamaica

I drove straight to get me something to eat at KFC. I wasn't in the mood to eat anything but to keep my stomach from making all that noise, I made the stop.

I finished the 2-piece meal with fries before I even made it home. Arriving at my house made me feel good, but sad. I was lonely.

I called Murda's phone but he forward me to voicemail. I hung up and sent him a message: *I know I fuck'd up, I fuckin' get it, I should have told you first, but I didn't. I'm sorry! This is my last time texting you, if you don't hit me back, then I know what we had is a wrap. By the way, I moved my shit out ya house.*

A minute later, my phone was ringing. It was Murda.

"Hello," I said happy as hell, thinking if that was all I had to say for him to call me, I would've done it from get go. I heard him breathing into the phone, so I said what I had to say. "Your silence whooped my ass more than Murdoc's hands did. You should see me." I heard him laugh, "I need you." I sighed. "Please."

Not a word from him. "I'm gonna text you the address, there is a Charger in the driveway. It's mine. The door will be unlocked."

Still nothing, so I ended the call and text him my address.

Tired as hell from the day's work, all I wanted and needed was a shower. But before I took one, I called Ms. Julia to talk to Tameia. She was asleep, so I advised her quickly that I was okay and I would see her tomorrow.

Then I hit Dre up to tell him to have that shit ready for me first thing in the morning. No excuses.

I ran the shower water as I took my clothes off and then in I went in. I let the water cascade from my head to the bottom of my feet.

I washed my hair and my body, slowly. My breasts hurt to touch them. My stomach was still flat even though I had a little seed in there. My hips looked like they were spreading, but I wasn't for sure.

I took my time in the shower, reflecting on all the crazy shit that had happened since I got home from jail.

Tears escaped from my eyes fast. I was in disbelief, but I knew life was a bitch so I shouldn't have been surprised.

122

As I composed myself, I washed the soap off of me and pulled the curtain back only to find Murda looking at me. I paused for a moment, gazing into his eyes.

He took a step toward me and said, "Love, I want you to know that I love you and I'm always gonna be there for you, lil' lady."

That was all I wanted to hear from him. I threw my wet naked body on his, as our lips moved as one.

I then pulled my lips from his and asked, "You really love me?"

"I do," he responded, but I wanted more.

"How do you know?"

"Love at first sight, lil' lady," that made my tears run harder. "And the day I saw you in person, I knew I had to have you." I couldn't stop crying. "You were created for me."

He kissed my tears away and then down my neck he went. His hands found my breasts and I threw my head back in pleasure. My body was on fire from his touch and only he could put it out.

His fingers pulled and stroked my hard nipples, causing my body to twitch. I let my hands explore his body. I unfastened his belt buckle as he pulled his white T shirt over his head.

He kicked his Timbs off fast, then he stepped out of his pants and boxers. His body was structured perfectly, with his muscles looking back at me. I placed kisses on his neck as my hand stroked him to full hardness.

He pushed me against the wall and fell to his knees. I looked down at him and stopped breathing when he stuck his tongue inside of me. I grabbed his head with both of my hands and I clamped my eyes shut and held him there.

I bounced back and forth off of the wall with the way he was pleasing me, but I wanted to feel him inside of me, so I told him. "I want you," I exhaled, "inside of me, please."

He stopped and stood up to face me. He kissed me and I tasted my juices. I took his hand and led him to the bedroom. My legs were shaking like they were going to give out on me. I pushed the door open and walked backwards to the bed with our lips locked together. "Fuck me," I said.

He pushed me on the bed and climbed between my legs pushing them apart as wide as possible. Our mouths danced again, together. I was extra slippery and super wet. I dug my nails into his back when he slammed into me.

The reunion of our bodies was everything. We continued on for an hour, making hot and sticky love.

After we finished, we held one another and nothing else mattered. That was until less than an hour later when I had got a call from Dre.

"I'm pulling in now."

"Pull all the way to the back beside the Charger. I'm opening the back door now."

I was still getting dressed. Murda was knocked the hell out with his mouth open and I had to laugh. That was what good pussy did.

I heard the sound of a door slam and I bolted to open the door. That nigga Dre was in all black from head to toe, so I had to ask him, "You gotta funeral to attend, nigga?"

He burst out laughing at me before he responded. "Hell no! You gonna move out the way or nah?"

I stepped to the side so he could come in. This nigga even had a black book bag on his back. I moved around him and signaled with my right hand for him to follow me to the kitchen.

I took the cereal box off the top of the fridge and opened it. "That's 10 bands right there," I said, pouring the money out on the counter.

A smile manifested itself on his face.

"I owe you 10 and as soon as I get it, you will get it."

He took the bag off of his back and sat it on top of the counter beside the money. I was so excited that my hands started sweating, so I rubbed them together. He started unzipping the bag, but stopped mid-way.

"Love, you just..." I cut him off.

"Nigga, save that preaching shit for when you become a pastor!"

He closed his eyes and laughed out real loud.

"I'm dead ass serious, how the hell you gonna preach to me, but you doing the same shit? Selling drugs!" I said, looking at his ass and laughing, too.

"No matter what I say you gonna do you." He never wanted me to be in the game although he knew my hustle would take me far, but it was too late for that.

"Stop talking and open the bag, my nigga. I got mouths to feed and I have to pay you your end."

He opened the bag and pulled a package out wrapped in foil. He pushed it over to me.

"That shit better not be stepped on either or you can cancel that 10 that I owe you." I was serious.

"Mane, have I ever sold you any garbage?" He picked the money up and dumped it into the bag, zipping it up.

His dope was always official when I copped from him back then.

"Naw, you ain't sell me no garbage back then, so I hope you ain't change up like the weather."

"Yo ass got jokes," he said, laughing again at me. "Holla at me when you ready," he said, dapping me up like I was a nigga.

Murda was standing in the living room in his pants looking at us. I saw his pistol on his waist. I let Dre's hand go and spoke, "Babe, this is Dre, the one I told you about."

Dre turned around to see who the hell I was talking to.

"Oh, this dude?" Murda said, walking toward us in the kitchen.

I stepped to the side of Dre and said, "Dre this is my baby, Murda."

I moved from beside Dre and stood beside my man. I looked up at him and smiled, wrapping my hand around his abdomen. He lifted his right hand over my head and moved so he could dap Dre up.

After their man shake, Dre spoke, "You got ya hands full with her."

He leaned his head in my direction.

Murda pulled me in front of him and replied. "She don't give me no problems, my nigga."

After a few more words, Dre said he had to bounce, so I let him go and then I turned my attention to my man.

"I've got a lot to do today, what you got planned?"

"You. If you let me," he said, picking me up and spinning me around in his arms.

"Imma be sick, Murda. Let me down," I said soft tapping him on his back.

"No, lil' lady," he stopped spinning me around and walked back to my bedroom.

He threw me on the bed and I bounced up like I was on a trampoline. That was his soft side for me and I loved it. When I was around him, I got all of his attention no matter what was going on around u s .

He took his pistol from his waist and put it on the floor, then he laid beside me, with his hands on my stomach.

"I made an appointment to have an abortion," I put my hands on top of his. "but I can't go through with it!" He didn't say a word. He'd always been a good listener so I continued. "Everything happens for a reason, right?" I turned my face to his but his eyes were still closed.

I moved his hands and turned on my side facing him. "I know I was wrong for not telling you and I'm sorry." I was tearing up again. I closed my eyes and spoke from by heart. "I'm scared to death."

"Of that nigga?" His voice was serious so I opened my eyes to find him looking at me with no fear in them.

"No, I'm not scared of Murdoc." Tears were running down my face into my mouth. "I'm scared because I have to raise them by myself."

He used his fingers to wipe my tears away but they wouldn't stop running.

"Lil' lady, I got you!" I kissed his fingers.

"I already got nine, two more ain't gonna hurt. They yours, they mine." Him saying that had me sobbing. He pulled me into his arms and told me to stop crying before the baby came out a cry baby. That made me laugh. I was so happy to have him in my life at that moment.

"You got money to make. You better hit the kitchen, lil' lady." Just like that my tears stopped. I jumped up off the bed and ran into the kitchen.

I pulled everything out that I needed to whip that chicken up and to work I went. Murda stood to the side and watched me work.

He never said a word until his phone rang but by that time, I had the whole bird cooked up and drying on Bounty paper towels.

126

I dailed Flowsicka's number and waited for her to pick up.

"I'm back, shawty," I said as soon as she answered.

"Say no more. I'ma holla at you in a few."

What was understood didn't need to be explained.

I'd met this bitch named April in prison while I was doing time. She said she and her nigga be slinging and shit, so I called her and told her I would be hitting her up in a few from a different number so answer, she said cool.

I made a few more calls as I bagged the crack up into 8 balls, quarters, 1/2's and ounces.

"I gotta get a trap phone," I said to Murda who was fully dressed.

"And some furniture," he said, pointing at the empty space.

"Well that can wait 'cause I got a crib on Greene Street." He walked off, shaking his head at me. "Right?" I yelled.

"You know it, lil' lady!"

An hour later, I'd gotten a straight talk phone from Walmart. I got it set up under a name that I couldn't even remember.

Murda was driving the Charger as I made my calls.

April said her nigga, Mike, wanted an ounce. I told her $1,400 and she said he said that shit better be all that for that price. I didn't put anything extra on that shit, so my shit was the fire.

Flowsicka hit me up and said that she needed 4 ounces and 2 quarters all separate.

I had ran into this nigga from when I used to be on the block in the old days when I'd first gotten home and he gave me his number 'cause I told him I would be trapping, so I hit him up, too.

"My nigga, what it do?" I said when he answered.

"Who this?"

"This Love, Polo."

He recognized my name, so I told him everything was a go as promised. All he had to do was holla and I would stop by like Santa at Christmas.

"Go to the crib, daddy, so I can pick all this shit up and make all the stops."

"Anything for you, lil' lady."

April hit me back up and said her nigga's brother wanted 2 ounces, too. I let her know that she was the one that I was giving the work to 'cause I didn't know either of the niggas, and she said cool.

I told Flowsicka the same shit, too, and shawty said, "Bitch, you know if I fucks with a muthafucka they legit."

I told her, "Yea, they might be loyal to you but not me so for right now you are the middle man."

Midday had come and I hadn't eaten shit but I made $9,800.

Everything went smoothly with the transactions and all the money was straight. I stopped at Ms. Julia's house to see my daughter. Tameia didn't want me leaving her so I ended up taking her with me to the car, with a bag of her things. That was her first time seeing Murda.

She looked at him the whole time he was driving. I couldn't stop laughing 'cause she was the replica of me and she was very observant with everything around her.

At the stoplight, before we got to the house, Murda turned around and spoke to her.

"Hey there, pretty lady." Tameia didn't even budge much less smile. He looked at me and mouthed, *"I don't think she likes me."*

"In due time, she will."

I called Dre and told him to come get his money right then or consider it a donation. His ass kept telling me how I was bullshitting about having his money. I told him don't show up and see what I do. He said give him twenty minutes so I told Murda to go to KFC so we could get something to eat.

When I pulled into my driveway, Dre was already there. I gave him his 10 bands. "Don't ever underestimate me again."

"Yo ass is the truth!" Was all he said with a happy face.

Chapter 19
March 2010
4 Real

Tameia had clicked with Murda real well. He spoiled her rotten, too. I was getting jealous. Anything she wanted, she got, the same with me, though.

I had yet to run into Murdoc, but I heard through the streets that the nigga had gotten three bitches pregnant and that didn't include me. I couldn't help but wonder if it was force or consensual.

"Girl, you gettin' thick," Flowsicka told me as I was delivering the 6 duce that she requested.

"Hell yea, all I do is eat, sleep, shit and count money all day." I rapped like a rapper.

"I hear you, but don't give hustlin' up for rapping," and I couldn't help but to laugh 'cause she was right. "Leave that rapping shit to me and you do the trapping."

"Well flow something for me then, Flowsicka." I told her with the six duce in her lap.

"Every day I'm hustlin'
Cuz I'm sick and tired of struggling
Street shit I got medals in
In Lynchburg I'm a veteran"

"Ohhh," I said and she smiled and kept going.

"I was really peddling
Like bitches up in Medellin
Use to stick that shit up in my tit
Making chicken is what I special in
My shit be dope I'm the dealer..."

"Bitch, get the hell out of my car," I told her laughing.

"Not before I kiss my god baby," she said, leaning over and kissing Tameia in the backseat.

"Love you, baby girl," she said.

"I love you, too." Tameia told her from her car seat.

"And you too in there," she said as she touched my little bun belly.

Everywhere I went, I took Tameia. Shit, she was mines, plus I wanted Ms. Julia to have a break. Murda said it was okay for her to stay with him sometimes, but she wasn't his responsibility, so anywhere I went, my girl did, too. She loved to drive around all day anyway.

Me, Murda and Tameia were out one-day trapping hard as hell when Ms. Julia called me and told me Tamaine was at her house and wanted to see his daughter. That would be the first time I would see him since that horrible night.

"Babe, drive over by Ms. Julia's house 'cause Tameia's daddy is over there. She said he wants to see her." His facial expression looked like he wanted to kill someone. I rubbed his leg, "In due time."

I turned around in my seat to speak to my baby girl, "Ready to see DaDa?"

Her face lit up, "Yea, Ma!"

They say little girls were daddy's girls and boys are momma's boys and in this case, it was true with Tameia. She loved her father.

A while later, we pulled up and that nigga Murdoc was standing outside when we drove up in front of the house on the street curb. I opened my door, then I took Tameia out of the backseat.

Murda opened his door, also. I walked around the car with Tameia in my arms, then I put her down. She ran to her father.

Murda stepped out of the car and closed the door as he leaned on it. I moved back into my man's arms as Murdoc looked at us.

Ms. Julia was standing outside with a broom in her hand as she swept her porch.

Murda had his hands on my stomach. I was six weeks pregnant now.

Murdoc picked Tameia up and took her inside.

Ms. Julia walked over to me and Murda.

"How are you two doing?" She was always sweet.

"You mean the three of us." That broke the tension enough for us all to laugh.

"I'm doing good, thanks for asking. How are you doing?" Murda was very calm and respectful. I loved hat about him, but I knew he had a lot on his mind behind that smile.

"I'm doing well, can't complain. God is good." She looked up at the sky and then back at us.

"I'm good, Ma. Can't wait to have this baby." I was rubbing my stomach.

"You look beautiful, Love. Pregnancy fits you well," she said and Murda had to put his piece in.

"Yes, she is beautiful."

Tamaine came back outside, but he never stepped off of the porch. "Imma keep her tonight. You can come get her tomorrow."

I didn't even reply.

The two men looked at each other with clear hate, but neither one of them moved. Murda kept whatever he was feeling to himself for that second.

I told Ms. Julia to call me, then I told Murda I would drive, so he walked around to the passenger side.

"Give Tameia a kiss for me, please, Ma."

"I will."

Tamaine didn't move until I pulled off.

"I can't wait to catch that nigga," Murda said as he punched the glove box. I knew he was mad as hell, so I didn't say one word. I just drove to our house on Greene Street.

After I contemplated on my man's thoughts against my ex, I refocused on the money.

I was paying $25,000 for a bird, but I was making close to $70,000 off that bitch, so I was eating real good. That night I went through a whole brick and a ½.

As I drove around the city collecting money, Murda rode with me. I couldn't stop thinking how much money this small ass city had in it.

We didn't hit the sheets until 3 a.m. "I gotta take a trip up top with my brother in two days," Murda said after he'd just finished dicking me down real damn good.

"How long you staying for?"

"Probably a day and a half. Right after I see my daughter, I'm out."

Murda had kids in eight different states. One was in New York City. He got along with all of his kids' mothers except Kandi. She was the last baby ma and the only one he'd married.

I overheard him one night talking to her.

"Kandi, every time I call to talk to my lil' man, you bring this shit up."

I had just gotten out of the shower and he was in the living room, so I left my bedroom door open to hear his conversation.

"That shit you pulled is unforgiveable." He wasn't screaming or yelling, just calm as water on a lake. *"Yea, you right. I was in the streets hard, trying to provide for my family and giving you the world when you fucked my worst enemy."*

Damn, I thought. He never told me why he left her and I hadn't asked.

"So because the nigga dead you think I should just forget it ever happened and start over?"

I don't know what she said but whatever it was he was laughing his ass off. I couldn't help but wonder *how did the nigga die?*

"Well, don't keep that pussy on ice for me 'cause I don't want it. Even getting plastic surgery on it couldn't change my mind." I was cracking up in the bedroom. Murda was crazy with his words. *"Yea, yea, yea. Kiss my son for me and let me know when you get that package for him that I sent and sign them divorce papers, too."*

"Well, Imma hold shit down here. You already know how I do." I wanted to reassure him that I'd be aite with him being away.

"This I know."

Chapter 20
July 2010

I had just found out that I was having a boy. Murda was staring at the screen with the baby on the monitor.

"I wanted another girl, but I guess not."

The nurse wiped the gel off of my stomach.

"Don't worry, we can work on that after you heal up," he said, facing me.

The nurse's cheeks turned pink and I had to laugh.

"Congrats," the nurse said and we both said thank you.

I had gained twenty-five pounds in five months and the baby was due in November. I couldn't wait.

After leaving my doctor's appointment, I called my probation officer for the month. Then I rang Ms. Julia's line.

"I'm having a boy."

"Ain't you just lucky? A girl and a boy! You don't have to have any more if you don't want to."

"I want two more and then I'm done."

Murda was shaking his finger at me. I looked at him but continued to talk to Ms. Julia, wondering what Murda was thinking.

"I'll be over there tomorrow to get Tameia."

"Love, QBanga said he needs to holla at you."

I told her it was okay to give him my number. I talked to Tameia for a minute because she was too busy watching cartoons so she didn't have any time for me, so I let her go and ended the call.

Murda's cell phone rang. "Yo."

I leaned back into the seat and text Snow.

"What the fuck?" he said, running the red light.

She text back. *Nuthin'*

"Mane, I'm on my way right now, bruh."

He hit the gas pedal and the car reacted, causing my body to jerk. "What's wrong, baby?" I asked him as he made a right unto Old Forest Road.

"They just robbed Maurice."

"Who?" I sat straight the fuck up.

"These two niggas name Face and Mookie!"

I never forgot a name, so I immediately remembered they were the same niggas who had robbed Murdoc.

"Them the same niggas that got Tamaine."

"Well they touched the wrong nigga now!" His grip on the steering wheel was tight. I saw the veins in his fingers pulsing.

"I'm dropping you off at home."

"No the fuck you not." I was sitting in the seat sideways looking at him.

The look he gave me told me to rephrase my statement and calm my voice down.

"I'm sorry for talking to you like that, but I am going with you whether you like it or not."

"You five months."

"So what I'm five months pregnant? That don't mean nothing."

He shook his head at me and put his phone to his ear. "Have them things ready, I'm 'bout to pull up."

When we got there, Maurice was standing outside of his house with a nigga I didn't know. Murda hopped out of the car before the engine had time to turn off, and I was right behind him.

"What them niggas got you for, yo?" He barked at his brother. Murda never raised his voice, so for him to do it then showed how mad he was.

"Two bands and an ounce!" He headed toward the entrance to the house and we followed him.

I heard Murda address the other nigga as A-Town while we were walking into the house.

"Where Flowsicka at?" Murda asked his brother.

He made his way to the sofa to sit down in front of a black machine gun.

"Shawdy either in the trap or the studio," he replied as he took a seat on the opposite side of the room.

I closed the door and looked around. Two flat screen TV's were hanging from the ceiling and the carpet was jet black, while the rest of the room had everything white, from the walls to the sofa.

"Love," Murda spoke in a calm tone to me.

I looked at him as he tapped the seat beside him with his left hand. He didn't have to say anything else. He wanted me beside him.

"Yo, Murda, I already told Maurice we can hit them niggas now or later, it doesn't matter. I'm down to ride, you feel me?" A-Town said, pulling out a .357 from his waist and placing it on the table in front of me. That nigga A-Town was 5'6", a good 160 pounds, with tatts all over his hands.

"Bruh, you best believe them niggas, gonna get touched before tomorrow gets here!" Murda said in a deadly tone that made the hairs on my arms stand up. He looked at me, then from A-Town to his brother.

Over the next twenty minutes, they had everything figured out. A-Town gave them the run down about where them niggas, Face and Mookie, were laying their heads.

"They got another nigga on their team named Scando, too. That nigga on the run for a gun charge," A-Town said as he walked back and forth within the room.

Face, Mookie and Scando all grew up together in College Hill. Face was the oldest and Scando was the baby. They all were best friends and they got a hustle taking other street niggas' shit.

"Tonight get ready to roll around 12." Murda told them as he pulled me up off of the sofa.

***

Later that evening

"I don't care what you saying Murda. I'm coming!" I was watching him get dressed.

He kept saying I was staying home, but I wasn't going for that shit.

Finally, he said, "Since your ass already dressed, let's go!"

It was 12 a.m. when we got to A-Town's apartment on Hillside Circle.

Maurice was shocked as hell seeing me.

"Love?" He looked at Murda and then back at me. A-Town was loading up his gun at the table with gloves on his hands.

"Don't even question it. I'm here now!" I was looking at him and Murda.

Maurice was Murda's blood and Murda was my man so damn right I had their backs.

"You heard the lady, brute!" Murda told Maurice with a laugh.

"Wife her," A-Town spoke with his fingers at Murda then to me.

"I already did!"

I watched them load their guns up feeling some type of way.

"Why ya face like that?" Maurice asked me as he tucked the heat into the waist of his pants.

"'Cause y'all got me feeling naked without one."

A-Town threw his head back as laughter escaped from his body. Murda just kept shaking his head from side to side in disbelief.

"I got you something, hold on," A-Town said, leaving the room.

When he got back he pushed a .38 across the table to me. I picked it up and cocked the hammer back.

"Yo! Yo!" Maurice said, jumping out of the way.

"Nigga, I know what I am doing!" I screamed at him. Them niggas acted like they never had a real gangsta bitch in their presence before.

I took my finger off of the trigger as I eased the hammer back.

All six eyes were glued on me, hoping I didn't fire off. A-Town was just shaking his head with a smile on his face.

"I'm driving, so let's go!" I said, stuffing the gun inside my shorts on the right side beside my big ass belly after I'd finished loading it up.

"Bruh, she's a handful." I heard Maurice telling his brother.

"You don't think I know?"

"You bring beef to one, you bringing beef to a family! I'll ride or die fa mine!" I told my boo when we got in the car.

"I see that, lil' lady!"

A-Town said the nigga Face had a bitch that he was fucking with on Kemper Street, so that was my first stop.

When I pulled into the parking lot to the apartment complex, A-Town told me to drive over to the building with the dumpster beside it and park.

"Stay here, we'll be back." Murda said as he kissed me on my lips. I gave him that look that questioned why?

"'Cause I said so."

Then all three of them exited the car.

I had the lights off, but kept the car running.

They had been gone for 20 minutes according to the time on the dash board and I was getting impatient, plus I had to pee. The baby was sitting on my bladder.

Against my better judgment, I got out and went beside the dumpster to pee. And that's when shit popped off. I heard a round of shots fired. I didn't even get my shorts down, but my .38 was out and ready to bark.

As I came out from beside the dumpster a nigga ran past me holding his stomach but he was letting his hammer talk, too.

He didn't even see me. And since it wasn't Murda, Maurice or A-Town, I aimed at his ass and fired. The first round caught him in the arm, causing him to drop the weapon. I ran over to him and kicked the gun away. He was hollering out in pain, drawing too much attention in the already quiet complex.

I heard Murda's voice from afar so I finger fucked the trigger again, shutting the nigga up, with one to the head. His dome opened up and shit went everywhere. I watched his body jerk and then stop.

By then, the car door flew open and I jumped inside as A-Town pulled out of the parking lot.

"Y'all good?" I asked like I hadn't just sent a nigga to his maker.

My baby moved in my stomach, I still had the burning .38 in my hand so I ran the other hand over my belly.

"What the fuck am I gonna do with you?" Murda said from the front seat.

"Nothing!"

A-Town made a right and hit the highway, back to his crib. Murda climbed into the back seat with me as Maurice took shotgun over.

"Lil' Lady," he said, taking the gun out of my hand and holding me in his arms, never finishing what he wanted to say.

A-Town had gotten a pipehead's car to use for the hit, so we left the guns with Maurice and headed home.

I had to pee so damn bad that it hurt. Before the car even stopped fully in our driveway I was out and opening the front door to our house.

I heard Murda laughing behind me but I paid him no mind as I rushed to empty my bladder. It felt so damn good.

"I thought you was in here throwing up."

"Ha-ha, I had to piss," I said, looking up at him laughing. "That's what I was trying to do behind the dumpster when that nigga ran past me."

Murda never asked me how I learned to use a gun or if I'd ever killed before but thanks to Tamaine, I knew a lil' something.

He took his clothes off and entered the shower, with me right behind him. He washed me from head to toe and then himself as he told me how he caught the nigga Face sitting on the second floor by himself smoking a blunt.

Maurice shot the nigga in the stomach but he managed to take off to the other side of the building, down the stairs and out of the back door. They'd wanted to punish the nigga in a cruel way but he got away from them. But not from me.

"So I guess my reward is some good loving." I grabbed his extra leg.

"You ain't said shit, lil' lady."

That night, the dick put me to sleep, and I slept like a baby.

The next morning, Murda woke me up with breakfast in bed. As I ate, I turned the TV on the news channel just in time.

"Early this morning, police received a call reporting gunfire at the Kemper Stone Apartments on Kemper Street. After searching the area, they found a dead male in the parking lot. He has been identified as 38-year-old Hunter 'Face' Brown. Crime stoppers are asking anyone with information to please call us!"

I turned the TV off and continued to eat my breakfast.

"Yo, babe, ya phone in here going off," Murda hollered from the kitchen.

"Answer it for me!" I was getting up to bring my dish to the kitchen.

I heard him say, "Hello."

He handed me the phone with a *who the fuck is that* look as I got in there with him. I glanced at the screen, but the number was new to me. I didn't have anything to hide so I pressed the speaker icon so he could hear, too.

"Yo!" I yelled as I placed the dish in the sink.

"Sis, this QBanga." Murda's face stayed the same, so I whispered loud only for Murda to hear.

"It's Tameia's uncle." The lines in his forehead disappeared. "What it do with you?"

"Slide through Ma Dukes' house so we can talk."

"You there now?"

"Yea, I'm playing with Tameia." I heard her voice in the background giggling.

"Aite, I'm on my way."

Jamaica

Chapter 21
I'm Da Plug

We went our separate ways. Murda went to check up on his brother, plus he needed to find out if he could get a location on Mookie and Scando. And I stopped over by Ms. Julia's.

QBanga was playing with Tameia when I walked inside.

"When you gonna drop that load?" That's how QBanga greeted me. I flipped him the bird and picked my daughter up to give her a kiss.

"Mommie, Uncle Q said my daddy ain't shit!"

My mouth dropped open. My little girl was cussing like she was a grown up. QBanga was laughing his ass off.

"Tameia, shit is a no no word for you."

"Huh?" My little princess was confused, so I had to sit her down and explain to her that she just couldn't say certain words. It took forever for her to get what I was saying. I kept giving QBanga my middle finger every time Tameia wasn't looking at me.

"Go get some of your toys so we can play." Once she was out of sight, I asked Q what was Tamaine *ain't shit* ass about this time.

"Mane, that nigga just ain't shit, yo! If he wasn't my dad's wife's son, I swear his ass would be dead right now!" I saw anger all over his face.

"What the fuck?" I was lost.

"So I'm fuckin' with this bitch name Lotoya, but shawdy ain't my main joint, you feel me?" I nodded my head *yes*.

"Shawdy got a baby daddy that's locked up in the Feds so I was just knocking her walls down until her nigga, Cake, touch land. Anyway two nights in a row, I've been calling the bitch, but she ain't been answering. This bitch lives out in Timberlake so I'm like what the fuck is up with her? Remind you, I've got a key to her crib, so I let myself in and guess who I see dicking her down?"

"Tamaine?"

"Yea, that nigga!"

Damn, that nigga can't keep his dick to himself.

"What happened?"

Tameia walked in the room with two dolls, so I told her to go get a brush and comb from her grandma so I could hear the rest of the story.

"They didn't even hear me until I cocked that hammer on my .9."

"Oh, mane, I wish I was there to see that shit!"

"Shawdy was on her back begging for her life. Your fucking baby daddy was just looking at me. It took everything in me not to fucking pull the trigger!"

"I don't know what to say."

"Oh, it gets better! So I leave right then and there and go home. I didn't tell my real shawdy, Kiara, shit about what happened. So anyway, two days later, I'm out handling some business when Kiara called me talking 'bout our house on fire."

"What?" I couldn't believe the shit I was hearing.

"I rush to the crib only to find the place flooded with police and firefighters and the house flat to the ground." He was shaking his head. "Kiara is not tripping, but I'm losing it 'cause I had 45,000 in that bitch! All the fucking money to my name! Do you hear me?"

I nodded my head.

"Well Tamaine calls me the next day and says, 'Nigga, next time you pull a pistol on me you betta use it'. I told that pussy to fuck himself and hung up on him. The bitch, Lotoya, text me right after I ended the call and said: *I'm the wrong 1 2 fuck with. That's why I burnt ya shit down.*

QBanga was so mad, he kept walking back and forth in front of me cracking his knuckles one by one. "That bitch ass nigga brought the bitch over to my shit and let her burn my shit down!"

"Mommie, who is a bitch ass nigga?"

We both jumped at Tameia's voice. That little girl didn't miss nothing for her age.

"Tameia, go to grandma!" But she didn't move until I got up. She was testing me.

QBanga couldn't stop pacing the damn floor. "Kiara staying with her parents. I can't stay there! I feel like I'm less than a man. My dick caused all of this shit to happen in the first place."

I listened to Q talk his soul out. That nigga was selling drugs the whole damn time. Said he heard my name ringing but he didn't want me to know he was selling 'cause he thought I would have said something to Ms. Julia and she would then tell his father. I cussed that nigga out about me possibly running my mouth to Ms. Julia.

"I need help, sis?" His face was in his hands.

"Nigga, that's all you had to say long time ago. I'm da plug, nigga!" And with that we talked business on the way to my Leesville house.

I gave him a brick and charged him $28,000. He wasn't tripping on the price, but I did let his ass know. "Nigga, I better have mines!"

After we got back to Ms. Julia's house. I packed Tameia up and called my P.O. Everything was solid on that end so me and my baby girl hit the streets hard.

Murda was out looking for Scando and Mookie while I drove all over the city distributing crack. Flowsicka wanted 4 ounces for herself and 3 for her peoples. April's people wanted 3 ounces, The nigga, Polo, finally called me and said how him and a few of his niggas had put their bread together and wanted an ounce, so I gave him that and fronted him one.

Sometimes all muthafuckas needed was that extra hand to push them. If a nigga wanted to eat and showed me they were hungry, I helped them.

That's what a muthafuckin' plug does!

Jamaica

Chapter 22
October 2010

I had one more month before my baby boy would arrive when me and my girls decided to hit up Phase 2 for a girl's night out.

Flowsicka, Shauna, April, Snow and myself were stunting hard in that muthafucka until I seen Tamaine and his bitch, Keisha, at the bar.

Keisha had it coming from me so when I ran up on her bitch ass, she jumped behind Tamaine.

"Bitch, get from behind him!" I yelled over the music.

The nigga, Tamaine, was protecting her scary ass but when A-Town came from out from nowhere and told that nigga to move with the strap, he moved and I attacked the bitch like a wild bear.

By the time security got to me, I had the bitch's weave on the floor and my knuckles were red, so I knew I had drawn blood.

A-Town made Tamaine watch me trash his bitch. Shauna was so hyped that after security pulled me off of the bitch that she jumped on her ass. A-Town made April and Snow run Tamaine's pocket, too.

Flowsicka was videotaping that shit on her phone. Security put us all out that night and banned us for a month. We didn't give a fuck, though.

***

When I got home that night, Murda was up waiting on me at the door.

"You out there beating up bitches and you 8 months pregnant? Is you thinking?" That was the second time he'd raised his voice at me and it scared me. Tameia was asleep in her bed, so I closed the door. "I know you hear me talking to you, Love!"

I heard him, but I kept ignoring him. Damn right I was out there fighting. That bitch wore my clothes, slept in my house, probably was pretending to be mommie to Tameia when I was locked up, so she had it coming.

"Yes, I hear you." I was taking my clothes off to take a shower.

"You must still love that nigga." His voice was low and cold, but I heard him.

I grabbed his arm. He didn't look at me, but he had his eyes on my hand on his arm.

"Don't fucking try to play me." My tone was just like his. "It's the principle to this shit, and I'm pretty sure you know what I am saying." His eyes were locked with mines. "Just like how you killed the nigga that fucked Kandi!"

He pulled his arm out of my hand and left me standing there. I wanted to run after him and tell him how sorry I was once again, but I wasn't. Keisha had it coming just like that nigga he'd smoked!

Inside the shower, I replayed the whole club show in my head. I couldn't wait to drop the baby so I could pay Tamaine's ass back. What I had for him was special.

When A-Town had that burner in his back, he was standing straight as an arrow. I wished QBanga was out there to see it.

Murda was in the bed when I got out of the shower. I dried myself off and threw one of his 4x T-shirts on and got in bed with him.

"Baby," he rolled over to face me after I called him. "Don't be mad at me, please." I gave him my sad puppy face.

The flat screen was on so I knew he saw it.

"Love..." I stopped him with a kiss.

"I stopped loving that nigga a long time ago. I know what it looks like but it is not. That bitch was supposed to get that ass beating long, long, long, time ago." I kissed him again. "And you know I didn't mean to say that other shit, either."

He licked his lips. "Can I show you how sorry I am?" He just kept licking them sexy ass lips of his so I turned around so my ass was on his dick. I lifted my leg and waited for him to take his pussy, which he did from the side.

I fell asleep with the dick in me, and my man was not mad anymore.

Beating Keisha's ass and getting some dick had my body sore as hell the next morning. Tameia woke me up saying how she was hungry, so I got my sore, fat, pregnant ass up to make my babies something to eat.

Murda was already up and in the shower. I turned the TV on in the living room for Tameia, so she could watch cartoons as I made her something to eat.

My trap phone was ringing off the damn hook so I took orders as I made breakfast. Polo had my money plus he wanted 2 ounces. QBanga had my money, too, all of it.

Murda was out the shower when I flipped the last pancake. The scrambled eggs were already done.

"Tameia, go brush ya teeth, baby, and then come eat." She got up and went to do her.

"Morning, daddy!" I said when he got in my presence with a smile.

Silence. "I thought we made up last night?" Nothing from him.

"Okay, I deserve it, just don't stay mad forever!"

He opened the fridge and got a bottle of water, then he slapped my ass. hard. I wanted to smack his ass with the hot skillet. He burst out laughing as he took a seat at the table.

My personal cell phone started ringing, so I told him to get it for me.

"It's your P.O."

I dropped the fork and took the phone out of his hands. "Hello?"

"Hello, Ms. Jenkins."

I was wondering what the hell she wanted 'cause I'd already called her for the month.

"I got a call this morning," I held my breath and rubbed my belly, "from Tamaine, saying that you've been smoking weed and selling drugs."

"What?" I was so shocked that I had to take a seat. Murda was looking at me.

"So I need you to come down here in an hour and do a drug a test," she said.

"I'll see you then." I hung the phone up and told Murda exactly what the bitch said.

"Damn, that nigga is the police fa real, Love."

"If I fail the test, kill that nigga!" I meant that from my heart. All those ass beatings he gave me, not one time did I call the police, but as soon as I touched his dust bucket bitch he ran to the cops on me.

He would rather see me in jail than free with his babies. I knew his pride was crushed, but to run to the police on me was a different story.

"Was it worth it?" Murda said.

I knew he was referring to last night. Tamaine wanted revenge. Tameia walked in so I didn't get to answer him. I sat my baby on my lap and kissed her all over her face.

After I fed Tameia, I drank a whole gallon of water and cranberry juice mixed together, while I soaked my hands in some bleach. Ms. Julia was on the phone. She couldn't believe her son did that.

Tamaine's daddy had to be a bitch made nigga 'cause his mom didn't have no bitch in her blood. His mom said she would meet me down there so she could get Tameia and wait to see what happened.

Murda drove me downtown to my P.O.'s office and Ms. Julia was in the parking lot, as promised.

"Tameia, you have to stay with grandma for a little while so I can in the building." I pointed at the building and her eyes followed my finger.

"Okay, Mommie."

I gave my baby girl a kiss and thanked Ms. Julia. She put Tameia in the car and closed the door so we could talk for a minute.

"I can't believe he is doing this to you," she was holding my hands in hers.

"It's all good. I'm Jeezy. I've never called the police on him. Never! But I do see that he'd rather have me in jail than out here with our children." I took my eyes from hers and looked at Tameia in the car and then at my stomach.

"You have me," she said so sincerely.

I kissed her and walked back to Murda's car. I waved at her and Tameia as they pulled out of the parking lot.

Murda was leaning on the car.

"You sure you want me to do that to that nigga if you don't make it back out?" He pulled me into his arms but my belly was so big that I didn't get far. I looked up at him with my lips poked out.

His head fell and our lips touched.

"Before you kill him, make him suffer!"

One final kiss and then I walked into the building. My Probation Officer was waiting on me in the lobby.

"Ms. Jenkins how are you doing?" She greeted me.

"I'm fine, ready to drop this baby."

She smiled and told me to follow her to her office.

I just couldn't believe Tamaine would do me like that, but I truly hoped he would be ready for what I had planned for him.

We went over a few papers to make some changes before she escorted me to the bathroom to do my piss test. She stood in the bathroom with me while I emptied my bladder into a cup. She removed a color strip from a tube and placed it inside of the cup that contained my urine. I washed my hands and dried them.

"Your results are," she looked at me and then back at the cup, "negative."

"I already knew," I said with confidence.

She dumped the urine, disposed of the cup and then removed her gloves from her hands.

"Take a seat in the waiting area. I'll be out to see you in a few," she said as she left me in the bathroom.

When the door closed behind her, I exhaled. I was praying the whole time I was pissing in the cup. Even though I used gloves and a face mask when I was cooking didn't mean anything 'cause the dope that I'd been getting from Dre was pure fish scale.

As I waited on her return, I was reading an article about Lock Down Publications.

She entered the room. "So you're due next month?"

"Yes, I am."

"Well, call me after you have the baby."

"I sure will."

Moments later, I stepped out of the building and found that Murda was in the same spot I left him in on his phone talking.

A big ass smile was on his face when he saw me walking toward him as I gave him one back, winking my eye. He ended the call and walked to meet me.

"I just told A-Town to take his finger off of the trigger," he said as he kissed my forehead.

"Huh?" I was lost.

"He had Tamaine in sight," he said, leading me a. around to the passenger side of the Chrysler 300. I guess I had just saved his life.

Damn, my man moved hella quick.

I rang Ms. Julia's cell number and told her to meet me at her crib. She was so happy to hear my voice, and I was just as glad to hear hers.

I text Flowsicka and Snow and let them know about the fuckery that Tamaine had tried to pull. They both said they expected it from him 'cause he was worse than a bleeding bitch.

Murda's cell phone rang and he answered it as I continued to text my bitches about my sorry ass baby daddy.

"What? Hold on let me put you on speaker phone." He took the phone from his ear and touched speaker.

"The nigga, Dre, that be pushing the black and blue 760 got slumped by the nigga, Scando, last night on Rivermont Avenue, yo."

My heart stopped for a second. My mouth felt dry as Dre's name played over and over in my head.

"Scando caught the nigga coming out of Miles Store. Dre wasn't coming up off no money, so Scando shot the nigga four times close range and then shot his baby ma in the head twice in the car."

I grew an instant headache.

"How they know that nigga, Scando, that did it?" I asked the caller.

"The video from the store. The shit is all over the news, yo."

I closed my eyes, saying a prayer for my nigga, Dre, and his family. That nigga had just fronted me 5 bricks. I felt myself getting sick. My baby was kicking up such a storm in my belly that I could see his movements.

Murda took the phone off of speaker and told the caller he would hit him back later.

"I gotta get that nigga, Scando, before the police get him!" I was so mad that I was crying.

Dre had a good heart. The nigga was there to show me love in the game from the start. Because of him, I was where I was at.

He went out like a true gangsta, though. I smiled through my tears thinking about his words to Scando. *"Nigga, I ain't giving you shit that I done worked my ass off for, pussy!"* A true gangsta always goes out like one.

Murda knew I was hurting bad. He rubbed my leg as he drove to Ms. Julia's house. I'd told him all about how I'd met Dre and he had mad respect for him just because of how he treated me in the game.

Dre didn't look down or take advantage of me because I was a female. He treated me like a nigga. He kept shit real with me all the damn time, no matter if I liked it or not!

"Lil' lady," I turned my head in his direction, "Imma help you find that nigga, on everything that I love." His words were enough.

"I know you will, killa!"

QBanga was at Ms. Julia's house talking to his father outside when I pulled up. Tameia and her grandma hadn't arrived as yet, so I introduced Murda to them. We took the conversation inside of the house 'cause it was cold outside.

QBanga told me what I had already heard about Dre. I just couldn't believe that nigga was dead.

I sat back and listened to Murda, Mr.Gates and QBanga talk. My man had a good personality, so they clicked to him instantly.

My trap phone rang, so I excused myself to handle my business. I still had to get money even though I wanted to mourn the death of a real live trill nigga.

"Yo!" I answered not recognizing the number.

"Yo, this Nutz from 16th Street," the caller said in my ear.

"And?" I heard about the nigga from around the way. They said the nigga was about his paper without bullshit.

"Damn, they did say you was mean," he said, laughing.

I didn't find shit funny so I ended the call only for it ring right back. Same number.

"What?"

"All I'm tryna do is holla at you, shawdy."

"First of all I'm not ya shawdy. Address me as Love!" Silence, so I continued, "Now what can I help you with?"

"I got ya digits from Flowsicka."

"Okay," I said as I let my guard down just a little.

"Can we meet up and talk in person?"

"Yea, Z Market at the Top College Hill!" I was calling the shots.

"Aite, how long?"

"Twenty minutes."

"Bet."

Tameia and her grandma came through the door. My baby girl ran into my legs and wrapped her little arms around them.

"Mommie, I can't wait for you to have the baby, so I can get a real hug."

That made me smile. She always knew what to say to make me smile.

"Brother, will be here soon. You excited?"

She rubbed my big belly with her little hands. "Yes, I'm ready!"

"Good, big sister," I kissed her forehead.

"Can I stay over here with grandma and grandpa tonight?"

Ms. Julia was standing there watching us, so I glanced up at her to see if it was okay and she nodded her head.

"Yes, you can, spoil butt." That made her giggle as she ran into the living room where the men were.

"Uncle Banga!" I heard her yelled.

"Thanks. Thank you for being here for me, Ms. Julia."

"Don't mention it. It's my job just like it's yours."

I loved that lady. I just didn't see how she had a devil as a son.

We walked into the living room together. Mr. Gates got up when he saw his wife. I saw pure love in his eyes when he looked at her.

Murda saw it, too, 'cause he blew me a kiss.

QBanga was playing with Tameia.

"Aite, love birds, I've gotta go. Tameia, come give me some sugar."

I said goodbye and hit the door with QBanga on my heels.

"Sis, I got that for you in the car."

I collected my money and told Murda to stop at Z Market so I could holla at that nigga, Nutz.

We pulled up right in front of the store. The Philly Muslims were posted outside selling all kinds of shit. I hit Nutz' phone and told him I was there. He said he was, too.

"What you driving?" I asked him as I scanned the small parking lot.

"A white Crown Vick."

I spotted it on the side of the building so I pointed it out to Murda.

"I see you." I ended the call as Murda drove us over to him.

When the car was parked, Murda and I got out. The nigga, Nutz, was still sitting in his car. So I called him with my right hand to come over.

The nigga was black as dark night, only thing white on him were his teeth. He was rocking Adidas from his hoodie to his shoes, with a VA fitted hat. He was tall, but not taller than Murda, so he had to be around 5'11".

He nodded his head at my baby, and Murda returned one. I had my hand out so he could shake it, which he did. We chopped it up. The nigga seemed cool overall. I told him the only reason I was fucking with him was because of Flowsicka. He said he understood.

I hit Flowsicka up when I pulled away from the meeting. She said the nigga was one hunnid all the way, so I took her word for it.

An hour later, I was linking back up with the nigga at Miller Park. He wanted two birds untouched, not cooked, so just like I'd got them from Dre, he got them from me. The only thing that was different was the price. I charged him 64,000, and he paid it.

"You not gonna count it?" He asked me after he gave me the money. "Believe me, if it is short, I'll find you!"

The nigga's money was straight, though.

Sitting at the kitchen table watching Murda cook me something to eat, reality hit me that I had to find me a connect. Fast. Dre had given me 5 birds that I paid for plus he fronted me 5. Out of the 10 I had 3 left.

"Babe, I need to find me a plug."

"That's all you need me to find you?" His reply threw me off.

"What you mean by that?"

He turned around to look at me.

"I'm asking you, is that all you want?" I didn't say nothing, just looked at him. "Get ya panties out ya ass," he said, laughing, "and don't over think shit." He turned his attention to the food on the stove.

The curry chicken smelled so damn good. I couldn't wait to tear it up.

"You want to take a trip with me to New York next week?" He was sharing the food out.

"Hell yeah!"

"Well, gather up all ya bread, then, so I can plug you in."

That's all he had to tell me.

Within the next three days, I had two of the bricks gone.

Not long after that, Dre's funeral was that Saturday at the community center on Fifth Street. Dre's farewell was so packed that the lined was wrapped around the block and the police had to shut the traffic down.

It hurt me to see that nigga, Dre, in front of me not talking or joking. His mom was crying so damn hard that I couldn't even look at her in that moment. I knew she was hurting 'cause I'd lost someone that I'd loved, too.

He was buried in the same cemetery as my mom and that was packed, too. When his coffin was going down in the ground, his mom fell to her knees. Family and friends were trying to hold her up, but it was no use.

After the hole was covered, she sat beside it rubbing the ground and pouring her heart out when I walked up to her. Her eyes were red and swollen from all of the tears she had shed and her black dress had dirt all over it.

"He was a real man, cool, funny, loyal, real, just full of life."

Her tears ran down her face as I spoke. "The nigga that did this to him, his momma gonna be just like you." That made her look up at me. Her eyes landed on my big ass belly and she covered her chest with her dirty hands. "I'm just a friend, nothing more." She smiled through her tears. I gave her my hand to help pull her up. She took it and stood. "I'm pretty sure you knew the life your son was living?" She looked down at his grave and nodded her head, so I continued. "Before he died he'd given me a package. I know if the shoe was on the other foot he would have done the same for me."

She looked at me and smiled. We walked off hand in hand to her car, where there were people waiting on her. Murda was parked behind them. He took the duffel bag out of the back seat and marched it to us.

"Sorry for your loss," he said as he dropped the bag at my feet. "Watch the news, though, 'cause the nigga who did this is a dead man walking and don't even know." His word made both me and her smile.

"That's the $125,000 that I owed him. I know it can't bring him back but it can help out with his kids. And if you need anything my number is in the bag. Feel free to call me at any time."

"Love, you were the realest friend he had!" Her response made me shed some thug tears.

Jamaica

Chapter 23
November 2010

I took that trip to New York with Murda and Maurice a few weeks before it was time for me to give birth.

The nigga who they were selling the choppas to had a brother who was a kingpin in the Bronx, so they set it up for us to meet.

Murda was in the hotel room with me when a nigga his height walked in. They gave each other that street nigga hug.

"Baby, this is Moe." I stood up out of the chair and Moe's eyes grilled me. "Moe, this is Love, my lady."

He tried to hug me, but I stopped him, "Don't take it personal. I only hug my man," I said, looking at Murda. Moe smiled and shook my hand.

"She's a handful, son," Moe told Murda.

"Oh, I know," was his reply.

We sat at the table to discuss business and got straight to the point. Money.

"You want it cooked or raw?" he asked.

"I fuck her myself." I wanted it raw, so I could see how good it was myself.

He smiled and both top and bottom was bling'd out with diamonds. All his jewelry weighed more than him 'cause he was a stick. Tall, skinny with a bald head.

"How much you want?"

"Whatever I can pay for!"

Murda was laughing, but I didn't find shit funny. I didn't go for a handout. What I paid for was what I needed.

"She is one of a kind. You better marry her, son," his New York accent was heavy.

"I intend to," was Murda's come back.

I cut the small talk out and got right to the point. "I need to know ya price!" He leaned back in the chair and looked at my belly.

"Twenty-five." I got up and headed for the door 'cause the shit he was saying wasn't cutting it. "Twenty-two." I stopped when he said that. I knew I could talk him down.

"Twenty." I was facing the door as I gave my price.

I heard him laugh. "I can do that!"

I turned around and walked back over to the table with him. "And it better be that fish scale, too."

"Believe me you won't be disappointed."

"Good 'cause I can get real ugly!"

The rental we pushed to the Big Apple was loaded with 6 bricks, all of my money. The nigga wanted to front me six to match what I got, but I didn't want it.

Firstly, I had to find out if the shit was legit first. Secondly, I didn't want to owe a nigga that I'd just started copping from. Plus, I had to show that nigga that it didn't matter what was between my legs, I had principles, too.

We took turns driving back, just like we did on the way there. Murda and Maurice came off real good, too. They each had 15 guns apiece, each gun going for $250-400.

I couldn't wait to hit the 'Burg. I had two things on my mind: Getting paid and killing Scando.

When I saw the VA sign. I was so damn happy. Fucking State troopers had me feeling stupid sick. I wasn't even supposed to leave the State of VA., but how was I to feed my family if I didn't?

The baby was due on the 20th and I had only nine days to finish the package. I stretched the 6 birds into 9 and added some color to make the shit different.

I bought 2 boxes of food coloring. The first color I used was blue.

"Love, why this shit look like this?" Flowsicka asked me when I handed her what she asked for.

"Mane, that's Blue Magic!"

She left with it and then called me back two hours later, telling me to save it all for her.

"Mane, that shit is the fiya, all the fiends want is that shit, yo!" She was happy as hell.

"I told you!"

Six days later, I ran through the 9 chickens like water. Niggas were blowing up my phone like crazy. My dope was everywhere like roaches.

"Babe, hit that nigga up and tell him we coming over for a 20 piece Popeye's chicken."

"Damn, Love!" Murda already knew, but he was surprised. I hardly got to sleep or gave him some pussy the way my phone was ringing.

Me and Murda hit New York by ourselves, this time. Maurice and A-Town were hunting for them niggas, Mookie and Scando, hard.

Moe wasn't surprised to see me back so fast but when I told the nigga I wanted 20 birds, his jaw dropped open.

"You a female and you pushing like that?"

"I'm not supposed to? Because this is a man's game or something?"

"I'm not gonna debate with you."

"Please don't, I'm due in 4 days," I said, rubbing my stomach, "so don't force me into labor now."

He and Murda cracked up at my joke.

On the way back home, no stops were made unless it was for gas. We would use the bathroom, then.

When Murda drove I slept. I slept, he drove.

The 2011 Jeep was loaded with bricks like a Mexican van and we had to get it home. When we got on the NJ turnpike heading back to Lynchburg, my doctor called and told me I had to show up at Virginia Baptist on the 19th instead of the 20th because they didn't want me to go over my due date. I told her I would be there.

As soon as my feet crossed over the threshold of my front door, I went to work. Murda hit the sofa checking up on Maurice and A-Town.

I planned to use pink food coloring this time. Pink Panther would be the name I called it. The 20 bricks were gonna end up being thirty. I wasn't trying to be greedy and sell garbage, I wanted to keep pushing the fiya.

By the time I finished cooking 15 chickens it was 8 a.m. Dope was everywhere being dried.

Jamaica

Murda woke me up around 2 p.m. the next day with Tameia on the phone. "Mommie, come get me!"

"Okay, I'm on my way."

There was a drought on the streets with work, but not for me.

Flowsicka hit me up and I told her to swing through and get her shit 'cause I was spending that day with Tameia.

"How the fuck this shit pink?" She held the 2 bricks up to the light.

"Pure Pink Panther shit, my nigga!"

"Well, I hope it is just like that Blue Magic you had!"

"Believe me, it is and probably better!"

That bitch had down bottom on lock for real, with the mic and the work.

"Oh, you know that nigga, Cell, from White Rock told me to holla at you for him."

"Ain't that Nelle's baby daddy or some shit?"

"Something like that, I'm not sure, so don't quote me."

"What the fuck he wants?"

"This shit you pushing!"

"Ha-ha." It was a man's game but he looking for me. A female.

Flowsicka gave me my bread and bounced and Murda had left to go meet up with Maurice and A-Town, so I dipped behind Flowsicka to go get my princess with a package for her Uncle QBanga.

"Mane, that shit last time was a killa, sis!" QBanga greeted me at Ms. Julia's door.

"Well, I got another one for you," I said, throwing him the book bag.

"G lookin' out, sis."

After I packed and swooped up my daughter, I took her and hit the cemetery to see my mom. It had been a minute since I spent time with her.

"This is my mom," I told Tameia once we arrived at her plot.

"In there?" she asked, pointing to the dirt.

"Yea, baby."

"Grandma her name, too?"

I nodded my head *yes*.

160

"Ma, tell the man to watch over me, guide and protect me, please." Tameia was looking at me like I was crazy for real, but I continued, "Our love is bulletproof!"

I walked ten graves over to my nigga, Dre. His dirt was still fresh. "Dawg, you nailed it on the head when you said I would be the Queen of the 'Burg! I'm just mad as hell you ain't here with me." Tameia was walking around looking at and touching tombstones. "But don't worry, my nigga, Imma send that nigga to hell when I meet him. I put that on my life. As long as I live ya mom's gonna get love from me along with ya seeds. Thanks for showing me mad love when I ain't had shit, real talk!"

Damn! I still couldn't believe that nigga was gone.

"Tameia, come on, baby, let's go," I yelled before I turned back to look at my nigga's grave. "Damn!"

Later, me and Tameia hit the mall up real hard. I got her everything her little fingers touched. I even got Murda some J's and a few fitted hats, 'cause he loved them. I got my baby boy a few things, also.

On my way out the door, I felt a sharp pain in my stomach that caused me to stop.

"Mommie, are you okay?"

I was holding onto the side of the wall. "Yes, baby." Then the pain was gone. I had one more day left before I welcomed another life on earth, but I had to go in that night. So, I dropped Tameia off at her grandma and she was mad as hell 'cause she wanted to stay with me. Baby girl was screaming, kicking and hollering for me to take her with me and it broke me down having to leave her.

I got home and packed a bag for my three-day stay.

Around 7 p.m. my phone rang. It was the hospital reminding me I had to be there at 9 p.m.

As soon as I hung the phone up, Murda called. "I'm texting you an address, get there now!"

Him: 7:04 p.m.: 906 Hill Street. Last house on the left.

I was out the door in two minutes flat with my baby bag in my hand. It felt like the baby was ready to come out. The sharp pain hit me again when I pulled up in front of an abandoned house, on a dead end street.

I got out of the jeep and walked in the grass to the front door.

I called Murda's phone. "I'm at the door."

The knob turned and there he stood with sweat dripping down his face. "Got a surprise for you, baby."

I walked inside. The windows were boarded up. I heard a knocking so I followed the sound, candles were on the floor giving light.

A-Town and Maurice and another nigga were present but the other nigga was tied the fuck up and beaten badly.

"Who the fuck is that?" I pointed at the nigga on the floor. He had a rope in his mouth tied behind his head. Blood and teeth were everywhere.

"Scando," all three voices bounced back at me. That made my day.

All I wanted to do was stop his life, we all wanted to, so we did it as a team. We each had .9 mil with a silencer. I counted down and we fired off into Scando's body. Pieces of flesh flew everywhere.

His body jerked from one spot to the next with bullet holes.

Dre had to be smiling.

"Baby, I've got to take a shower before I have this baby." I told Murda when we stopped firing.

"Burn this bitch down," he told Maurice and A-Town before leading me to the front door.

"You drive, I can't!" He opened the door for me and made sure I was secured. I looked at the house and saw smoke. By the time we pulled off, it was on fire.

Chapter 24
Baby Time

Murda drove me directly home so I could get out of the gun smoked clothes and take a shower. The sharp pain from earlier had returned, causing me to hold unto the furniture in the bedroom as I got dressed.

"Babe, what time is it?" I asked as I picked out an outfit.

"It's 9:02."

"Shit!" I was supposed to be at the hospital at nine, but Scando had to be dealt with.

Murda jumped into the shower as I got myself together. As the seconds turned into minutes, the sharp pains got worse.

I called Ms. Julia to let her know that I was on my way to give birth. Tameia was in a deep sleep, so Mr. Gates kept an eye on her as Ms. Julia met me at the hospital.

I got to the hospital, but my doctor wasn't there. The staff notified me that she was on her way. They had my room already set up, so all I had to do was get ready to deliver Tamaine Jenkins.

They checked my cervix and I was dilated by 4 centimeters.

The pain was so strong I was sweating a river. But then I got an epidural and felt so much better.

Murda was by my side the entire time. He never left.

I was in labor for 8 hours and 46 minutes before lil' man entered the world at 5:46 a.m., weighing in at 7 lbs 10oz and 21 inches long.

Ms. Julia cut the umbilical cord, again, as I admired Baby Tamaine who was the spitting image of Big Tamaine.

Snow and Flowsicka showed up an hour later after I was cleaned up, gushing over my new bundle of joy.

"Girl, you sure that's your baby?" Snow asked me as she reached for him. Flowsicka was shaking her head and smiling at Snow's remark.

"Hell yeah, he mine!" I knew why she asked because lil' man was white as toilet paper.

"He is his daddy's twin," Ms. Julia added her piece.

"Why the hell he ain't here?" Flowsicka asked.

Jamaica

I didn't know why he wasn't. I had told his mom to let him know I was in labor, and she said she had talked to him. He said he would get here when he gets here. So I just changed the subject.

"Ya'll should have seen Murda's face when I was pushing." He was sitting in the chair beside me on his phone.

"How was it, brother-in-law?" Flowsicka questioned him.

"Twisted all up." I answered for him.

"And you wanna know why?" He chipped in. "'Cause she was breaking my arm with her hand."

One of his hands held one of my legs up while I held the other one and pushed. The entire room was cracking the fuck up, but when big Tamaine walked in, we stopped.

He walked over to his mom on the sofa and kissed her on her forehead. Murda was standing up with his hands on his hip. My baby was strapped.

I told Snow to walk over to him with the baby, so he could see his son. His mom put a towel over his shirt so he could hold Baby Tamaine.

I tried to pull Murda down beside me on the bed but his feet weren't moving. I looked up at him, pleading with my eyes not to hurt Big Tamaine in here.

"What's his name?" I heard the dead beat ask.

Snow and Flowsicka looked at me to respond.

"Tamaine Jenkins."

He was just staring at the baby in his arms. A few seconds passed before he spoke again. "So, why you ain't give him my whole name?"

That's all it took for him to say. Murda escaped from my grasp and stood over him with the .45 at his temple. Neither Snow or Flowsicka moved. I was praying that the nurses didn't walk in.

I heard Ms. Julia's soft cries, and I watched as tears ran down her face. I couldn't do anything, the pain pills they had given me had me dizzy and weak.

Big Tamaine didn't even look up. He just kept rocking Baby Tamaine, with the burner at his head. For a second, I wondered if the nigga was high.

164

"Pussy nigga, you raped her!" He pushed Big Tamaine's head with the gun.

"Snow, get my baby," I said in a very low tone, but she didn't move.

No one did.

"Nigga, you lucky!" Murda's voice was low but it sounded like it echoed off of the wall. That's how strong and powerful it was when he spoke.

"Next time we meet..."

"Smoke the pussy!" Flowsicka had the nerve to say, cutting Murda off.

They all hated him for how he did me and I didn't blame them, but I didn't want Murda to go to jail over his bitch ass, plus Tameia and Tamaine needed to have a father.

Ms. Julia looked at me wanting and hoping that I would say something to Murda to save her only child's life. I saw hurt, pain and love in her eyes, as I gazed back at her.

"Murda!" I shouted. His eyes and hands were still on his prey. Nothing was happening so I called out his real name. "Martin!"

He glanced at me and I shook my head. Little by little, he removed the gun from Tamaine's temple and walked backwards until he got to the door. He tucked the gun back into place and exited the room.

Big Tamaine looked at me with pure hate. His hands were shaking so bad I thought he was going to drop my baby.

Ms. Julia took my son out of his arms and walked out the room, too.

Tamaine got up and Flowsicka spoke, "Yo ass ain't shit!" He was walking toward my bed, so she got in his way. "Nigga," her hand was under her shirt. My bitch was packing heat, too, "I'll body you and won't think about it!" Standing at 4'11", that bitch was 6'11" with that pistol. "You saw ya seed, now leave!" Her voice clapped like thunder.

That nigga didn't say one fucking thing else. He looked from Snow to me and then to Flowsicka before he headed to the door with his dick tucked between his legs. I prayed he wouldn't turn around at the last minute and get smart.

Minutes later, me and my bitches chopped it up for a few hours before they bounced. Ms. Julia left also, but she let me know that she would be bringing Tameia tomorrow to see us.

I was so tired that I fell asleep the moment she walked out.

When I woke up some time later, Murda was feeding Baby Tamaine a bottle. I watched him burp and change his diaper. He handled my son gently and with so much love. I wished I was one of Murda's baby ma's.

Right then, I was beaming with joy seeing him interact with my blood.

Tameia arrived later in the day with a balloon for her brother. Her grandma and grandpa plus Uncle QBanga trailed in behind her.

"Let me hold him," Tameia asked. Ms. Julia had her sitting on the sofa holding her brother. "Awww, he my baby," she sang. Baby Tamaine was awake just looking up at his big sister.

Murda was in the bed with me, as QBanga and Mr. Gates snapped pictures.

Big Tamaine didn't call or show back up.

Just like on my daughter's birth certificate, the father's signature was blank on Tamaine's, also.

"I told you, fuck that nigga!" Murda said to me seeing the tears in my eyes. "He don't want to be their father? That's cool. They mines now. I know I'm not their blood, but I'll treat them like my very own!" His voice was soothing, mellow and soft.

I threw my arms around his neck and thanked God for him. The world still had some real niggas left, and I had one.

Chapter 25
January 2011

I took a week off from the streets after I got home with Lil' TJ, while Tameia took care of her brother like she was the mother, for real.

"Let me feed him. Let me bathe him. Let me do that, Mom. Let me do this, Mom." That was all she would say and I would let her help me out. She was the perfect big sister.

After a week was up, I dropped the kids off at their grandma's house every morning at 9 a.m. and hustled my ass off until 7 p.m. at night.

Big Tamaine was coming around seeing his kids more, thanks to the ass whopping Murda gave him. Flowsicka witnessed that one up close.

She was coming out of Buffalo Wild Wings one night with Maurice and Murda when they ran into Tamaine. Flowsicka said Tamaine swung on Murda first but he ducked the blow and hooked Tamaine up with a 6-piece combo like he was Kimbo Slice.

"Girl, that shit was so funny," she said, telling me the story. "Murda was beating him and talking to him, at the same time. When Tamaine lost his balance and fell, Murda kept sticking him with blows. *Wham! Wham! Wham!*" She demonstrated with her body. "Murda gave the nigga a chance to get up and fight but that nigga couldn't see the ol' head, Murda!" I shoved her for calling my man old.

"I bet them blows wasn't old." We were crying laughing.

When Murda got home that night he said he'd run into Tamaine but nothing else. I truly think that what he gave Tamaine helped him become a father. Even Ms. Julia said she saw the change in Big Tamaine, too, but I didn't give her any details.

Word around the city was that Scando had ran off 'cause his nigga Face's killers were looking for him and Mookie.

"Yea, girl that shit is crazy," Snow was telling me over the phone.

"The streets are not talking at all." The corners of my mouth expanded into a smile. "They say Scando's mother is taking it hard because it's not likely for him to disappear without telling her."

167

Jamaica

I had pleasure in killing that nigga. Scando could have just robbed Dre and pistol whipped him instead of killing him and his wifey.

"I heard there are posters and flyers of Scando posted all over the city, thanks to his mom."

His momma was mourning just like Dre's mom but worse 'cause she just didn't know.

Me and Snow rattled on about Lil' TJ and Tameia plus a few other things. Everything was straight with her except that Pedee wanted to get her pregnant. I tried to talk my bitch into letting him drop his liquid off in that thing, but she said she wasn't ready.

"Do you love him?"

"Hell yeah!"

"So, what you waiting on?" I qizzed her.

"Time, Love, just that perfect time."

I listened to her tell me how she was feeling, but I also took her man's side, letting her know that what she didn't do another bitch would, plus he was a good nigga to her. But her hardheaded ass kept saying the timing wasn't right.

By the time she got off of the phone with me, she was mad as hell because I told her she was selfish. When bitches got themselves a good man, they tend to just drag them instead of appreciating them and giving them what they wanted.

I knew from learning experience.

I'd tried to give Tamaine the world even though he treated me like shit. So why not give Murda the world? He loved me and my two. If he wanted another baby, I damn sure planned to give him one. No questions asked!

My trap phone rang, bringing me out of my thoughts. It was Nutz.

Out of the 30 bricks I had only 17 left, so I answered to see what he wanted.

"Mane, that shit I got from you was the truth, yo!"

I heard the excitement all in his voice.

"I'm glad you happy."

"Hell yeah! So I need to see what kind of deal you can give me if I get 10."

There was a drought. I was the only person with the work in the city and he asking for a deal? I was driving across the states to get that shit, gambling with my life and that nigga wanted a deal.

"A deal, my nigga?" I asked him to make sure I heard him correct.

"I'm just saying, I am spending bread with you." He had the guts to say like I didn't have other people spending their money, too.

So, I went in on that nigga.

"Yea, you spending that moola, but I'm providing you with the real deal! My shit is official. You can do whatever you want to do with it. But listen, my nigga, I've got mouths to feed, so if you ain't liking what you hearing, you can delete the number."

Murda had his palm over his face but a smile was there, too, as he shook his head from side to side listening to me.

The nigga, Nutz, told me he would call me back, so I hung the call up.

"That shit right there is a fucking shame! How the fuck you gonna complain on my prices?" I was standing in front of Murda. "I could see if the shit was garbage then say something, but I am giving this nigga the real deal!" Murda was such a good listener. He didn't say a word and that was a good thing 'cause my trap phone rang.

"Yo."

"You remember that nigga Cell from White Rock, that I told you about?"

I rubbed Murda's head listening to Flowsicka. "Yea!"

"Well, I linked up with that nigga an hour ago. He wanted to know if 10 birds can fly without stopping." He wanted 10 brick off top, untouched.

"You know the birds can fly down South to Georgia for the summer anytime." Murda pulled me onto his lap.

"But 32 is the number I am wearing on my shirt." I wanted $32,000 for one brick.

"Oh yea, he said he don't care as long as the birds fly straight." He didn't care about the price as long as the coke was straight. "Aite, let me know when you ready."

"Get the bread and I'll come to you straight from the grocery store."

What's understood doesn't need to be explained so the call ended. Meanwhile, Murda was placing soft kisses on my neck, that got my body hot.

I'd just stopped bleeding, too. I pushed his head back from my neck, pulled his dick out of his pants as I slide my panties to the side and gave my man a quickie 'cause I had to pack up the work for Flowsicka and get that money.

Not long after my quickie with my man, my phone rang and it was Flowsicka telling me everything was a go.

"Meet me at the Food Lion on Campbell Ave.," I told her as I put the bricks in a Food Lion grocery bag.

"Say no more," was her response.

I turned to face Murda, "You riding with me?"

"The way you just rode me," he said with a laugh, "hell yeah! I'm riding with you!"

***

The nigga, Cell, was the passenger in a Suburban. Flowsicka got in the back of our Chrysler with a black book bag on her back. She spoke to Murda as I passed the grocery bag back to her.

"I ain't count the bread 'cause I just picked the nigga up." She relayed to me.

"If the money ain't straight, I'll go find him!" Murda said, looking at the Suburban.

"Oh, I already know," Flowsicka said with an evil laugh. And I wondered if Maurice had told her some stories.

I gave her 5 bands and told her good looking out with me sale. The bitch didn't want to take the money for shit, so I had to literally stuff the shit in her shirt for her to take it.

"Real bitches do real things!" I sang to her out my window as I pulled off.

"Real bitches is all I fucks with!" She yelled at me.

I ran the greenbacks through the money machine, as soon as I got back to the crib.

"Is it all there?" Murda asked me from the bedroom.

"It sure is!"

A few more sales hit my line up. April's nigga wanted a 6 duce, Polo wanted 4 zones. The nigga, Nutz, hit me back and requested 5 birds, at the same price that I told him the 1st time.

The way the money was coming in by the time I finished the rest of the chickens, I would be looking at a milli and change.

QBanga called me on my way out of the door so I had to turn back around and get what he wanted, too.

"I'm going up top next week so let me know what you want me to tell that nigga, Moe." Murda told me as I shut the passenger door.

"Okay."

We talked about finding Mookie, the third nigga of the Dead Robin Hood Gang. The nigga had gone into hiding, but A-Town was looking for him day in, day out, nonstop.

Delivering the pies were successful and after the last stop, we went to Ms. Julia house to pick up the babies.

Big Tamaine was there with his bitch, Keisha, and she was pregnant.

We were all under the same roof. Murda was standing beside the nigga, grilling him and waiting for him to say something stupid so he could fuck him up, again.

Tameia was playing with her brother in his car seat in the living room with Mr. Gates.

Keisha was looking me up and down like she wanted to go another round, but I wouldn't disrespect Ms. Julia's house like that. So, I let the bitch live.

"Are they ready, Ma?" I asked Ms. Julia.

Tamaine's face was red. He was mad. There was a scar above his right eye and I wondered if Murda had blessed him with that.

"Yes, they are."

Murda walked off, leaving us there to go get Lil' TJ's car seat.

"Tameia, tell grandpa bye-bye and go give grandma a kiss." I yelled to her.

I heard Murda and Mr. Gates exchange a few friendly words and then Tameia telling him good bye. Murda took Lil' TJ out to the car as Tameia said goodbye to her grandma and her dead beat daddy.

I looked back at Keisha at the door and noticed a wedding ring on her finger. I shook my head as I closed the door behind me with my daughter in front of me.

The bitch, Keisha, turned him into the police and he wifed her up, plus she had an older child by a nigga that was doing 10 years for robbery. She left dude before the judge even gave him his time. She was a neighborhood's whore. So many niggas hit that pussy according to the word on the streets.

As I saw it, a nigga would wife a hoe before a real bitch. Tamaine's union with her proved my point.

Chapter 26
April 2011

I heard my phone ringing back to back, but my bed was feeling so warm that I just didn't want to move. After it stopped, seconds later, it resumed again. So, I lifted Murda's arms off my chest and got up to get my phone.

"Hello?"

"Love!" I heard a lot of noise in the background as Flowsicka called my name. Hearing the urgency in her voice woke me all the way up. I picked my trap phone up to see the time. It was 4:50 a.m.

"What's up?" I whispered, trying not to wake Murda up.

"Mane," her voice was shaky, like she had been crying. "I'm over at Shauna's mom's crib." I got up and went to the bathroom and closed the door so I wouldn't wake the kids up. "They just killed Timmy, yo!" She hollered into the phone.

Timmy was Shauna's little and only brother.

"What?"

My girl was hurting, she was sobbing so hard in my ear and I could only imagine how Shauna and her mom, Hana, were coping.

Timmy had just had a little boy a few months back. *Damn!*

"That lil' nigga dead, yo!" Flowsicka kept saying that over and over. After she calmed down a little, Flowsicka gave me the details.

Two niggas ran up in Timmy's baby mother's crib behind the skating ring off of Odd Fellows Road and demanded money. After Timmy gave the bread up, the niggas shot him in the head, in front of his son.

"Mane, I know the streets talking, huh?" I said, hoping she would say *yes.*

"Hell yeah, you know the streets gonna talk 'cause that lil' nigga didn't deserve that shit! All he was doing was feeding his family, yo!"

"Mane, that lil' nigga is gone, Love."

I had to sit down on the side of the tub 'cause my legs were getting weak from the early morning news.

"Have you heard any name linked to that shit?"

My bitch was so fucked up she could barely breathe. Her and Shauna went way back before me and her, so I understood how she was feeling.

Timmy was like a brother to her.

"They saying Mookie and some other nigga named Goon."

"Mookie that was down with Face and Scando?"

"Yea, that nigga!"

Well, that nigga Mookie came out of hiding only to kill someone that would be missed by all and that made my blood boil.

"Let me get the kids dressed and drop them off at their grandma's so I can get up with you."

I ended the call without waiting for her to respond. I called Ms. Julia's house phone and she answered thinking the worst had happened.

She said okay to me bringing the kids over after I got them dressed.

"Murda." I said, shaking his arm to wake him up. He opened his eyes but closed them right back. "That nigga, Mookie," his eyes opened up when I said that nigga's name. "Him and another dude named Goon killed Shauna's brother, Timmy!"

"When?" His early morning voice was deep.

"Flowsicka said a few hours ago, in front of his son, in his baby ma's crib behind the skating ring."

"Where my phone at?"

I got up and got his phone for him off of the charger on the floor and handed it to him as he sat up in the bed.

I packed Tameia and Lil' TJ a bag of clothes and supplies to stay over at their grandma's house. I wasn't gonna go back to get them until that nigga, Mookie, was dead along with Goon.

The kids were still asleep when I dropped them off at their grandma's house, a short time later. I gave Ms. Julia a tiny version of the story and she told me to be safe as I left her.

Murda had called and woke up both A-Town and Maurice. Flowsicka was still at Timmy's mom's house with Shauna, so when I called her, I talked to Shauna for a few minutes. Shawdy couldn't even get a complete sentence out to me the way she was bawling.

"I want that nigga, Mookie, to flock like Face and Scando. Dead!" I said to Murda as we pulled up at A-Town's crib.

"That won't be hard!'

A-Town was wiping the sleep out of his eyes when he opened the door. Maurice was already there blazing up a Bob Marley.

"My shawdy fucked up, yo!" Maurice said, releasing a cloud of smoke from his mouth, referring to Flowsicka.

"That shit just happened so the nigga, Mookie, can't be far," Murda said as I crashed on the sofa beside Maurice.

"The nigga ain't smart enough to move. Right now he probably scared. He did that shit in an apartment complex," A-Town was lacing up his Timbs.

Dre and Timmy lost their lives behind them Robin Hood niggas over their hard earned money.

"Fa real, I don't give a fuck who we got to body for this nigga to show up. I'm ready to do his momma, baby ma and his seed." Maurice pulled on the blunt before he continued. "My shawdy hurting over this shit and when she hurt, I hurt, too!" That comment made me realize how much Maurice truly loved Flowsicka.

I was doing my part because of Flowsicka *and* Shauna. Shauna let me use her information to get around town without question and I had to live by the code and keep it true by smoking the nigga that killed her loved one.

"So, let's visit his momma's crib. She still living in College Hill at the bottom," A-town said, reaching for the blunt from Maurice.

"Just don't kill the baby," I finally said.

"Why not?" He killed Timmy's little man's heart when he killed his daddy, so fuck that!" Maurice said with venom in his voice.

I couldn't say anything to defend Mookie's child's life.

Maurice's cellphone went off, so we got quiet as he answered.

"Babe," he said, so it had to be Flowsicka.

A-Town had returned with some hammers for our mission. Murda grabbed the Mac 11 with the banana clip up off of the table and admired it. Maurice picked up a Glock .40 as he listened to Flowsicka. A-Town threw me a .22, and I threw that bitch back to him.

"What the fuck am I going to do with that?" I grimaced as I reached for a bigger toolie.

A-Town shook his head at me, as he continued loading up.

Murda was wiping his toy down with a towel.

"Aite. I love you, too, babe," Maurice said as he let the cellphone fall into his lap.

"Flowsicka said the police caught the nigga, Goon, in the apartment, next door, with the murder weapon. A 12 gauge shotgun." *Damn! I knew they left Timmy real dirty.* "Goon told the boys that he didn't pull the trigger but Mookie did and how it was all his idea," Maurice relayed.

In less than 24 hours, one nigga was caught as the other ran for his life.

"So you see what I'm saying? That nigga, Mookie, can't be far!" Murda said, putting on some gloves to fill his joint up with bullets.

The police were at Mookie's mom and baby ma's house when we rolled through, so we kept it moving.

"He still in the muthafuckin' city!" A-Town yelled from the back seat.

"Ecoco Lodge on Main Street have cameras?" Murda asked with the Mac on his lap.

"Hell naw!" Maurice responded.

"Babe, drive that way." I turned left onto Maddison Street, passing Blue Ridge Jail and then left at the stop sign to hit Main Street.

I circled the parking lot twice before I parked on the left side of the pool in front of the rooms. Murda pressed the window button on the door handle, letting the window down to let some fresh air inside.

"They said that Mookie had left town after he came up off of a lick he pulled by himself a couple months ago." A-Town informed us. "But the nigga must have run through that change."

"Who did he hit?" I asked.

"Some nigga named AD for seventy bands!"

"Seventy bands and that nigga couldn't flip that?" My eyes were roaming the parking lot.

"Babe, that nigga is not a hustler, he is a taker!" Murda placed his left hand on the gear stick so I hit the brake and put the car in drive.

176

I pulled out of the parking spot toward the main office when A-Town yelled from the back seat. "That's that nigga right there!"

The nigga was on my side. And since Maurice was seated behind me, I let my window down as I drove up to office. Apparently, Mookie had just got himself a room.

Then all hell broke loose.

Murda was laying on my arm against the steering wheel, letting the Mac bark, while Maurice and A-Town lit him up from behind me.

I saw Mookie's body rock from side to side and then back and forth.

The noise that the Mac was making had my ears ringing. Glass shattered from the office building, as Mookie's body finally hit the pavement.

The shells from the Mac dropped on my legs, between my thighs, all inside and outside the car, and I was hella glad that Murda had used gloves to load that bitch up.

Ain't no way in heaven could that nigga still be breathing with all them bullets in him.

I exited the parking lot and made a left taking me up Main Street.

I hit White Rock and then passed Jubilee, where Shauna lived. I saw Murda's lips moving but I couldn't hear shit he was saying.

My ears were still ringing.

I passed Greenfield Apts., then I ended up at Burger King on Campbell Ave. I made a left at the light to hit 460 to take me to Leesville Rd.

Murda's lips kept moving. "Go to the crib on Leesville Rd."

I pulled up in my driveway twenty minutes later. I unlocked the door for the house so Maurice and A-Town could go inside as Murda searched the car for the shells.

My hearing was coming back, but slowly.

"How the fuck the Mac didn't jam, baby?" I asked him as he opened the back door.

We were picking up the shells from everyone's heat from out of the car.

"I kept my finger on the trigger lightly," was all he said.

He had to be a pro.

***

A week later, Shauna laid her brother to rest.

I was getting tired of attending funerals, so I didn't go, but I did send my condolences with Flowsicka.

Flowsicka said the entire block showed up with Timmy's picture on their shirts, as they remembered the little young nigga.

On another note, the police didn't even broadcast Mookie's murder. I guess they figured justice was served so why look for the people that took his life when he had taken one, himself.

Chapter 27
June 2011

Summertime in the South was all about ol' school cars. So I bought this 1973 Buick Centurion from an old white man in Maddison Heights for $1,700. I had the title in Ms. Julia's name, as I got it worked on in the chop shop.

My favorite colors were black, green and yellow, just like the Jamaican flag. So those were the colors I told the shop I wanted on it. Instead of having two tones, I would have three.

I'd pushed my weight up in the game with the dope to 40 bricks a month. So every month me, Maurice and Murda were taking trips to New York to both supply and demand. Maurice and Murda supplied the choppas and I demanded the work.

Cell was coping ten every month from me, so was Nutz, at 32 apiece.

I was turning the 40 bricks into 50, still keeping it fire. I would change my color up every time I had a new batch.

My name was the only thing singing around the 'Burg. Even Tamaine was buying from me. Funny how the tables had turned.

"Damn, you can't let me get it for twenty-five, yo?" Tamaine asked me as Murda and I was picking up the kids.

"Twenty-five? Shit, you lucky I'm not taxing you thirty-two, like the rest of them niggas!" I was charging him thirty.

"I'm your baby daddy."

Murda was strapping Tameia in her car seat as I watched how soft he was with her.

"And?" I turned around to look at him.

Keisha was having a little girl, all the other bitches that claimed to be pregnant weren't. She was standing on the porch with shades on and I figured she had a black eye.

Ms. Julia told me how he was beating on her, still.

Murda was then standing beside me waiting on Tamaine to respond to me, so we could leave.

"Because I'm your baby daddy!"

I had to laugh 'cause the only reason I was serving the nigga in the first place was because I was scared if I didn't he would run to my P.O. again or even the police.

"That doesn't mean shit, Tamaine!"

Murda had my hand pulling me to the car so we could leave 'cause Tamaine had turned slow, unable to understand what I was saying.

"Holla at me, if you want it or not," I said over my shoulder to him.

Murda opened the driver's door. I got in and let the window down as Murda entered the car. I knew Tamaine felt some type of way 'cause of how he was looking back and forth between me and Keisha.

He had two baby mothers. One was broke and the other was moneyed.

We pulled off, rocking that nigga Jeezy's song *Streets On Lock* 'cause that's how I had the 'Burg.

A while later, I was waiting to pick up my ol' school when I ran into Kenny's Burger to get me something to drink. I had Murda drop me off, so he and the kids didn't have to wait.

"Excuse me." I was busy texting Murda how I was gonna fuck him when I put the kids to sleep that night. Then I heard the same voice say the same shit again. "Excuse me."

I lifted my head up from the phone screen to see a tall, brown skinned, heavy set, curly headed nigga in front of me.

"You talking to me?" I asked him with an attitude 'cause I didn't talk to niggas I didn't know. His eyes were roaming over my body.

I'd just gotten Lil' TJ's name and original footprints on my thigh like I had did Tameia's.

"Is you Tamaine's baby mother?"

I hated being referred to as his baby ma by anyone but that was how they were saying it in the streets. Tamaine's first baby ma this and that.

"Yea!" The lady had rung my drink up, so I was taking the money out of my pocket to pay for it.

"I'm Fat Boy. You be hollering at my people, Nutz, all the time."

Niggas just couldn't keep their mouths shut, for shit. That nigga had to be talking for this nigga to know I was serving him.

"And who told you I be hollering at Nutz?" I asked and took a sip of my coke.

"Nutz told me," he said exactly what I was thinking.

I walked around him to go to the door so I could walk back across the street to the chop shop to pick my car up. He was behind me when I got outside.

"What do you want?" The heat had me frustrated enough, now he added to it.

"That nigga's prices ain't right. I'm paying $1,500 for an ounce."

Damn, I thought. Nutz was making bread so why was he complaining about paying the 32?

"And it ain't even fire, for real." He continued.

I served the nigga, Nutz, the shit without stepping on it so he could do him with it, but he was taxing and cutting it, too. Not a good look for him.

"I'm tryna get my hands on that shit, the good shit!" I took another sip of my drink.

"If you ain't calling my phone with a stack or more, then I can't help you."

"Love, right?" I nodded my head. The nigga knew my name. Hell no!

"I got brick money, shawdy." I put my hands up to stop him.

"First of all, I'm not ya shawdy. Second of all, I gotta verify ya info. You got a number I can reach you at?"

I didn't know what type of bitches those niggas were used to but I was cut from a different cloth and that shawdy shit I was not feeling.

He called his number out as I stored it in my trap phone. I told him once I figured out what was what, I'd hit him up. He claimed he understood so I walked away.

When Ricky, the car man, pulled my car out the shop, my mouth dropped in awe. The top of my ride was black then green with the yellow on the bottom. The Jamaican flag was on the hood and trunk.

The 26 inch rims had that thing sitting up like a bus. The inside was just like the outside. Black, green and yellow. A 32-inch flat

Jamaica

screen was in the middle of the ceiling, hanging down. The one stop shop had done everything from the paint job to the sound. Inside the trunk was 2 15's with a 3200-amp watt. A loud horn was inside the grill so when the music played inside it would sound outside, too. Everything together cost me $5,500 but I gave Ricky $6,000 and an ounce of powder. He was a nose runner.

On my way home, I got pulled over by the police.

"License and registration, please," the black male officer asked me when he got to the driver window. I pushed my hand into my pocket.

"I think I left it at home." He was admiring the paint job.

"Do you have the registration?"

I leaned over and opened the glove box to get it. He had a note-pad and a pen in his hand, as he received the paper out of my hand.

"Name, date of birth and social security number." He demanded.

I had Shauna's information all memorized, so I wasn't worried.

I gave him the info that he requested and watched him walk back to his squad car in my rearview mirror.

Murda called while I was waiting for the officer to return. I told him what was up and he said to call him as soon as I pulled off.

Minutes later, the officer was back at my window. "Everything is good," he said, handing me back the registration. "The only problem that needs to be fixed is the color description." I was looking at the paper. "You need to have black, green and yellow, or you're gonna get stopped all the time. Get it fixed so it will be in our system when we pull it up in case you are pulled over again."

I assured him that I would get it fixed and apologized for the inconvenience. I waited for him to pull off before I moved.

As I turned on Memorial Ave., heads turned 'cause I had the music blasting inside and outside.

The sun was shining bright and the breeze was blowing so it wasn't as bad as earlier.

When I pulled up at the house, Murda was outside waiting on me without the kids. I figured they were taking a nap.

"That shit nice, but you drawing too much attention to yourself with that," he said, pointing to my ride as I moved toward him.

"You act like I'm gonna drive it every day."

"I never said you was, Love, but the streets do talk!" I wasn't in the mood to hear his speech so I headed in the house to see my babies.

Both Tameia and Lil' Tj were knocked out together in my bed. I closed the door, as I dialed Nutz' number.

My new year's resolution for 2012 was to give the streets up and invest in a restaurant, but for now, I trapped.

"Yo!" I'd forgotten that I had dialed that nigga's number until he screamed into my ear.

"Who the hell is Fat Boy?" I heard a lot of talking in the background.

"Fat Boy?" He repeated and I said *yea.*

Nutz claimed the nigga, Fat Boy, was a blood nigga from Greenfield who was trying to come up. He said he'd been serving the nigga for like nine months and so far, shit was gucci. He asked me what was up, but I didn't disclose anything that me and Fat Boy talked about.

"I heard his name around, that's all," I said.

Murda was now inside of the house, looking at me as I made my way around the kitchen.

"Well, I'ma holla at you in a few days."

"Aite. Do that." I pressed end and placed the phone on the counter.

I was taking the frozen chicken breast out of the freezer when I heard Murda's voice, "Babe."

"Yes." I answered. He entered the kitchen and took a seat at the table.

"I'm not tryna be on ya back about the shit that you do, but that joint outside is calling the police to fuck with you, hard. You still on paper but yet you pushing that without a job." Everything he was saying was the truth, so I didn't interrupt him. "Have you thought about going back to school?" I had to stop what I was doing and look at my hardcore man. "Have you?" He asked me again.

"No." I wasn't in the mood to talk about school or anything beside my kids and money, right then. I wanted to finish the rest of the brick that I had left so I could take another trip to the Big Apple.

"You need to start thinking about doing something positive. As I said, I'm not tryna run your life or tell you what to do. You're only 24 and sitting on a good mill and a half." I was thinking about doing the right thing, but not right then. "I'm just saying, you have two beautiful kids and a man who loves you. You've been locked up before so you already know how that other side looks and I know damn well you ain't tryna go back there."

I had to walk over to him and check his temperature on his forehead. He felt a little warm.

I'd been married to the streets since '06 and there it was five years later, and I was still faithful to it. "I was thinking about divorcing the streets come the beginning of the New Year," I told him as I walked back over to the sink to start dinner.

"I'm giving my end up." I turned around to face him. "I've got a good amount of money to open up a barber shop and a car wash detail shop and eat from that." Murda's tone was serious.

I had to blink my eyes to make sure this was the same man that just killed Mookie, sitting in front of me.

It was.

Chapter 28
September 2011

Summertime was winding down, but my money was still climbing the charts. TJ was learning how to walk and I had registered Tameia for preschool. Murda and his brother were still collecting all of the guns they could find and taking them to New York.

Snow and Pedee were expecting a new bundle of joy, finally. My girl gave up and listened to my advice. Flowsicka was still still the mic and the work.

April's nigga, Mike, had caught a body charge in in SC and got caught. The news said he committed the murder in front of a gas station. When I asked April about it, she said how a nigga tried to rob his brother, so he bodied the Robin Hood nigga.

A-Town, on the other hand, ended up getting his high school sweetheart pregnant, even though she was fucking with another nigga.

I was surprised that he hadn't touched the nigga, yet.

Tamaine and QBanga got into a shootout but none of them got injured.

Ms. Julia had a huge break down and she had to go the hospital. Her husband, Mr. Gates, was livid. He said Tamaine nor QBanga couldn't visit his house.

Fat Boy was a new client of mine along with a wild, young nigga named Jeremiah Scott aka Mr. Lynchburg. He had niggas scared of him. He was fucking nigga's bitches like pussy was going out of style. And let a nigga try to approach him about fucking their bitch, that nigga would shoot first and not even ask questions later.

A-Town told me that Mr. Lynchburg had fucked Keisha back in the day, I wondered if Tamaine knew.

Mr. Lynchburg also had a habit of jacking niggas for their shit, so I had to tell him one day when he met up with me to buy a brick.

"What you do on your end is on you but don't try to do that shit with me!"

"Come one, Love! It ain't that type of party with me. Niggas just be thinking their bitches all that and their money so long that it can't get repo'd." He was licking his lips talking to me outside of my car.

We were in his hood, White Rock. "I'm just looking for my Mrs. Lynchburg!"

"Even if you find her, you wouldn't know what to do with her 'cause you too wild." My kids were in the back seat in their car seats playing with each other.

He was walking off to his ride but I heard what he said, "We'd be the King and Queen of the 'Burg if I had you!"

I didn't call him out on his comment, I just pretended that I hadn't heard him.

Tamaine's baby ma, Keisha, was getting ready to drop their child in January. Ms. Julia said they had gone downtown to the city hall and gotten married. He was spending less time with Tameia and Lil' TJ, but that wasn't new to me.

Shauna had a lil' boy by this light skinned dude. Little man was so handsome even though he looked like his momma. Shauna was still taking it hard with losing her brother, but she spent a lot of time with her nephew, trying to ease the pain.

Dre's mom finally called and thanked me for removing her son's killer from the earth. I didn't say nothing.

I had eight more months before I got off papers and I couldn't wait. My probation officer wasn't tripping. I was still calling in once a month.

I'd found a building on Memorial Ave. for rent so I could open up my restaurant in January. My trips to New York were still regular but I wasn't getting as much product as I was before 'cause I was leaving the game alone.

I never thought I would have accomplished that much in that little time, but I did.

Before I made my exit, Fat Boy and QBanga wanted me to teach them how to cook up, so I taught them the lesson in my Leesville house.

There I was, a female showing niggas how to cook crack, but real bitches did real things. Just saying.

"Damn so that's what you do?" Fat Boy asked me. Tameia was in the living room watching cartoons. Lil' TJ was at home with Murda doing men things 'cause Murda said, "You a woman! You can't raise no boy into a man!"

Fat Boy was talking about me melting the crack back down and adding more baking soda to it and letting it get hard so it could be more.

"Yea! Just keep mixing it. Eventually it gets hard." I was showing him exactly what I was doing. QBanga was looking on, taking it all in his brain.

Tameia walked into the kitchen but I didn't run her out, she already knew what was what. She called the crack *Mommie's candy*. She'd seen me so many times in the kitchen cooking it up that it wasn't new to her anymore.

"You the police." My baby girl said. I stopped whipping the crack and looked to see who my kid was talking to. Her finger was pointed at Fat Boy.

"Why you say that Tameia?" I asked her as she let her hand fall to her side.

"'Cause he is, Mom!"

I thought my little girl had seen a cartoon with the police so I brushed her statement off as I looked at Fat Boy.

"Go watch TV, girl." I told her and returned my attention back to my students, but I couldn't keep her words out of my head.

I continued schooling QBanga and Fat Boy on everything that they needed to know, but Tameia's words echoed repeatedly.

They said kids could see things, but mine had to be imagining things up.

Jamaica

Chapter 29
January 2012

I'd taken my last trip in November. I was finishing up the last of the bricks so I could open up the restaurant. Murda's barber shop was open for business and things were going well.

A lot of niggas was mad as hell that I was leaving the game for good, but I had to for my family. Mr. Lynchburg kept saying how he would pay me 35 for a brick, that shit was tempting, but I couldn't go back on my word to take that trip.

I had 16 zones left and I couldn't wait to get rid of that.

Murda was out with his brother and a few niggas at the bar. So it was just me and Lil' TJ at home, since Tameia was at Ms. Julia's with the flu. My little man was fast asleep and I had just finished cooking the 16 ounces around 1 am that night.

I was so tired that I left all of the crack out to dry on the paper towels as I took a spot beside my son in my bed. I had fell asleep but I wasn't so gone that I couldn't hear what was going on around me.

I heard them muthafuckers before they even hit my front porch, thanks to the outside house alarm beeping.

I jumped off of my bed and sprinted like a track star, leaving my son behind.

Once I made it into the kitchen, I grabbed most of the crack cookies and dashed to the bathroom.

By the time they entered my house, I had flushed the toilet and was leaving the bathroom when I heard the explosion of my front door.

"Lay down! Lay down!" They all screamed. "FBI. Lynchburg Police Department!"

I laid right by my sofa on the floor in the living room in my white Hanes shirt and pink Victoria Secrets underwear.

It looked like a hundred of them was in my house. They had black masks all the way up their faces and the only thing that could be seen were their eyes.

"She needs a blanket or something to cover her up." One of them yelled. A foot was on my lower back as a gun was aimed at my head.

"Who else is here with you?" A male voice asked me while one of them helped me up and sat me on the sofa beside my shorts from earlier.

"My little boy." I put both of my feet inside of my shorts and reached down and pulled them up over my ass. "He's in the bedroom." Right after I said *bedroom*, I heard Lil' TJ crying. "Damn!" I said out loud. It broke my heart hearing him hollering.

"Do you know your rights?" A man without a masked face asked me as he took a seat beside me.

"Am I supposed to know them?"

His facial expression said he wanted to slap me. "I'm going to read them to you," he said to me.

"You have a fucking search warrant?"

"Yes, we do, Miss Jenkins!"

"Show it to me, then!"

He gave me the paper that he had in his hand.

As I read the warrant, he read me my rights. As he was doing that, another masked officer brought Lil' TJ out to me. He stopped crying when he got in my arms. I rocked him back and forth, trying to put him back to sleep but he wouldn't go. Too much was going on around him.

When the white man stopped talking, I spoke. "Can you call my son's grandma so she can come get him?"

"Yes, I can. What is the number?"

"434-401 ..."

He got up and picked my house phone up off of the base and dialed Ms. Julia's number.

"Damn!" I said, kissing Lil' TJ's wet face. He wrapped his arms around my neck.

Ms. Julia didn't answer so he hung the phone up. I knew she was asleep. When I glanced at the time on the cable box, I saw it was two-thirty in the fucking morning.

As soon as he put the phone back down it rang.

"Hello, this is Cobbs with the Lynchburg Drug Task Force Police."

I knew Ms. Julia was saying, *"What the fuck? Not again!"*

"We are at Love's house and she requested that you come and pick your grandson up."

As he talked on the phone, I watched the other officers ransack my house. I mean, they were taking pictures off of the walls, pulling vents off, lifting and pulling shit all out.

He hung the phone up and sat beside me.

"How old is your son? Is that the only child you have?"

"You the police, you should be telling me. That's what y;all get paid to do. Investigate shit, right?"

"I'm here to help you, Love," he said like we were old friends.

"Help me?" I asked him with a smirk on my face.

"I'm going to get you a piece of paper and I want you to answer these questions the best way you can."

He found a notebook on my computer desk with a blue ink pen and handed it to me. Lil' TJ's eyes were looking at the officers tear the house apart.

"Whose drugs is that in your kitchen?"

I look toward the kitchen at the crack cookies on the table, then I wrote the question down and waited for the next question.

"Who do you get your drugs from?"

Now I am thinking to myself like how the fuck you gonna arrest me if you don't know where I am getting my drugs from, unless someone talking. So, I wrote that question down, too.

"Where is the rest of the drugs and money at?"

Yea, I wrote that question down, too, thinking this motherfucker had to be on some good drugs thinking I was ready to spill my guts to him.

"It's your job to find it." I reminded him.

"You playing hard now, but think about not seeing your son until he is 20 years old."

I looked at Lil' TJ. He leaned over and kissed my cheek. I felt like he was telling me to be strong.

That was the police's game. They used children to break their parents down so they can sell their souls. But they damn sure didn't do enough surveillance on me because if they had, they'd know that I wasn't saying shit!

"Is that all of the questions you have for me, dude?" Fuck addressing that pussy ass cracker by his government.

"Yes, I'll give you some time to answer them." With that said, he walked off into the kitchen.

I closed my eyes and leaned my head back on the sofa as I pulled Lil' TJ's head onto my chest, wondering how did I fuck up? My paths were clear.

My mother used to always tell me, "It's the love of money that destroys everything."

It made sense to me now.

Me being a female with the mentality of a man and the intentions to get money beyond anything attracted nothing but haters and enemies, even though I made sure everyone ate with me and off of my plate.

"Your mother is here to pick your son up," he said, bringing me back to reality.

When Ms. Julia appeared through the door, her eyes said it all.

She had my back. Just seeing that made me smile.

"I owe you a lot!" I told her once she was in front of me.

"Girl, don't worry about your babies. They are in good hands." I knew that came from her heart.

"I know and I love you for that, Ms. Julia."

She bent down and took Lil' TJ out of my arms. He went to his grandma easily. I stood up and gave her a hug and let the tears stream down my face. Not tears of fear but tears of joy, knowing that she was willing to raise my children for me at the price of nothing.

"Take care of yourself, Love. You will be okay." I kissed her and TJ before they left me.

As I took my seat on the sofa, I realized how lucky I was to have Ms. Julia in my life.

When I caught my first drug charge in 2008, she took my daughter and raised her for me until I came home. Now here I was again, in 2012, leaving her with my son, too.

There was no loyalty in the streets but there was loyalty in me. I'd rather die in jail than tell on the next. I wanted my kids' heads to always he held high no matter what and I knew loyalty prevailed.

"Here goes the paper with your questions." I had only written the questions that he asked me plus I added a sentence of my own.

"Take her ass to the 9 West Building," he told one of the officers after he read the paper.

My sentence was, *What the fuck y'all muthafuckas take me for?*

They cuffed my hands behind my back. Brown paper bags were everywhere lined up.

"You will be gone for a long time if you don't co-operate with us," Cobbs informed me.

"Well, then, tell the Feds make my bed up 'cause I'm on my way!" I yelled back to him.

His fucking weak threats didn't scare me and I wanted him to know that.

They had called for a police officer to take me downtown.

The entire street was lit the fuck up but it was worse than my first time. One would have thought I had sent a bomb to the White House, the way they came for me.

The white male officer escorted me out into the cold air and placed me in the back of the police car. I could see my neighbors looking out of their windows at the excitement.

Truth be told I didn't give a fuck! This was my life. Who were they to judge me?

I closed my eyes and asked God to help me through this journey that I was about to take. I begged him to watch over my children and to remind them that I'd love them no matter what. I also thanked God for Ms. Julia.

Once the police car started, the officer spoke. "You need to think about this. You're only 25 years old, you have children that you need to raise. So cooperate and they'll help you."

I knew that muthafucka wasn't telling me the same shit, too? "Let me make this clear to you so you can pass it along. I've never snitched and I don't plan on starting now!" I was yelling through the little section of the glass so he could hear me good. "I don't give a fuck about witness protection or any of that shit they have to offer."

My statement had him stuck. I wanted him to understand me, but how could he? He was one of them. A cop and I was a female supplier, so he'd never comprehend.

"Well, I would tell, if I were in your shoes."

"That's 'cause you're a bitch! You couldn't walk a mile in my shoes. I am Love Jenkins! One of a kind, there is no more like me!"

He got the picture and shut the fuck up.

The ride to the 9 West Building was awful. I wanted to know who told on me and what they said. My head was pounding.

I was ushered into the building through the side door. I'd been there back in '08 and the only thing about the room that had changed was a clock on the wall with a map of Lynchburg Virginia.

My cuffs were removed.

I was thinking. *Damn, why do they have me down here at 3:40 a.m.?* But knowing them, they wanted to question me more.

I sat in one of the chairs and put my head on the desk waiting to see what was going to happen. So many thoughts were running through my head. My kids, Murda, my freedom. My fucking life!

At 4 a.m., a white lady walked in. "Hello, my name is Sarah Roberts. I'm with social services."

"Social service?" I shook my head, thinking: *not again.*

"Yes. The reason for this visit is because your son is in an unstable environment."

"Unstable?" I slammed my fist on the desk, causing her to jump.

"When drugs and guns are around a child, that becomes dangerous. Do you have someone that will take care of him?"

I'd been through that procedure before so I gave her Ms. Julia's name and address. And then, just like she appeared, she disappeared.

At 4:30 a.m., the door opened up again. This time I knew the face.

"So, Miss Jenkins, are you going to talk?" Cobbs must have gotten a hell of a salary because he wanted me to talk hella bad.

"Look, I ain't tryna waste ya time so could you please have me booked into Blue Ridge so I can get some sleep." I was still seated.

"Let me run something by you, Love. There is always someone that is going to talk," he said.

194

My legs were shaking, "I don't give a fuck who tell you what! I. Ain't. Telling. You. Shit!" I was kicking the table. "So can you please leave me the fuck alone?" I was screaming.

"Do as you please, but I'm telling you this. You are going to suffer!" He left with a smile on his face.

Fuck everything that cracker was saying, I was tired as hell. I'd been up cooking crack until 1:45 a.m., all I wanted to do was close my eyes and regroup my thoughts.

Ten minutes later, I heard two male voices talking out by the door but I couldn't figure out what they were saying. I got up out of the chair and made my way to the door so I could look out of the little glass part.

Our eyes locked and the officer pushed him through the other door.

My mind was doing a 360. *What the fuck?* I was questioning myself. *What the fuck was that nigga doing here at that time of the morning? What the fuck he doing down here, period?*

I knew what I was seeing was real. I didn't have to second guess myself. I could only co-sign for myself that I was loyal but for anyone else, I couldn't.

Jamaica

Chapter 30
My City

I was booked into Blue Ridge jail and my bond was denied. I didn't call home during intake much less shed a fucking tear. I slept.

The next day, they sent me to general population. When I entered the cell block everyone knew of me or about me, and they showed me nothing but respect, guards included.

My first call was to Snow. "My nigga, this shit is crazy!" I said as soon as she accepted my call.

"I know, Love, I know." She was crying. I heard her sniffing through the handset.

"Listen! I need you to stop crying and listen to me," I told her, hoping she would put the tears on hold for what I had to say. "I need you to go to Leesville and handle something for me."

I told her what I needed done and she said it would be taken care of, ASAP. Then I told her to call my other half on three-way.

When Murda answered the phone, I could hear the pain he was feeling for me through his voice.

"What they charge you with, baby?" he asked.

"Possessions with the intent to distribute. Abuse or Neglect of a child and possession of a firearm."

"What the fuck?" Murda yelled with rage.

I had to calm him down, just to find out what the police had confiscated. He said they cleaned the crib, all of the flat screens and furniture. My Jamaican car and the Chevy Caprice were both taken.

"Everything, Love. All our clothes and jewelry, gone!"

I'd expected that. I told him not to stress, that shit could be replaced.

My visitation was on Friday, so I told him to make sure he was there with Ms. Julia and my kids to see me.

"You know I'm gonna be there, lil' lady." Even in that stressful moment, he made me smile with his words.

After I talked to him and Snow, I called Ms. Julia. She said my arrest wasn't on the news, and I wondered why. QBanag told her they had picked up Nutz, Cell and someone else, but she couldn't remember the name. I told her to kiss my kids for me and please make sure I saw them on Friday.

"Only death can stop me from showing up, Love!"

For the next few days, all I did was sleep. I couldn't even get up to get a tray, that's how I tired I was.

Friday came fast. Ms. Julia and the kids were there at 8 a.m., waiting to see me. Tameia was standing on the ledge in the window of the booth, talking to me.

"Ma, what's this place called?"

"Jail." She wanted to know what jail was so I had to explain it to her. "When people do bad things, they put them here."

"What you did bad?"

Tameia wanted to know everything, and I never lied to her about anything and I damn sure wasn't about to start. So I told her.

"For selling candy."

"Your candy?" She placed one hand on her little hip, which made me smile.

I wondered just for a second if that was how smart I was growing up.

"Yea, the candy that buys you and brother everything!"

"That's just crazy, Mommie." My little girl was a handful and more.

I talked to her for a minute or two more before I baby talked to Lil' TJ. He was teething and it made him cranky. Ms. Julia sat him down on the floor so him and Tameia could walk around and we could talk, privately.

"What they saying, Love?" Tears started running down her face.

"You gotta stop crying," I told her but the water kept running.

For the few days that I'd been there, not one person came to see me. One of the officers I knew from the streets because her nigga was in the game said the Feds came to see Cell and Nutz, and I relayed that info to her. I told her not to worry, but I knew better than that.

"Keep the money that you have for me and use it for you and the kids."

Last of a Dying Breed

She started crying harder when I said that. We talked about much but time flew and our visit went by fast.

Tameia was raising hell when it was time to go.

"I wanna stay with my mommie, Grandma!" She was yelling with both hands on her hip. I had to tell her she couldn't, but that I would be home soon and with that the tears came. "Promise?" Snot was running down her face and that was the first time I'd cried since I'd gotten arrested.

"I'll try, Tameia." The words took forever to leave my mouth 'cause I knew soon was gonna be later. "Kiss brother for me. I love you!"

"Okay and I love you, too."

When they left, I threw the phone at the glass, but it bounced back at me.

Miss Allen, the female guard ran to my booth after hearing all of the noise. She asked me if I was okay and I told her I was straight.

"You have another visit on the way up to see you, Ms. Jenkins."

She was a cool officer, and I could tell the only reason why she had the job was because of the pay check. She didn't let the authority get to her head. She treated the inmates like they were humans instead of criminals.

Minutes later, Murda took his seat before me.

"Baby," I said, putting my left palm on the glass. He lifted his and placed it on the other side of it.

I'd never seen Murda cry until then, I knew he was hurting, but I needed and wanted him strong so I could be strong. I leaned my head on the glass and the tears dropped from my eyes, as I held onto the phone.

"I need you out here with me!" Seeing and hearing him like that fucked me up. I'd always seen him strong.

"I need you to be strong for me, pleasse." My tears were still running.

I lifted my head up so I could see him. Our hand palms were still on the window.

"Imma try, lil' lady." His voice was weak, but it was a start.

He informed me on what the streets were saying.

A nigga named Marquees got picked up for a gun charge. It was the nigga's 3rd time, so he told on Fat Boy and Fat Boy told on me, Nutz, Cell, and some other out of town cat.

I told him how I'd seen Fat Boy down at the 9 West Building that night talking to them crackers. Come to find out Fat Boy's house got kicked in at 1 a.m. and he told them about me that same hour.

Murda let me know that Snow had called him and dropped off the bag to him so he had it all put up.

"When I know what's going on, I'll let you know what to do next." I told him as we both took a seat.

"How you holding up?"

"Shit, you know, missing my babies, you and my freedom." If I didn't have my kids then it would have been easy, but with them it was harder.

Murda wanted me to call him all of the time but he knew how much I hated using the phone from my last bid. It was bittersweet, but I did promise I would write a lot.

"I love you!"

"I love you too, lil' lady."

Seeing my kids, Ms. Julia, and my man had my spirits up that day, but not for long.

When I hit my bed that night, I cried myself to sleep under the covers. I didn't want anyone to see me shed a tear.

"Jenkins!" The morning officer yelled.

I sat up, rubbing my eyes. "Yes?"

"You have a visit," she said, walking to the door.

On a Saturday? I thought.

It had to be early 'cause most of the inmates were asleep. I put my orange jumper over my T-shirt and boxers and slid my shower shoes on as I headed for the door.

"What time is it?" I asked the officer at the door.

"It's 7:45," she said as she called control over the radio to unlock the door.

I buttoned up the jumper as she placed me in the visiting booth.

No one was on the opposite side, so I sat and waited.

A few minutes passed before two white men appeared in front of me. One took a seat as the other stood behind him. When the bald headed one picked the phone up, I picked mine up, too.

"Hello and good morning, Ms. Jenkins."

"Morning," I said, yawning and rubbing my eyes. They hurt from all the tears that I'd cried the night before.

"I'm Surtees and this is my partner, Stevens," he said as he pointed to the blonde headed dude behind him. "We're with the FBI and Drug Task Force for Lynchburg."

"Okay." I was wondering what took them so damn long to come see me.

"You are involved in the biggest drug bust ever in Lynchburg," he said, looking into my eyes, trying to intimidate me with his sneer. "We know you know a lot of people."

I didn't say a word, but I did yawn again. It was early as hell, and I was tired from doing nothing.

"You're facing a lot of time here, but you could change all that!"

I moved my eyes from his and looked up at his partner. Dude was just standing there nodding his head, and I had to laugh out loud.

"Did I say something funny?" He asked and I returned my attention back to him. "A few CI's said you know the city pretty well."

Right then, I knew a few people were talking. Fat Boy and who, though?

"You wake me up on Saturday morning, early as hell to find out some information?" I asked him, pointing to him and his other half.

They both nodded their heads, and once again I had to laugh. I dropped my head but picked it back up. "Y'all know Cobbs?" I asked, knowing they probably did. The one holding the phone signaled with his head *yes*. "Ask him if he got an answer out of me!" My face was literally touching the glass when I spoke. "And let that pussy know I still ain't cracked, either!"

I dropped the phone, got up and banged on the glass trying to get the officer to let me the fuck out of the booth. I looked back and FBI Surtees flicked me the middle finger.

I unzipped my jumper, pulling it, my boxers and under wear down before telling him to kiss my black ass.

Steven's face was beat red like a stop sign.

When the guard got to the door, I was snapping the last button closed. I turned around and flipped Surtees the finger just to top it off. The officer's face was priceless. The officer knew who they were, so witnessing me flipping them off had her doing a double take.

When I got back to the pod, I took a piss and went back to sleep like nothing happened. I didn't wake up until it was dinner and shower time.

The food was nasty but the commissary was okay, so I made myself a swoll: *noodles and cheese nips*. After that, I called my kids and talked to them before I returned to bed to write Murda a letter.

Artist: Jeezy
Song: Takin' It There

Baby
I got that song in my, head, thinking about you. :) How are you doing? I got ya letter, it was exactly what I needed to hear but we both have to face reality. I am not tripping about the time. I can do whatever they give me on my head. The only thing is not being there to raise Tameia and Lil' Tamaine, fuck everything else! Real Talk.

What am about to say to you might sound crazy, but I have to say it 'cause it is real shit. If I get 5 or more years, I don't expect you to sit around and beat ya dick, but I expect to not hear about it.

When I call, answer ya phone. I don't give a fuck if you have ya balls in deep, pull out and tell that bitch hold on you gotta take my call.

I know you're not the kids' father and you don't have to do shit for them, but please do it for me. Help Ms. Julia raise them 'cause we both know their daddy ain't shit.

Whatever you do, don't have no more babies. Lol, but I'm fa real and don't give ya heart away. Fuck all you want, but don't get attached. I know that's very selfish of me, but I need that from you.

Let the streets go and do the right thing, don't think I'm getting soft 'cause I'm far from that. There's no loyalty in the streets no more. A muthafucka will tell on his own momma to walk free.

I love you and what you stand for as a man. Real Nigga Shit! Until my casket drops, ya other half.

Loyalty is my lifestyle.

Mizz Murda

P.S. And you know if the shoe was on the other foot, could nan nigga grab my attention and I put that on my life, and you already know!

I closed his letter up and wrote on the back of the envelope: *Sealed with a kiss.*

I dropped his letter in the box and went to bed to eat my food.

Afterwards, I washed my face, brushed my teeth and hit the sheets, thinking about what the FBI had said to me.

I didn't talk to anyone in there. I stayed to myself so to take my thoughts away.

I reached under my bed and grabbed *Love Knows No Boundaries* by *Coffee*. Snow had it sent to me so I'd have something to occupy my mind. I woke up with the book covering my face and the officer hitting my bed with her flashlight.

"Jenkins!" It was Miss. Allen. "You have a visit," she said leaning down beside my bed trying not to wake the inmate beside me up.

"On a Sunday?" I closed the book and tucked it back under my bed.

"It can only be three people." She held three fingers. "Your lawyer, clergy or the police."

She walked toward the door as I got up and put my jumper on to go see who the hell it was.

"How are you doing?" Miss Allen asked me when I got near her.

"I'm good, can't complain! I'm breathing." A smile appeared on her face.

"How are you doing?" I asked her in return.

"Good." She nodded her head before she called control to open the door.

Jamaica

My visitor was already there when I entered the booth, with the phone at his ear. Ms. Allen opened the door and I walked in. She locked it back and left.

He gestured with his hand for me to take a seat but I wasn't trying to get comfortable. I picked the phone up and spoke, "What the fuck do you want?"

"Love, I'm here again today, by myself to help you," I opened my mouth but he held his hands up. "Hear me out."

I placed my left foot onto the seat and waited for him to continued. "I left my partner outside today. He can be such an asshole sometimes," Stevens said. "You're facing a lot of time. Time that can't be replaced with your kids! You help us and we will help you." I licked my dry lips as the pussy spoke. "You know a lot of things that I want to know and what you tell me can help you. We both will win in the long haul. I'll make sure your kids get witness protection and everything we discuss will not be disclosed to anyone." I'd heard enough.

"I don't give a fuck about anything that you are saying! I could care less about what you want to know or what you don't know! Stop coming to see me. I'm tired of getting up to see ya faces. I might be a bitch but there is no bitch in my blood!" I dropped the phone, took my foot down and turned around to face the door.

Before I could even bang on it, Ms. Allen was walking past, so I mouthed to her *"I'm Ready!"* I didn't scream like yesterday or drop my jumper, but my tone and demeanor were direct.

The cracker was still there even after she took me out and closed the door. He just kept shaking his head.

She took me back to the pod and I hit the shower. It had to be around 9 a.m. 'cause the television was on.

After my shower and handling my other business, I made my bed before I went to watch whatever the other two females were watching.

Ms. Allen was in the podium on the phone, she wasn't talking just listening to the other end.

I spoke to both of the ladies before I took a seat. "Good morning," they replied in unison.

As soon as my ass hit the chair, Ms. Allen called me over to her, she was no longer on the phone.

"I need you to pack all your things up," she said.

"Where I'm going?"

"Twenty-three and one."

I didn't even argue or say another word. Twenty-three and one was lock down. I would be able to come out of the room for one hour every day to take a shower and use the phone. I knew them muthafuckin' FBI crackers were mad, so they wanted to make my life a living hell, but hey just didn't know who I was.

I packed all of my shit up and put it into the gray box that they gave us to put our commissary and whatever else in.

I folded my bed in half and tossed it on top of the box. I pushed it in front of the door and waited for Ms. Allen to direct me to my new spot.

The entire pod was up and looking at me, but I wanted a bitch to say something to me about making all the noise with the box.

The way I was feeling, I probably would have caught me a body with my bare hands.

Minutes later, she moved me into B unit down the hall, that was 20 and 4 and also lock down 23 and 1.

She put me in cell number 23 on the second floor and left to get me some cleaning supplies so I could clean the room.

Other inmates were in their doors, looking out of the glass at me.

Them FBI agents wanted to break me all the way down, but that shit wasn't happening.

Ms. Allen returned with cleaning fluid in two bottles. She opened my slot and handed them to me.

"I'm sorry I had to do this to you," she said before she closed the trap.

"No need to apologize, I'm Jeezy!"

I cleaned the cell, using pads to wipe everything down. I did the walls, sink, toilet, bed and vent. By the time I was finished, I was tired and hot.

I laid my bed down on the steel, taped Tameia's, Lil' Tamaine's and Murda's pics on the wall beside my head and relaxed.

It was super quiet and truth be told, I liked it. I didn't have to lace the toilet all of the time before I used it.

Minutes later, off to sleep I went.

I woke up hearing a nigga's voice. "Hell yeah, baby."

"I'm just saying, though," that was a female's voice and it was all coming through my vent.

"Sing to me one more time and I'll let you go back to sleep," he said.

"Ms. Allen 'bout to do the lunch trays. After she done, I'll hit you up!" The female replied.

It didn't take long for me to realize what was what. The men's pod was on top of ours, and we could talk to them through the vent by standing on the sink and toilet.

Lunch was served afterwards shortly after that.

Ms. Allen was a ghost when shawty sang to the nigga. I laid in my bed and listened. She had a nice voice and she was singing Trey Songz, *Holla If You Need Me*.

I got used to my living arrangement quickly.

Every day, I got an hour out to take a shower and use the phone.

My mail and meals was delivered to me every day.

I told Murda all about what had taken place. He was so mad but when I assured him I was okay, he eased up a little.

Every week, Ms. Julia, my kids, Murda and Snow came to see me.

I told Murda to tell Flowsicka to lay low and not to visit me. If she needed to reach out to me she needed to do it through him or Snow.

I hadn't heard anything else from them FBI pussies until I read the newspaper one morning on my hour out.

FRONT COVER
BUSTS NET $10.5m IN DRUGS IN HILL CITY
Dozens of guns seized; investigation reaches to Cleveland, OH.
A federal drug task force seized more than $10.5 million in cocaine and marijuana in Lynchburg along with more than 4 dozen weapons and arrested several residents in an alleged cross country drug conspiracy.

The local arrests were made in February. Word did not get out until Tuesday because the Common Wealth's Attorney used the busts to make a plea to spare his office and the city police department from funding cuts during the city council meeting.

I couldn't believe the shit I was reading, I turned the page over to continue reading the article. There was a picture of myself, Nutz, Cell, Fat Boy and a nigga I'd never seen before.

US Attorney's office spokesman refused to comment, including as to why information about the arrests had not been released, citing policy not to talk about cases until defendants are indicted.

The system was so fucked up! I hadn't even been to court yet. *Damn!*

The task force targeted Fat Boy, 26, of the 200 block of Warren Street in March 2010 using informants to buy more than a brick of crack cocaine.

They were watching that nigga from 2010? What the fuck? I kept reading.

When they arrested Fat Boy at his home, they found 1 brick of cocaine, 4 ounces of crack, about $12,000 in cash and a stolen handgun. He was charged in Lynchburg General District Court with possession with the intent to sell cocaine, possession of a firearm with a schedule 1 or 2 drug.

My time was up to be out so I asked the officer if I could bring the newspaper to my room, and she said *yes.*

At the same time, Love Jenkins, a female, 25, of the 2000 block of Greene Street was arrested and charged with child neglect, a second or subsequent offense of possession of schedule 1 or 2 drug with the intent to distribute and being a felon in possession of a firearm. The total yield was more than $3.6 in cocaine, a carbon 15, 1 handgun and $1.5 in cash.

I was mad reading that shit, but not too mad 'cause they hadn't found all of my hard earned money.

Nutz, resident of 16th Street had 467 pounds of marijuana, 26 firearms, 11 ounces of crack and almost a million in cash.

I had to laugh 'cause that nigga had enough heat to go to war by himself.

A search of Cell's apartment on Taylor Street turned up $2 million in marijuana, and $987, 000 in cash.

The out of town nigga were identified as 42-year-old- Brad Morriston from Cleveland, OH. He was arrested at Wingate's Inn near the airport with 4 million in cash, 110 pounds of marijuana.

All of those charged are jailed in the Lynchburg Adult Detention Center without bond.

I fold the paper up and pushed it under my door after I finished reading it. I had to rest my eyes after seeing all those numbers.

Chapter 31
1 Hunnid

Two days later, I was in court but I didn't even know what was going on. The judge said the state dismissed my charges, but the FEDS had picked it up. Instead of taking me back to Blue Ridge Jail, they drove me to Roanoke, Virginia, to be indicted.

When I got there I was given a court appointed lawyer before I went in front of the judge. Inside of the court room, there was a sign over the Judge's head: *Why Do Ten When You Can Tell On A Friend?*

The judge read me my charges and asked my lawyer how I wanted to plea, but he didn't answer 'cause I did.

"Not Guilty!" I was then booked into the Roanoke City Jail.

I called Murda when they gave me my one-time free phone call, to update him on my status. I told him to tell Ms. Julia to go pick all of my shit up from Blue Ridge, food and all. He said he would be up there every day to see me because they had visits every day.

When I got to the cell, it was smaller than the ones in Lynchburg.

The block that I was placed in had only ten cells, with two to a room, but not every room had two people.

I was stuck in #6 with a white girl named Mickey. The shower and two toilets were in the same section and the shower didn't have a curtain, much less a door, so whoever used the bathroom would be seen.

The next day, my lawyer came early to see me. He introduced himself to me but I told him there wasn't no need to go into details, since I was replacing him. I didn't want a nigga to represent me that that worked in the same building as the District Attorney.

Hell No!

That same day, Murda came to see me as promised. He told me that he'd gotten in touch with a Jewish lawyer for me and that the man would be down to see me on Thursday. I told Murda he didn't have to come every day to see me 'cause it was a waste of time, but my man was not trying to hear that shit, plus he got onto my ass about that damn letter I sent him.

"What makes you think I can't beat my dick until you come home?" he asked me gripping it through his pants. I licked my lips as my pussy jumped.

"I'm just saying..."

"Love," he stopped me, "your pussy," he pointed at it. "Is the only one that can quench my thirst!" That made me smile and I let the subject go.

Mail, money, visits, I got them all from him since day one. Whenever I called, he answered. Maybe, just maybe he'd be the one to prove me wrong about men.

I told him to let Ms. Julia know that I was okay and not to worry about driving with the kids to come see me and for her to just wait until they brought me back to the 'Burg.

That Thursday, my new lawyer showed up with two hands full of paper work. He sat down across from me and gave me a quick rundown about him and his work.

He was from New Jersey and had been in business for 6 years. But all that shit wasn't important to me.

"When I got the call to represent you, I contacted the District Attorney and asked for all the evidence and paper work they had on you."

I leaned back into the chair. Roanoke's attorney visit rooms were big. There was glass all around us. I could see the officers and they could see us.

He said he had my motion of discovery with all of the people who were telling on me.

"Only one person's information is solid." He pushed a stack of papers in front of me before he continued. "You're facing life, Love."

"Yea," I lifted my head up at him. "I'm facing life! But my fucking people paid you, so what the fuck you gonna do?" I slammed my fist on the stack of paper.

He adjusted his yarmulke on his head before he pulled on his long beard. "I'm going to try and get you a deal for 15 years."

"Did you say 15 years?"

"Look at the paper with all the evidence on you and tell me what you think. Life or 15?"

In the United States District Court for The Western District of Virginia Lynchburg Division.
United States of America
Vs
Love Jenkins
Comes now the Defendant, Love Jenkins was joined in the conspiracy by Superseding Indictment dated May 20, 2012, but not arraigned until June 15, 2012.

I flipped the page over 'cause that wasn't nothing important. The page had all of our names, mine, Fat Boy, Cell, Nutz and the Cleveland nigga.

The Grand Jury Charges:

1. That from a date unknown, but no later than early 2010, and continuing through February 23, 2012, in the Western Judicial District of Virginia, the defendants listed about, did knowingly and intentionally combine, conspire and agree with other persons, both known and unknown to the Grand Jury, to knowingly and intentionally distribute and possess with intent to distribute 980 kilograms or more of a mixture or substance containing a detectable amount of cocaine, a schedule 2 controlled substance; and 460 kilograms or more of marijuana a schedule 1 controlled substance, in violation of title 21, United States Code... section with a bunch of fucking numbers in brackets.

"What the fuck?" I looked up from the paper at my lawyer.

"Continue reading," he said.

"What the fuck? That is your job. That's what you get paid for." I was mad that this kangaroo muthafucka was trying to come off on me.

"Ms. Jenkins," he said like he wished he didn't take the case. "I want you to read what they are charging you with yourself, then I'll explain it all to you."

I looked at him and rolled my eyes, before I continued reading.

So far I was in count, 1, 9, 16, 17, 18, 19, and 20. Seven counts all against me.

In count 20, it stated that I had a package shipped or transported in interstate or foreign commerce. They were talking about the package I asked Snow to move for me, but they didn't know what it was. But fuck if they didn't charge me anyway.

"You can beat that, right?" I slid the paper across to him. He read it over before he spoke.

"Did your friend get arrested?"

"No!"

"Well, that will be dropped!" His tone was confident when he replied. The next document was the amount of currency that they found between us all.

Approximately 12,000 in U.S. Currency

Approximately 1.5 million in U.S. Currency

Approximately 1 million in U.S. Currency

Approximately 987,000 in U.S. Currency

Approximately 4 million in U.S. Currency and coins

It wasn't no point of us slinging drugs if we weren't banking, I thought.

Lynchburg was so small, but so much money was floating around. Plus, all of the money that was still out there.

I was glad that Murda had invested his share into a business.

My lawyer's voice brought me back from my thoughts, so I continued to read the file.

Firearms:

2-Hi-Point handgun

4-.380 cal

6-Springfield Armory .40 cal handgun

2-Carbon 15

6-.357 Ruger Revolver

9-Smith & Wesson .40 cal handgun

3-SKS rifle

4-12-gauge Shotgun

5-9mm

5-Keltec 556 mm caliber rifle

Then there was all of the ammunition and magazines associated with the weapons. Fucking Feds had hit real big with this sting.

"You believe they found all that shit?" I pushed the firearm paper over to him. He glanced at it and shook his head.

Damn, I thought Murda and Maurice had cleaned the city, but they hadn't.

"Oh, before I forget to show you," he said, reaching into his carryon bag.

He pulled out two sheets of paper and pushed them across to me. I sat the other paper down and started to read what he gave me.

I understand that this is a voluntary interview, subject to the conditions set forth in this agreement. If I agree, I will make collective information at the U.S Attorney's office in Roanoke, Virginia.

"What the fuck is this?" I said, waving it in the air.

"On my way over here to see you, the Assistant U.S Attorney of the Western District of Virginia faxed it to me." He placed his elbows on the table. "It's called a proffer!"

I was confused, so I asked him what a proffer was and he started to explain it to me, but he didn't finish before I started ripping the two sheets up and spoke real slow so his Jewish ass could understand me.

"You work for me, that's what I pay you for!" I was so mad I was seeing spots in my vision. I kept ripping the paper up into smaller pieces. "Fax that shit," I pushed the tiny pieces of paper over to him, "back to that dick licker U.S. Attorney!" His face turned red like he wanted to crawl under the table and hide, He was so embarrassed. "Ain't. No. Snitching. In. My. Blood!" I was slapping my palms against the table.

The female guard knocked on the glass and asked if everything was okay, and he replied. "Everything is fine. Thank you."

I picked the papers that I had before he pissed me off back up and continued to read them, only to be pissed of way more by that snitch nigga.

On 3/21/2012, C. "Fat Boy" Wood was interviewed at the United States Attorney Office. Prior to the interview, Wood and his attorney, a Federal Public Defender, signed a proffer letter which provided by the Assistant Attorney. Thereafter, Wood provided the following information.

*   Fat Boy, age 25, has been buying/selling drugs basically cocaine and cocaine base (crack) since he was 15-16 years of age.

Well, damn, that nigga started the movie off with himself. My lawyer was leaned back into his chair as one of his legs was on the desk.

    *   *In the past, Fat Boy purchased crack cocaine from Nutz. The transaction amount was typically an 8 ball Or 1/8 ounce.*

Well, there goes Nutz. Mane, I couldn't believe this shit I was reading. But black and white didn't lie!

    *   *Around 2004, Fat Boy purchased from DP a member of the TWS crew. The transaction amount was typically an ounce every day. Fat Boy believed DP is currently incarcerated on a gun charge. Fat Boy explained 'TWS' stood for "Together We Stand' but the streets said it was 'Together We Snitch'.*

I knew that nigga wasn't calling another nigga a snitch, especially when he was selling his soul. But a snitch always knew a snitch. *Damn!*

    *   *Fat Boy confirmed he had just gotten convicted of a drug distribution in Amherst VA. As a favor, he wore a wire on Love Jenkins for his freedom.*

My heart stopped. I closed my eyes, hoping I didn't read what I read. I opened it back up and read that section again. *What the fuck?*

    *   *For the past three years, Fat Boy said he went back to Nutz and the transaction amount grew.*

This nigga was telling them everything under the sun and more.

"Just keep reading," my lawyer said.

    *   *Fat Boy described 17 first and last name unknown as a close associate of Nutz.*

This nigga had it out for Nutz bad. I wondered if Nutz fucked his momma.

    *   *Fat Boy believed JT may be a drug associate of Nutz. JT, a light skinned black male in his early 30's lives in the Dearington area and drives a blue Infinity.*

Mane, he was describing niggas and their ride. Oh, mane! My head was pounding with a headache from hell.

    *   *Fat Boy clearly advised that Love Jenkins manufactured crack cocaine at his residence on Warren Ave. Occasionally, he manufactured it at her house, also.*

"What! I never went to this nigga's place!" I was looking at my lawyer, hoping he could see the truth through me.

"It doesn't matter what you say, Love!" He stood up, "Love, with all the information he had given them, they have you, Nutz, Cell and they picking up more as we speak, thanks to Fat Boy!"

He made sense. Hell of a lot of sense! I was fucked, plus they had found drugs in my house and the wire he wore on me that day when I was teaching him and QBanga how to cook up. *Fuck!*

* *Fat Boy stated that Love manufactured crack cocaine and often used food coloring during the process. Fat Boy confirmed that Love always had a weapon on her at all times.*

I felt like I wanted to throw up. My stomach was in knots. I couldn't stop shaking my head.

* *Fat Boy purchased crack cocaine from TB at a gas station on Campbell Ave.*

* *Fat Boy purchased crack from Q, another TWS member.*

* *Fat Boy said that Maurice is a drug dealer.*

If that nigga was under the radar, now he was not!

* *Fat Boy said that Big P is also a drug dealer and burns the highway up with drugs.*

* *Fat Boy sold to Milles 1-2 times per day.*

* *Fat Boy sold to Marquees for a year. Fat Boy claim Marquees is presently locked up.*

* *Fat Boy believed that Cell is selling quantities of cocaine.*

The more I read, the worse I felt. My mouth was dry and my head was hurting.

* *Fat Boy said that BS is on the run because of a murder charge.*

* *Fat Boy believed TT who is was incarcerated in '98 is selling Cocaine. Again.*

* *Fat Boy identified Lala as a Blood gang member.*

* *Fat Boy believes NY, a native of New York was involved in some murder.*

* *Fat Boy has a strong feeling that Murda is a drug dealer.*

Reading about Murda had me hot. My nigga never touched a package! If he did, I would tell them people that I did it. *What's the point of having the both of us locked up for?* If I could have gotten my hands on that snitch bitch, I would have killed him.

*   *Fat Boy believes A-Town is a real killer.*

*   *Fat Boy believes Polo is Gangsta Disciple and a drug dealer.*

"That nigga told on almost twenty fucking people!"

My lawyer was walking behind me. "And they believe him, even if it's a lie."

Real was a real word, but by definition of what it meant in the streets it was dying out at warp speed. The only thing about real was the definition switched with the user now. So what was real to one was nothing close to how the next person used it.

I had seen enough, and I didn't want to see or hear shit else but the time I was getting. I got up and headed toward the officers but before I turned the door handle, I faced my lawyer.

"A female is the only human that can bleed for 7 days, 24 hours nonstop and still live. I bleed for 10 days straight and my heart still beats. The time they gonna give me won't stop shit. Imma let them pussies know that real bitches do real thing!"

And that was 1 hunnid!

Chapter 32
Court Time

When Murda visited me that day, I told him everything.

"I'll sign a plea for fifteen. Anything more and they can take me to trial!" His eyes watered up. "Baby, them crackers ain't breaking me! The only thing changing will be my zip code!"

I watched as the tears rolled from his eyes and I wished I could have wiped them for him like he had done for me. But my days of crying were over. If it wasn't about my kids, then fuck it!

A few weeks later, on my son's birthday, I was back in court. They had shipped me back to Lynchburg.

Murda, Ms. Julia, Snow, Flowsicka, Shauna, April and even people I didn't know were there.

Channel 7 news station was also present.

My lawyer got all the charges dropped except for the Conspiracy to Possess with the intent to distribute cocaine base (crack) and cocaine, Possession with the intent to distribute cocaine base (crack) and cocaine, and possession of a firearm.

They offered a plea for fifteen years and I took it.

My lawyer whispered into my ear letting me know that Fat Boy was sentenced the day before to six years.

Rat ass eating cheese nigga snitched on the whole city and was still doing time.

I listened to the DA call off all of the weapons that they had linked between the five of us and I shook my head.

The Drug Task Force team wanted me to get more time even though I had signed my plea, so they stated their case in front of the judge hoping he would add more time to my sentence.

The DTF said they made approximately 26 cocaine buys from Fat Boy, thanks to Marquees. They identified Fat Boy's suppliers as Nutz and myself. At that point, in the investigation, it led them to seeing me meeting up with Cell. And Cell was messing with the out of town dude so that's how he got jammed up.

Loose lips sink ships.

The judge asked the DTF team questions about me.

Q: Is Love Jenkins in this court room, today?

Everyone turned and looked at me. I was bopping my head to Jeezy's *All White Everything* song in my head.

A: Yes, sir, that's correct.

Q: Where does she fit into this overall scheme of things?

The dude that was representing the DTF crew laughed before he answered. My head was still moving.

A: Miss Jenkins is a mastermind. In two of the last seven buys, Ms. Jenkins was the distributor.

Q: When you searched her house what did you find?

A: A lot! Metal cooking pots, sifters, food coloring. The pink food coloring was also present in the crack cocaine that was purchased by Fat Boy.

Q: You need these things to cook crack up with, right?

A: Yes, sir, that's correct. Ms. Jenkins had Pyrex bowls, metal knives, digital scales, everything!

Q: Is it fair to say that's sort of a unique thing with the food coloring?

A: Yes, it is!

Q: How many times before have you seen this?

A: This is my first time in the system seeing a different color of crack. She had the Blue Magic, Blue Motorcycle, The Jamaican Lizard, Hulk, Pink Panther, Bubble Gum. She had it all, sir.

The judge looked like he couldn't believe what he was hearing, especially coming from a female.

Q: What else did she do?

A: She contacted another female telling them to ship a bag for her.

They were talking about me calling Snow, they dropped that charge, so I didn't understand why they were bringing it back up.

By the time they were done trashing my name, I was still smiling. *Fuck them! They couldn't break me.*

Before the judge gave me my time, he asked me if I had anything to say. And I did.

I stood up with the handcuffs on my wrists attached to a chain that wrapped around my waist that attached to the shackles on my feet. I looked back at my people and winked. I had to let them fuckers know how I rolled.

"I'll *never* snitch, much less shed a tear! I'll *never* violate the code of the streets and I will *never* testify or surrender information that y'all need. You can give me anything, a bitch won't trip!" The judge's mouth was hanging open so I went in for the kill. "Y'all might lock my body up but y'all won't trap my mind." My lawyer was pulling my arm down so I could sit down and shut the fuck, but I yanked my arm away. "This shit, right here, is in my blood line. I'm the realest bitch ever bred!"

The judge was standing up, hammering his gavel away and screaming, "Get her out of my court room!"

Two white male guards lifted me off of my feet but my mouth kept going.

"I'm the last of a dying breed!"

Jamaica

Chapter 33
Years Later and Doing Fed Time

Laying down on my stiff ass bed, I was on my back listening to my mp3 player. The air that was blowing from the vent was frigid, and even though I had two blankets covering me along with my clothes, I was still fucking cold.

My eyes were shut, trying my best to picture myself somewhere other than here.

With one hand behind my head and the other on my pussy, I was thinking about the last time I was fucked real good.

Damn, I need a nut!

I shot up when someone touched my left foot. It's my neighbor, Heather. I hit pause to Jeezy's *Lost Soul.*

"Love, they calling your name for mail." She removed her hand from my foot. "And you have plenty!"

"Thank you." I replied.

She exited my room without saying another word. I pressed play and flung the blankets off of me.

I climbed off of the bunk and pulled my black and white Adidas flip flops from beneath the bed and slipped my feet into them, moving toward the door to my room.

I shoved it open and the first thing I smelled was Crystal's egg rolls. Just like I thought, she was at the microwave upstairs.

Crystal had been doing that for the past six months on every Friday. She utilized the trash can they allowed us to have in our rooms.

I overheard her telling one of her friends at the computer last week how she needed to get her hands on a new *frying pan* as she called it from the safety/warehouse.

I've seen the *frying pan.* It was not as tall as the regular trash can because she got another inmate who worked in facilities to cut it down so it would actually fit inside of the microwave perfectly.

"Pennixl" The officer yelled and Ja'Kala showed him her ID and he passed her mail to her.

"Jenkins, right here, sir," I said when I got to the desk with my right hand in the air.

"Where's your ID?"

Fuck! I left it in my room. Damn!

"I lost it," he was staring a hole through me. "I went to R&D to get a new one, today." I lied to the police all of the time with a straight face. *Fuck 'em!*

"What's your last three numbers?"

"It's 084." This officer was really on some police shit.

"Here you go, Ms. Jenkins," he said as he handed me a handful of mail.

"Thank you."

I zoned him and the noises around me out to see who took the time to show me some love.

Shawn, Pierre, Jolon, April, Flowsicka, Angela, Derrick, Jeremiah, Doneille, Moyan, Murda, Shauna and Tameia had all written me.

"Jenkins," his eyes spotted me again and he handed me my mail without any questions this time.

The return info grabbed my attention. *Wood?*

The only person I knew with the last name Wood was the nigga who told on me. *Hell no! I know that ain't him. Fuck the rest of the mail!*

At that point, I walked off trying to rip the envelope open. I glanced at the address, once again.

Washington, DC.

I was so focused on finding out who the fuck that was that I bump into Heather. "My bad, shawty."

"You good. I told you *you* had plenty mail," she said as she looked at the stack in my hand.

"Hell yeah!" I responded as I'm walked toward the stairs.

I was trying to get to my room, so I can see who the hell this was for real.

I opened up my door and my celly was not in the room.

I dropped the letters on my bed, holding onto the mysterious letter that was piquing my curiosity.

The mail room had used a lot of tape on one letter. Damn!

Finally, I got the motherfucker open.

Dear Love,

Hey there. How are you doing? I hope this letter finds you in good health. I hope all is well with you.

I know you're wondering why I'm writing you and I know I'm probably the last person you want to hear from, which I can understand but I need to get this off my chest.

I know I can't make you believe me, Love, but trust me I never meant for it to go down like that. I never knew they was gonna take what I said and use it against you. That shit fucks with me every day knowing you got all that time and you gonna be away from your kids that long. It eats me up like a muthafucka. I know you'll never stop hating me, although I pray you do.

I wish I could take the statements back. I swear it's not a day that goes by that I don't think about the wires I wore that day. I really wish I could turn back the hands of time and make it okay.

I debated asking you this, but do you regret meeting me? I hope you're able to say no despite it all.

Changing subjects, you know every time I cut on my mp3 player and listen to Jeezy, you're all I think about. I know you love him, that's your nigga!

On the real, I really think about you hard. I even asked my sister to get a picture off of your Facebook page and send it to me.

I hope I can gain your trust and we can link back up again. That's not out of the question, huh? Well, if I have a chance at redemption, I enclosed my info.

I ain't gonna hold you up too much longer. I probably took up too much time already. Until next time, keep your head up and stay strong. You a G so I already know you gonna be alright. I hope to hear back from you, even if you cussing me out.

Peace Out
Fat Boy

I could have burst a blood vessel after having read that fuck shit.
Nigga got me fucked up!
I paced the floors with his letter clutched in my hand, remembering every step that led me to *him*.
Do I regret meeting you? I replayed his question to myself.
"Fuck yea, bitch boy!" I answered out loud before I sat on the bed and fell backwards, staring up into nothingness.
I should have never shown love to that nigga, but the thorough bitch that I was *did*, so I wasn't about to cry about it now. I'd been solid from the womb and there wasn't a man alive that was capable of breaking me.
My eyes then shifted from one side of the room to the other as I processed the day we crossed paths.
I thought until I couldn't think no more before I shook my head at the idea of him reaching out to *me!*
Nigga sold his soul and I ended up with football numbers for selling drugs, now he wanted to write and cop a plea for being a snitch?
I tucked the snitch's letter under the foot of my bed 'cause I was going to write his ass back tonight before I went to sleep.
I then heard the officer yelling, "Lock down!"
I looked at my watch and it was 3:40 p.m. I had no plans to leave out so I sat in the chair at the desk to read the rest of my mail.
I tore my boo's letter open and I smiled just seeing his hand writing.

Love,

Conspiracy catches more play than Drake's new shit on the radio and the little journey you on ain't nothing but a minor set back for a major come back. Loyalty builds an empire and our foundation is set on respect. Can't nothing destroy us, let alone scratch our armor.
Yo, what's good? How are you doing? I'm peace, just thought of you so I decided to put pen to paper and give us both something to do because truth be told, I miss the fuck out of you!

The babies good! The business doing ok! Shit is just crazy out here, especially since you ain't here with me.

I heard about all them new drug laws, so you know I got my fingers crossed, right?

It's been 4 years 3 months and 10 days since you been gone. I can't believe you on the other side of the country, but don't trip, Imma find a way to visit you!

The picture we got together is perfect, the government wanted to destroy our love, but they only making it stronger. I love the 10 page letter you wrote me, it surprised me 'cause it was so real and raw, and hell yeah the Feds ain't watching 'cause these niggas telling.

I got an interview with Coffee to tell ya story because facts are stronger than fiction and most movies can't compare to ya life.

I keep a thought of you on replay, true story, and I'm glad that I can put a curve to your lips (smile). You know I only got a soft spot for you, nobody else! We picture perfect remember that.

Silence is golden, and a lion ain't got to roar for people to know it's a lion, I know what you stand for and best believe me the streets do too. I've learned a long time ago that a man is only as great as the woman who stands beside him, whether it be platonic or much more because like-minded individuals build empires!

It's a must that you stay strong and focused to win this battle, 'cause two things you have left to count on is the undivided love that ya seeds and I have for you!

I see you fucking with Jeezy and Boosie hard as hell (LOL) as long as them niggas know that I come first! (Smile) Oh yea I don't give a fuck how old I am gonna be when you touch down, I want two more babies, and I want them from you!

You know how desperate these bitches are. Literally. I throw them a bottle of water and a three pack condom box 'cause I know they thirsty. And I don't want something only Magic Johnson's got money to get rid of.

Imma beat my dick for 15 years, shit, Papoose did for Remy Ma for 7! I got this boo! I know what kind of woman I have and I refuse to fuck it up over some pussy! Can't nan bitch compare to you, so why am I gonna look? I don't move backwards.

Yo, it's late so I'll end this for now but not forever and until pen meets paper, I'll be thinking/missing/loving you!

You Already Know
Murda

I couldn't help but to smile, even from home he made me feel good. Yea, I got fifteen years but with him by my side, I felt like I could do thirty.

Who knows? Maybe we'll last til' my casket drops!

I was a lot of things. To one nigga, I was his first baby ma. To another nigga, I was his wife, his ride or die bitch. To the Police Department of Lynchburg, I was that bitch also known as Love. To my kids, I was the best mom ever! As my favorite rapper and motivational speaker, Jeezy, said, I'm was a T.R.A.P.S.T.A.R.

A better way of saying it, a brick layer, but not the shit where I was busting sweat all day in the sun or freezing in the winter. *Hell Naw!* I was a hustler.

A full time hustler at that and *yes,* all the while having two children. It was not to get twisted, my kids came first. I hustled my ass off so we could eat real good. There weren't too many female hustlers about that life, but with me, I *lived* that life! I did it because that was how me and my two ate.

Thinking on my purpose, I thumbed through the remaining letters until I came across baby girl's.

I ripped Tameia's letter open with tears in my eyes.

It took me almost an hour to read the two pages she wrote. All because I wanted to read each line, word for word to the letter.

I found myself laughing at times but my chest was swollen with pride. Baby girl was so grown to be so small. At eight years old, she closed her letter by saying that loyalty was her lifestyle, too.

Mane, I love her and Lil' Tamaine.

After rereading my baby girl's letter I couldn't help but to cry this time around. I wasn't shedding tears because of the time I was given, but for not been there to raise my kids!

226

Bitch ass crackers gave me all this time, but watch how I do this shit!

Jamaica

Chapter 34
Response Time

It took me some time to get my thoughts together, but I finally had the venom surging through my veins and prepped to pour through the ink of my pen. It was time to murk this nigga!

Snitch,

Ain't no better way to address you, the name fits you well. Yes, you're so correct, I was wondering why the fuck are you writing me. The only reason why I'm writing you back is to set the record straight. You got everything off your chest when you sold your soul to them devils! So miss me with that shit, nigga.

You claim you never meant to tell the feds anything, but yet you told on damn near the entire city! Black and White don't fucking lie! The feds wanted me, well they got me, thanks to you. Nigga, I am glad your conscience fucks with you, I hope you lay down and never get back up!

You wish you could take the statements back? Ha-ha! Well, this statement I'll never take it back! You need to be buried beside your momma 'cause she birthed a bitch! If I could turn back the hands of time, I would have killed you when Tameia called you the police in the kitchen that day.

And, nigga, please stop listening to Jeezy, that nigga don't fuck with snitches!

You don't want me to hate you but yet you told on me and all them other niggas. You want peace? Nigga, you is a snitch and snitches get no love from me, much less peace. Take that love you got for me and fuck yourself with it! I am a warrior. Get it straight, pussy! You are a confidential informant, remember that!

Fuck you!

Fuck ya momma!

And make sure you tell ya DEA friends I said fuck 'em, too.

I felt a little relief after I finished writing the letter, but nothing but a bullet to his head would make my heart skip a beat.

My headphones were on blast as I listened to underground music on the radio 105.7 Da Beat.

"We have a female artist from Lynchburg VA who goes by the name Flowsicka. Here is her new joint *Seen It All,*" the deejay broadcasted.

What? I couldn't believe that my bitch had finally made it. I heard her voice and I tried to cover my mouth to muffle the scream that was coming out of it.

My head started bobbing to the beat and her voice.

My bitch, Jamaica, she the real deal
Them boys gave her 15 she kept her lips sealed
She so trill, never told never fucking will
That nigga folded on her quick
That bitch tough as steel
Thinking how they did her dirty
Give me fucking chills

Hearing her spit fire brought a smile to my face. I replayed her last words to myself knowing they were true: *A nigga will tell faster than a bitch!*

But as for me, loyalty was a must! I couldn't live no other way.

I am the last of a dying breed!

The End

Acknowledgments

First of all, I gotta give thanks to **the man above** for giving me yet another gift of creativity. It is a gift that I'm truly grateful for. It brings me peace within this storm. Every trail/test I had to face you told me, it was already in me and I got what it takes to make it out. Protect me from my friends cause my enemies I can handle.

Tameia, baby girl, I love you and I miss you more than you'll ever know! I love all your letters, oh mane! You just don't even know how you be making my days. You are my twin in everything that you do and I know the world is not gonna be ready for you. Continue to do good in school. Take care of your brother, remember you're his KEEPER, so stop beating on him. I love you and know that when I get home mommie gonna try and make up for all the lost time. We bonded by blood, baby, and it's UNBREAKABLE!

Tamaine Jr., every time you get on the phone you be having me in tears with your words, "Mommie, how are you doing or Mommie, I love you sooooo much." In due time, baby boy, I will be home. I know Tameia fight you all the time but I have a feeling she tryna' make you tough, and you better not hit her back either. I love YOU and I miss you so much more. Take care of Tameia! Remember, OUR bond is UNBREAKABLE.

Oswald and **Julia James**, grandpa and grandma, I love and miss y'all so much. Every night I close my eyes I ask God to grant me one more wish and that's to see y'all again. Not too many people live to see 20 much less 94 and 95. Y'all are the TRUE meaning of LOVE. Y'all raised me with LOVE, y'all taught me the true meaning of being a woman. All the qualities I got now, I got them from the both of y'all. I love y'all with all of my heart!

Leather, you know how I am feeling! If it wasn't for you, I just don't even know where my babies would be. Thank you! I know you said you wasn't raising no more kids but I know if I had one more and things got sour for me you would be right there raising that one too. But don't worry, when I touch this time things gonna be way different. I love you!

Esha, Savon, Melik, Mya, thanks for sharing y'all grandma with my kids and helping her take care of them, too. I miss been there with y'all, but it's all good. Tammy, what's good my nigga? I am still waiting on them flicks, too.

Donna, mom, what it do? I hear everything that you saying too, don't think I don't. I am gonna get it together, soon, so don't worry. I love you!

Wilber, daddy, I don't have nothing nice to say, but know that you are DEAD wrong!

Chessan, what it do my little and favorite sister? I love YOU. No matter what you riding with me. Thanks for all your words of encouragements, you always know how to put a smile on my face. I love you and I love that picture from 98' of the both of US #throwback for real. I am praying that ya mom pull through this. Bobby, congrats and I love you! To the rest of my siblings, all I can do is SMFH!!! Y'all know how to find me!!!

To **my family in JAMAICA, WEST INDIES**, JJ (my little brother, I love you and I remember when you was a baby, ha-ha, stay out of trouble) Aunty Tats, Uncle Dennis, Chevelle, Nicky, Anna, Erica and Family, Tunkie, Kimmy, KJ, Uncle Kings, Aunty Bev, RIP Uncle Willie, I swear I can't even remember everyone right now, but know that I love YOU all. Y'all know the JAMES family is hella big!

Doneille, I swear you getting worse and worse with emailing me, damn, get it together my dawg. I see you trying me mad hard, when I get home you know we gonna get it craccin' so get ya game up. But 4 real though, thanks for standing with me on this journey, I don't know what I would have done without you. Aye yo, you are the greatest mom, don't ever forget that and a hell of a babyma. Stay strong and know that I love you bacc! These wires can't cut our bond!

Gevetta, I love you! You've been team JAMAICA since day 1! No matter how far they send me you always find a way to make it to come visit me... I just want you to know, that I LOVE YOU...

Leonardo, (Rocket) I guess 0-100 real quick, huh? As long as we stay a hundred steps ahead there is no competition. Let's keep them questioning, how did we do it. We sticking to the code so they will NEVER find out. Meesa and Maddie, y'all are Queens in the making!!!

La'Tasha aka Flowsicka, sissy, I know you going through it right now but you too strong to be broken down. I salute you for what you stand for as a female. WE go harder that any nigga put together! They don't come like US no more! Our bond is tougher than steel, always remember that! I love you and I miss you. The system can't stop REAL bitches! Remember Real Bitches DO Real Things ALWAYS. Maurice, my nigga you got a REAL 1, hold her down!!! Ya Love is 1Hunnid!

Jolon Carthorne, aka Boslyfe, I appreciate all the love and support that you show me, real talk! Keep ya head up, this too shall pass!!

Shauna, sissy, mane, I know you lost without US, but stay strong for sissy! I am Jeezy, this shit done worn on a bitch. You fell off the map but I am GLAD that you are back and riding this wave with me and Flow. You ready to take that trip to NJ, again? Ha-ha... I love you!!!

A-Town, I know you on a vacation too and I hope it ain't as bad as what the haters praying for. We gonna act fool when we link up.

Keep ya head up no matter what and know that I love you, bruh. I know YOU will NEVER rotate, cause REAL is all you know!

April, mane, I don't even know where to start sis. Thanks for having my back like you do. For going out ya way to make sure I see my kids, mane!!! Anything that I want you, you on it like white on rice. I love you and I miss you, Blue Ridge created such a hella bond with US. You know this shit ain't gonna break me, at all. Mike, I hope you know that you have a REAL bitch on ya side! Keep that head up, you at the door now.

Pierre, you get on my last damn nerve. You never email me back but you stay tripping. Anyway, I am here if you need to vent, I know y'all ladies comes first, it's all good though. Keep ya head up and know that the sky is only a view.

Kiara aka Keke, Sis, you at the door now. I am happy as hell for you, real talk. Remember what I told you, use all that info and do it right. You already know who is REAL and who is NOT. Stay focus and make sure the kids are first. I love you. Ha-ha 26's had me feeling like I was in the sky, lol, you know I am a damn beast in that kitchen. When I hit land make sure you READY! LOYALTY is a lifestyle for US!

Timothy aka Cake, I am so glad that you are home! We go ham on each other all the time for nothing, and true be told, nigga I am not scared of YOU...But 4 real though, stay real and do right by them kids! You are a solid nigga!

Nutz, what's good, my nigga? You are not forgotten, keep ya head up, yo. And I heard you going ham with that pen and paper, I can't wait to hear you on a track. Real Niggas Do Real Things, REAL BITCHES, do too!

Kemper, really? Where you at?

Jeremiah, I am not gonna sit here and preach to you, but you was dead wrong, and hell yeah I was in my feelings. I shouldn't huh? 4 women pregnant at the same time? Hmmm, you real heavy, anyway, keep ya head up! You are a handful, know that!

Gutta Pot, Yo every holiday, you make sure I hear from you. Stay Real!

Moe, I remember when you told me I was gonna make an impact. Can you see it now?

Tameka, (Geek) damn, I know it ain't like that?

QBanga, you is crazy! I am glad that shawty didn't put you on fire...Enough said! But I know the last few months have been down, but stay up. Buy 6 copies of this joint, too!

Peedie, nigga I am on ya ass hard!

Andre West, so I know you don't read no books, so continue to buy them for ya shorty.

Timothy (Pooh), you show love no matter what.

Hanna, hey there lady, I miss our old days! Know that ya baby boy is watching over you, gone but never forgotten! I love

Derrick, you are such a procrastinator, mane! Anyway make sure you get that all white 760 when I touch with Booise in the front seat! You owe me that!

Shante aka Shawn, mane ya words are always up lifting to me, you know it is grind time. Are you ready to travel on the road with me? Aye, in my Jeezy's voice. I love you and I know you focus, so continue to grind hard and don't ever quit.

Angella B., our friendship is a blessing and I can't wait to visit you in the A. Don't worry things will get better soon!

IPPC, my FB accountant, thanks. You guys are the greatest.

A. Kanell, you are the best celly ever!

Spegetti, let me say this, I LOVE YOU, kid!!! Real talk!!! Stay true and real no matter what, don't let this time change who you are as a person. Continue to pray, and keep the faith, God will always make a way. I don't know what I would have done without you. Thanks for always giving me your opinion on my work, I hate it when you get RAW.

Lucy D (Ma Lucy), first of all, thanks!!! You listen to me all the time, our talks are the best! I am soooooo happy that you are finally home with your babies, 13 and a 1/2, mane, I salute you!!! And lately, I've turned into a baby Lucy with all them heads that I have been doing. I am gonna get my hair licenses, too. I love you!!!

Nikki and **Antonio** (Dee) Williams, it is hard trying to get a hold of y'all, but as y'all can see, I am still showing LOVE!!!

Palk, you are one of the realest, don't ever change who you are and you need to keep up with the entertainment so I can know what it going on and you a Jeezy fan on the low(LOL). Duncan and Belser, y'all know Gotti and Future put together can't see Jeezy, that nigga is UNSEEABLE! B.Williams, I hate it when you take all that power to ya head, had me doing extra duty and shit!!! Black, them moves be hella crazy!!

To **my sperm donor**, nigga, all that shit you jaw jacking ain't shit, do for OUR kids! I am tired of arguing with a bitch, grow some balls, and get in touch with me, until then shut the fuck UP!

To **the nigga that told on me and the city**, bitch, you know who you are, so I am not gonna go into that! These niggas these days tell more than a bitch. Taking a stand on their own momma but still they getting love from the street. WHY? Because they ain't tell on you or your people. A snitch is a snitch! No matter how you put it. The word LOYALTY don't mean shit these days! I don't condone that shit, cause I was raised different. I am not selling my soul, I was born real and I'll die REAL. Both my middle fingers to all y'all fuck niggas and bitches!!!

LOCK DOWN PUBLICATIONS, as a TEAM we are the greatest! Too many to name, but we are a team that grinds together and as they can see we shine together. #TEAMLDP. We move as 1, so they better cut it. The Game is OURS!

Ca$h, yo, you are one of the realest niggas alive. Real Talk... I remember reading 'TRUST NO MAN', mane, I can't even tell you how you smoked that shit! I ended up catching feelings for YOUNG BLOOD (Ha-ha). But anyway, ever since day 1 you've kept it 1000 with me, real and raw. When I am down and out or just need to vent, I can always vibe with you. Sometimes I hate the shit you be saying, but deep down, I know you're right! Now with this book game. Thank you for giving me a chance, especially when I was on my knuckles. You didn't reject what I sent you, but you gave me a better understanding on how to do it better. I fucks with you the long, long, long way, and for that my Loyalty lies with #LDP. So, I'm end this like this. I played the game and lost. And I won't front like I chose the game to survive. I was already surviving when I stepped off in da game. But fuck that! I wanted to live and have big thangs. Money, cars, jewels and shit! And that is why I chose da game. Somebody just forgot to tell me that it would end with my ass in prison. You know, in this game there's some authors tryna write about shit they ain't lived. Maybe they witnessed it from their front porch or from the passenger seat of their man's whip. Real niggaz can tell the real from the fake. See, street fiction should be based on the writer's own experiences, thoughts, and painfully gained wisdom. Otherwise, they're just lying to kick it. Making a dollar off of shit niggaz are buried in graves and prisons for. Rufus shit is fiction but damn! Keep it believable! Me, I'ma keep it gutta fa y'all, always! Some publishers wouldn't give me a chance or they offered crack head money, tryna pimp me like I'm a ho! So, I chose to roll with LDP, shawdy. Now I'ma let the streets support one of its own. Feel me? Like bitches on lock with me say! This is about to be the realest shit you ever read!

I've got the best editor ever in the world, real talk! **Shawn Walker**, you're the greatest, no lie. LOADB, wouldn't be what it is without you. You wanted this story to be the ish and you pushed me to the limit. The respect I got for you is unexplainable! I can't say enough about you! Thank you! Thank you! Thank you so much. On every level, the support and love is real from you!

Coffee, my round what it do BM (inside joke). From day 1/2 you've been the same and I love that about you. We blow the email up like it's nothing, talking about everything under the sun. And with that we've created a bond that cannot and will not be broken. I know I tell you all the time but I love who you are as a person. Your LOYALTY is unmatchable! Real recognize real no matter what! Hey I am screaming to the world, I LOVE ME SOME COFFEE, no homo :)

To my **FANS**, what would I do without y'all? Thank you all for allowing me to be apart of y'all lives. Thanks for all the LOVE and SUPPORT y'all show me, I promise to never let y'all don't so, I will continue to drop nothing but bangerz! Make sure you leave ya reviews on Amazon and hit me up on FB @ Jamaica Tha Author or look me up at FBOP Locator: Julian James 16692084.

RIP--- **Tara, Skip, Timmy, Chris Austin, Whyte Mike, Swerve, Mario, Dre** and the rest... Gone but NEVER 4gotten!!!

I am not gonna remember everyone so I am gonna do it like this, A_____Z.

Write me: Julian "Jamaica" James 16692084
          Federal Prison Camp
          Box A Glen Ray Road
          Alderson, WV 24910

Jamaica

Coming Soon from Lock Down Publications/Ca$h Presents

TORN BETWEEN TWO

By **Coffee**

LAY IT DOWN **III**

By **Jamaica**

GANGSTA SHYT **III**

By **CATO**

BLOOD OF A BOSS **IV**

By **Askari**

BRIDE OF A HUSTLA **II**

By **Destiny Skai**

WHEN A GOOD GIRL GOES BAD **II**

By **Adrienne**

LOVE & CHASIN' PAPER

By **Qay Crockett**

I RIDE FOR MY HITTA **II**

By **Misty Holt**

A SAVAGE LOVE **II**

By **Aryanna**

THE HEART OF A GANGSTA **II**

By **Jerry Jackson**

Available Now

RESTRAING ORDER **I & II**

By **CA$H & Coffee**

LOVE KNOWS NO BOUNDARIES **I II & III**

By **Coffee**

LAY IT DOWN **I & II**

By **Jamaica**

PUSH IT TO THE LIMIT

By **Bre' Hayes**

BLOOD OF A BOSS **I II & III**

By **Askari**

THE STREETS BLEED MURDER **I, II & III**

By **Jerry Jackson**

CUM FOR ME

An **LDP Erotica Collaboration**

BRIDE OF A HUSTLA

By **Destiny Skai**

WHEN A GOOD GIRL GOES BAD

By **Adrienne**

A GANGSTER'S REVENGE **I II III & IV**

By **Aryanna**

WHAT ABOUT US **I & II**

NEVER LOVE AGAIN

THUG ADDICTION

By **Kim Kaye**

THE KING CARTEL **I, II & III**

By **Frank Gresham**

THESE NIGGAS AIN'T LOYAL **I, II & III**

By **Nikki Tee**

GANGSTA SHYT **I &II**

By **CATO**

THE ULTIMATE BETRAYAL

By **Phoenix**

DON'T FU#K WITH MY HEART **I & II**

By **Linnea**

BOSS'N UP **I & II**

By **Royal Nicole**

I LOVE YOU TO DEATH

By Destiny J

I RIDE FOR MY HITTA

By **Misty Holt**

BOOKS BY LDP'S CEO, CA$H

TRUST NO MAN

TRUST NO MAN 2

TRUST NO MAN 3

BONDED BY BLOOD

SHORTY GOT A THUG

A DIRTY SOUTH LOVE

THUGS CRY

THUGS CRY 2

TRUST NO BITCH

TRUST NO BITCH 2

TRUST NO BITCH 3

TIL MY CASKET DROPS

RESTRAINING ORDER

RESTRAINING ORDER 2

Coming Soon

TRUST NO BITCH (KIAM EYEZ' STORY)

THUGS CRY 3

BONDED BY BLOOD 2

IN LOVE WITH HIS GANGSTA

Jamaica